Keith Gessen is a founding editor of the magazine *n+1*. This is his first book.

Praise for *All the Sad Young Literary Men*

"Beginning with its risky yet playful title, *All the Sad Young Literary Men* is a rueful, undramatic, mordantly funny, and frequently poignant sequence of sketchlike stories loosely organized by chronology and place and the prevailing theme of youthful literary ideals vis-à-vis literary accomplishment. . . . Transposed to theater it would be not a conventional play in three dimensions intent upon simulating life, but an evening of linked monologues delivered with droll, deadpan humor and melancholy irony, with, perhaps, from time to time, images of historic figures projected against the back of the stage. . . . The predicament of Gessen's characters, as it is likely to be the preeminent predicament of Gessen's generation, is the disparity between what one has learned of history and the possibilities of making use of that knowledge in one's life."   —Joyce Carol Oates, *The New York Review of Books*

"[Gessen's] achingly comic command of the hopes, vanities, foibles, and quandaries of his peers has produced something better than fashionably maneuvered satire. It is irony (of a rare cosmopolitan sort) that this Russian-born writer brings to the New York scene, a pond that takes itself to be the ocean. He evokes the world's culture along with our own."   —*Los Angeles Times*

"Brilliantly painful . . . Gessen is shrewd, funny, and oddly compassionate; though consider yourself blessed if you're not like any of his characters. (A–)"   —*Entertainment Weekly*

"This interesting and agreeable first novel . . . can be good entertainment for readers, as the saying goes, of all ages. . . . A convincing portrait . . . Gessen has a deft satiric touch and a nice feel for irony."
—Jonathan Yardley, *The Washington Post*

"Before age thirty, Gessen made his mark as a public intellectual and literary critic. But his artistic debut may dwarf those other, considerable contributions. Gessen's fiction teases out subtle insights into travails both political and romantic, and with powerful humor. Heaven will take note."
—Mary Karr, author of *The Liars' Club* and *Cherry*

"Gessen is . . . a wunderkind of the literary scene."
—*The Houston Chronicle*

"Every generation has its clever young men, and Keith Gessen must be counted among his. . . . One of the pleasures of Gessen's novel is how well he reproduces the speech patterns of brainy, left-wing Ivy Leaguers—their sardonic deployment of social-theoretical jargon, their riffs on technology and capitalism, their anxiety about status."
—Judith Schulevitz, Slate.com

"[A] humorous and compassionate handle on the minds of anxious, overanalytical grads . . . an invigorating first novel."
—*The Cleveland Plain Dealer*

"Gessen's novel is studded with self-aware observations . . . [that] capture the inner lives of these expensively educated, romantically hapless men flailing in the dark."
—*Star Tribune* (Minneapolis)

"There is something weirdly fetching about *All the Sad Young Literary Men*—weird because the book describes such a tiny, occasionally infuriating world, one where progressive magazines and book reviews might save the world and crossing paths with the vice president's daughter is just a part of a Harvard education. . . . And yet there is something affecting about the impossibly great aspirations shared by Mr. Gessen's trio."
—*The New York Sun*

"A fiercely intelligent, darkly funny first novel."

—*Kirkus Reviews* (starred review)

"This book violates pretty much every principle you learned in writing school; it's about hypereducated twentysomethings who don't seem to have jobs or fixed locations, and who primarily engage in speculation about what might have happened between them and their ex-girlfriends. . . . ASYLM bears, in other words, the ring of truth to life as I know it, and probably as it is known by anyone reading this. It also conveys a startling amount of emotional honesty and (this may be the least fictiony of all) ambivalence, as well as the occasional nicely turned phrase. It's a good book, and for once it's suggestive of what might be possible in contemporary fiction, rather than of what we think has been done best by those who came before."   —Dan, Goodreads.com

"Rarely has a book pissed me off so much while simultaneously forbidding me from putting it down."   —Caitlin, Goodreads.com

To access Penguin Readers Guides online, visit our
Web sites at www.penguin.com or www.vpbookclub.com.

All the Sad Young Literary Men

Keith Gessen

Penguin Books

PENGUIN BOOKS

Published by the Penguin Group

Penguin Group (USA) Inc., 375 Hudson Street, New York, New York 10014, U.S.A.

Penguin Group (Canada), 90 Eglinton Avenue East, Suite 700, Toronto,

Ontario, Canada M4P 2Y3 (a division of Pearson Penguin Canada Inc.)

Penguin Books Ltd, 80 Strand, London WC2R 0RL, England

Penguin Ireland, 25 St Stephen's Green, Dublin 2, Ireland (a division of Penguin Books Ltd)

Penguin Group (Australia), 250 Camberwell Road, Camberwell,

Victoria 3124, Australia (a division of Pearson Australia Group Pty Ltd)

Penguin Books India Pvt Ltd, 11 Community Centre, Panchsheel Park, New Delhi – 110 017, India

Penguin Group (NZ), 67 Apollo Drive, Rosedale, North Shore 0632,

New Zealand (a division of Pearson New Zealand Ltd)

Penguin Books (South Africa) (Pty) Ltd, 24 Sturdee Avenue, Rosebank, Johannesburg 2196, South Africa

Penguin Books Ltd, Registered Offices:

80 Strand, London WC2R 0RL, England

First published in the United States of America by Viking Penguin,

a member of Penguin Group (USA) Inc. 2008

Published in Penguin Books 2009

1   3   5   7   9   10   8   6   4   2

PUBLISHER'S NOTE

This is a work of fiction. Names, characters, places, and incidents are either the product of the author's imagination or are used fictitiously, and any resemblance to actual persons, living or dead, business establishments, events, or locales is entirely coincidental.

THE LIBRARY OF CONGRESS HAS CATALOGED THE HARDCOVER EDITION AS FOLLOWS:

Gessen, Keith.

All the sad young literary men / Keith Gessen.

p.   cm.

ISBN 978-0-670-01855-0 (hc.)

ISBN 978-0-14-311477-2 (pbk.)

1. Young men—Fiction.   2. Authors—Fiction.   I. Title.

PS3607.E87A79 2008

813.'6—dc22   2007021009

Printed in the United States of America

Designed by Daniel Lagin

For Anya, Alison, and Anne

Contents

All the Sad Young Literary Men

Prologue

In New York, they saved.

They saved on orange juice, sliced bread, they saved on coffee. On movies, magazines, museum admission (Friday nights). Train fare, subway fare, their apartment out in Queens. It was a principle, of sorts, and they stuck to it. Mark and Sasha lived that year on the 7 train and when they got out, out in Queens, Mark would follow Sasha like a little boy as she checked the prices at the two Korean grocers, and cross-checked them, so they could save on fruits and vegetables and little Korean treats. They saved on clothes.

It was 1998 and they were in love. They were done with college, with the Moscow of Sasha's childhood, with the American suburbs of Mark's—and yet they'd somehow escaped these things with their youth intact. To be poor in New York was humiliating, a little, but to be young—to be young was divine. If you'd had more money than they had that year, you'd simply have grown old faster. And so, with smiles on their faces, they saved.

It was 1998 and they were angry. The U.S. had bombed a medicine factory in Sudan. The U.S. was inert on Kosovo—and then we started raining bombs. The Israelis continued to build settlements on the West Bank, endangering Oslo, and the Palestinians continued to arm. "Contingency and irony, sure," said Tom, in their kitchen. "But have we forgotten solidarity?" They hadn't. Mark and Sasha went to teach-ins, lectures, protests in Union Square. They attended free readings, second-run movies, eight-dollar plays. The readings were miserable, the plays were horrible, the lectures were nearly empty. Some of the movies were good.

Their friends came to visit, from Manhattan, from Brooklyn, from farther away. Val's real name was Vassily and he lived in Inwood; Nick wanted to be an art critic but worked for the moment at a bank, with expensive art on its walls. Tom was a fiery radical of the far left: in college he'd read Hegel's *Phenomenology;* in New York he mostly read the political writings of Lomaski. Toby came to visit from Milwaukee and wandered around the city, his head craned up to see the faraway tops of the buildings; he was gifted with computers but wanted to write. Sam came from Boston and couldn't stop talking about Israel; he even had an Israeli girlfriend now.

It was 1998. Mark and Sasha and their friends held down the following jobs: translator, gallery assistant, *New York Times* copy clerk, Web temp, investment banker, temp, temp, temp.

Mark had always been cheap, but in college he'd become radically cheap. He went to Russia to research a project and met a girl. She had enormous green eyes and held her back straight and walked like a ballerina, the heel just in front of the toe, and she spoke English with such a proper, Old World reserve that Mark wanted to help, to put his arms around her, to tell her it was OK. One day after classes they'd gone for coffee, sort of—there was no place to sit in all of Moscow, unless you sat outside, which is what they did, and then as it was dark he'd offered to ride the subway home with her.

"I don't believe this is something you would like to do, really," she replied, properly.

Oh, but he did! She was tiny, with her big green eyes, and they rode the train for over an hour—she lived at the very tip, the very southern tip, of the entire sprawling metropolis—and when they got out of the subway, Mark had to catch his breath. The rows of buildings, graying socialist high-rises, nine stories, thirteen stories, seventeen stories, each with its crumbling balconies, each grayer than the next, stretched into the horizon like a massed column. Mark was terrified.

"You live here?" he said to the girl, to Sasha, immediately regretting it.

"Yes," she said.

It was just a matter of time, after that, before he declared himself. Three years later, they were in New York.

So they saved! Mark cheated, a little. They had a 4Runner, a present from his father, and Mark would drive it to the big Pathmark on Northern Boulevard. Once there, he achieved the serenity of a Zen master. The people of Queens ran around this way and that, their shopping carts like externalized stomachs. Others had coupons and carefully they held them, like counterfeiting experts, up to the items they hoped to save on, to make sure they were the ones. Mark never did. He had emptied himself of any attachment to specific foods. The only items he saw were the items already on sale. In this way he kept his calm, he tried new foods, and he saved.

They kept a budget. At the beginning of the week they gave themselves seventy dollars for food and transport. Impossible?

Basically impossible, yes, but not if you never go for "drinks" at a bar, never walk into a restaurant, and never ever buy an item of clothing not at the Salvation Army on Spring Street and Lafayette. Sasha herself was perpetually amazed. "I see girls in there," she reported, "they have three-hundred-dollar shoes, but they are looking for a jacket, a blouse, they would like to look like me."

"Whereas you already do," said Mark.

"Tak," said Sasha. *"Imenno tak."* Exactly.

And, slowly, Mark's Russian was improving. He made his meager living now by translating industrial manuals into English. Sasha helped. The rest of the time he studied Soviet history and wondered if he should apply to graduate school. Sasha worked at a gallery and painted watercolors. She thought they should have children. It was 1998 and the rest of the world was rich.

Their friends came over and Sasha fed them. All together they argued and argued—there was so much to argue about! Val looked through their art books and gave talks about the painters—about Goya, about Rembrandt. Sasha told him about the Russian icon-painters, about the profound influence of religious anti-representationalism on Russian art. Tom explained the latest political developments. Sam talked about Israel and the writing world: who was publishing in the *New American,* who was publishing in *Debate.* Mark listened always and observed. It was clear what some of them would do with their lives; it was less clear about the others. In the case of Mark, for example, it was unclear.

Occasionally he and Sasha had terrible fights. She was so quiet; she was so small. One time they met up in the city to watch a free movie in Bryant Park. Mark was already at the library on 42nd Street, and Sasha was at home, so she was to bring some food. But she was in a hurry and forgot. Trying to hide his annoyance, Mark led them around midtown looking for a place to eat. Finally they walked into a deli. The salad bar was closed. The sandwiches cost six-fifty, seven dollars. Mark concluded to himself that he would have a Snickers bar, but Sasha should eat.

"That's all right," she said. "I don't need anything."

"You need to eat something," he insisted. "It's a long movie."

"No, I'm fine."

"ORDER A SANDWICH!"

"Bozhe moi," she said, my God, and without another word walked out the door. He followed her quietly and Snickers-less. They did not go to the movie.

Things like that. And sometimes Sasha would lie in bed for days and refuse to get up. But this passed, it usually passed, and anyway they were in this together. In an emergency, it was understood, Mark would be able to find a real job. So they were pledged to avoid emergency. Or maybe only Mark was pledged to avoid it. There were other issues, of course. There are always other issues.

But most of all Mark and Sasha and their friends worried about history and themselves. They read and listened and wrote and argued. What would happen to them? Were they good enough, strong enough, smart enough? Were they hard enough, mean enough, did they believe in themselves enough, and would they stick together when push came to shove, would they tell the truth despite all consequences? They were right about Al-Shifa; they were right about the settlements. About Kosovo they were right and wrong. But what if they were missing it? What if *it* was happening, in New York, not a few blocks from them, what if they knew someone to whom it was happening, or who was making it happen—what if they were blind to it? What if it wasn't them?

In their apartment, in their beautiful Queens apartment, Mark and Sasha knew only that they had each other. And they also knew—even in 1998, they knew—that this would not be enough.

I

The Vice President's Daughter

It was just at the point when things were finally cracking up for me that I ran into Lauren and her father on
Madison Avenue. Jillian, my fiancée, was visiting her family in
California and I, I had raced up to New York in our car. I didn't
know what I was going to do there, in fact the people I contacted to
announce my trip were people I barely knew—but the main thing
was to get out of our apartment. The life I had then was slipping
away, I could feel it, and I had developed the notion that some
nudge, some shift or alternately some miracle, might help me fit
everything back into place. I would hold on to Jillian, I hoped, and
last until the next election, and then we'd see.

I had just been to the Met and was now looking for a place to
get a coffee and check my e-mail when I first recognized Lauren
and then, without bodyguards and without ceremony, her father. I
had seen him at campaign stops, I had written and thought about

him almost without interruption for an entire year of my life, but I'd never been this close, and he'd never been so alone. I was carrying a book under my arm, and some papers, I think, with phone numbers and e-mails, and finally my cell phone was in my hand like a compass because I guess I was hoping some of the people I'd called would call me back. I stopped on the street and stood for a second before Lauren saw me. On Madison Avenue she looked happy, flushed, a walking advertisement for our civilization, while her father wore his beard, his infamous beard, and I was surprised by how substantial he looked, how physically powerful. I wanted to say to Lauren "I'm sorry," though she didn't look like she needed it, and "I wish you were President" to her father, who looked like he did. I saw him flinch from me a little—from the way I froze on the sidewalk he might have thought I was another ill-wisher, another nut—but soon it was all over: Lauren looked at me, shabby and scattered with my phone in my hand, and I looked at the former Vice President, and we all paused for a moment while I kissed the Vice President's daughter on the cheek, she assured me they were in a terrible hurry though it was nice to see me, and they crossed northward while I waited for the light.

I think I could have screamed. I walked down 80th Street, down the long hard residential blocks before Lexington, and I felt myself outside myself, and saw us all for what we were. Sorrow touched me; I was touched, on East 80th Street, by sorrow. My phone rang finally in my hand and it was Jillian, my Jillian, and I did not pick up.

I was hurt, of course, that I had not been introduced to the former Vice President, but I had no cause to be offended. Lauren's friendship with me was contingent on her friendship with Ferdinand, my old roommate, and Ferdinand was a complicated person. In his particular line, I always said, he was a genius. "You're an astute observer of history" is how I explained it to him once. According to Hegel, I said, for I had read fifty pages of Hegel, the world-historical hero is necessarily something of a philosopher, and sort of extrapolates—

"It's always like that," Ferdinand interrupted. It was our sophomore year, and we were gathered around a big circular table in the Leverett House dining hall, where day in and day out I tried to apply the lessons from my classes to the great sociorelational problems of our time—Ferdinand's sex life, usually. On this day I had a huge bowl of green peas in front of me, and a chicken parm sandwich, and I was sipping from a cranberry-grapefruit mixture, which I'd patented—swirling and sipping and discoursing on the higher thoughts. "It's always like that," said Ferdinand. "You tell a goat to draw God, he'll draw a goat. Philosophers are goats."

"Yeah, OK," I conceded. "But this is about you, the philosopher-stud. You've sensed something in the air, a shift in the historical mood of the female class, and you've acted. What is it?"

Ferdinand considered this, slowly, wondering whether I was making fun of him, and then began to laugh his deliberate, nobody's-fool laugh. It opened with a lengthy enunciated "ennhh," asking, waiting for you to come along, and then it burst forth like applause.

So he laughed now, he didn't answer, and that was OK. I knew I wouldn't learn the secrets of the world-spirit from Ferdinand, nor would I learn how to pick up women. I wouldn't even learn how to dress from him, because he was tall and narrow, he could order clothes directly from the catalogs, which with my build (I was a high school fullback) I couldn't do. About the only thing I learned from Ferdinand was that women were perspicacious, prophetic, for they saw in him what I at first did not. He struck me as vain, deluded, skinny. I didn't get it. "Boy, am I glad they gave me you," he said on the first day of college, after we'd moved ourselves into Matthews, sent our awkward parents home, and opened my bottle of peppermint schnapps (the best I could do) and his dime bag of mediocre weed (the best he could do). "I was afraid they'd stick me with some total nerd," he said. I was flattered. "Or an Asian."

"What?"

"Much bigger chance of their being a nerd. Don't you think?"

"I guess," I said. And, in short, when washed and J.Crewed Ferdinand suggested we hit the bars, I did not refuse—it seemed like just the thing to do before getting down, finally, to the books. And Ferdinand was a good companion, at first, though he was loud and obnoxious and I couldn't tell what sort of person he'd been in high school. His family had money but did not seem to come, so to speak, from education—whereas my forefathers had been huddled over Talmuds, then Soviet literary journals, for many generations. But I have always been attracted to cruel, acerbic people, and Ferdinand was fantastically acerbic. He knew right away that our classmates were a bunch of jerks. "Total douchebag" was about the extent of his commentary on most of the people we met over the next few days. "Major league DB." He referred to girls he didn't like as "assholes," and somehow this cracked me up. Intent on showing that my high school drinking had been significant, that first night I got absurdly drunk and threw up on the bushes next to Boylston Hall. "Dude," said a relatively sober Ferdinand as I rejoined him, "you've christened the Yard. *In nomine Patris.* And we only just got here." The next day he was relating the story to everyone we met. "Who's got the best roommate?" he'd demand. I was embarrassed and proud.

But there were also calculations going on in Ferdinand's mind. The bars were his business, the girls were his destiny, and on the fourth night of college we had our first conflict. That day we'd gone to the Salvation Army near Central Square and bought a monstrous yellow paisley couch for fifty dollars, and saved money by carrying it the mile back to our dorm. We took little rest stops in the heat and traffic of Mass Ave and sat down on our new couch, lounging. When we got back to Matthews we showered and then sat on the couch again, newly home, as Ferdinand smoked an illegal cigarette ("What's the point of college," he said, coughing, "if you can't smoke?") and I began to choose my classes. When he finished his smoke, Ferdinand announced it was time to go out.

"No thanks," I said. I had now spent three nights getting very drunk. I knew I'd held long conversations with people, including the prettiest of my new classmates, but I couldn't remember anyone's name, and in general I had a bad feeling about the whole thing. Now I was constructing a complicated chart, my first big assignment in college, which would tell me the classes that would most quickly fulfill the reading list with which my favorite high school history teacher had sent me off into the world. "Homer," it began. "Herodotus. Tacitus. Augustine. Lactantius."

"You can do that later," said Ferdinand. "Now is the time for the bars. You have to lay the groundwork. Tomorrow will be too late."

"Forty bucks a night for groundwork," I grumbled.

"Yeah," he admitted. "But you need to spend money to earn money. You coming?"

I told him no and he was out the door. I sat there that night, the course guide and the CUE guide and the Confi guide and my long, increasingly Anglocentric list—"Chaucer," it continued. "Jonson. Johnson. Sterne. Burke. Carlyle. Thackeray. Eliot."—all strewn across our paisley couch, and felt sad for myself, and sorry. To arrive at Harvard and find—Ferdinand! It was infuriating. It was absurd. Our dorm was in the very center of the Yard, our windows opened onto the little quadrangle between Matthews, Straus, and Massachusetts Hall. It was still warm and outside a few people were playing Frisbee. Were they douchebags? Maybe, but I could have gone out there and said hello, laid the groundwork, maybe now they were douchebags but later on they'd be geniuses? Then again, they kept dropping the Frisbee, those guys, and it was like they'd never played before. It was all too sad. I opened Ferdinand's CD book, having no CDs of my own—a few years earlier I'd made the determination, based on my extensive purchasing of cassette tapes throughout junior high, that the compact disc was a technology bound for speedy obsolescence, and decided to wait it out—but Ferdinand's collection was all greatest hits, greatest hits, Allman Brothers, greatest hits. All those hours, those irretrievable hours, I'd spent studying for the SATs. All those days, those irretrievable sunny days when I flipped through the catalogs, considered my applications, wondered at the roundedness of my character—and now Ferdinand was my roommate? He was the first in a series of disappointments at that bitter place, though eventually I think they formed a pattern, and I tried to read it.

Ferdinand	Me
Four nights a week in the Crimson Sports Grille, laying groundwork.	No interest in groundwork.
A moderate though consistent drinker, hardly ever drunk.	A streaky drinker, and a lousy drunk— a little busy with the hands, to begin with, and too quick with the lean-in, always, but worst of all too earnest, too ready to spill my guts in the old high school way.
Never felt sorry.	Felt tremendous guilt for even the smallest indiscretions. But as an apologizer I was a total failure.
Along with some of our classmates, destined to spend his life apologizing ingeniously, that is to say covering up, for global warming, the School of the Americas, the ravages of free trade and the inexorable march of mighty capital.	Could not even think what to do upon meeting a girl the next day to whom I'd said too much. And so I pretended not to see her, or walked across the dining hall, so that a few months into my freshman year the range of women whom I had not encountered in a drunken stupor narrowed and narrowed until I was reduced to just getting drunk again and hoping someone would meet me halfway. I had done well with girls in high school, considering all my studying, and I was miffed by the new dispensation. At first I basically thought: What the fuck? And then I thought: You've got to be kidding me. And then I began to sort of think, Oh no.

And I had grand notions, too. I had quit football because I was too small, but also so that I could read Kierkegaard. My history teacher's list was nice, but here was *Fear and Trembling*. Here *The Sickness Unto Death*. I considered dipping into Weber. Occasionally the word *Foucault* would float from my tongue, a trial balloon. In such moods I denounced Ferdinand—he was not Harvard!— but at the end of the year I stayed with him. We were hanging out with lacrosse players and their girlfriends, I was badly drunk three nights a week, and some of my morning classes went by unattended, went by anyway, while I lay in bed moaning. In the weeks before rooming groups were due, I made a few halfhearted sorties in the Freshman Union to some of the more articulate kids I'd met in my classes, but they were as wary as they were intelligent, their groups had congealed and they liked it that way, and anyhow I hadn't yet learned how to talk with them: instead of *Foucault* the word *douchebag* kept escaping, like a dark secret, from my lips. One late night in the basement of the Owl Club, Ben, a slight and drunken lacrosse player, asked shyly if he could room with Ferdinand and me, and we said OK. So that spring the three of us joined hands together for the housing lottery, and stepped over, without really knowing what we were doing, into the chasm of the rest of our lives.

That summer I failed to intern at the *Washington Post* or even to write travel copy for the student travel guide. Instead I went back to Maryland and worked as a camp counselor, and at the end of most every day, exhausted, I would drive to my mother's grave and water the tree my father and I had planted there. I don't know what significance this has, but it sticks in my mind from that time. Perhaps because memory is a faulty organ, or anyway a very mechanical one that works through repetition, I remember the nightly exhaustion, from carrying eight-year-old campers, and the heat, and the watering. Then I would go home and take a nap, and at night, when there wasn't much to do, I'd go driving just as I had in high school and try to figure things out. I used to think that by driving and driving through the suburbs of Maryland I'd finally just break through, break out; and then, finally, I did, I left. And now where was I? My mother's old Oldsmobile still ran, and I went up 32, I went down 32, and time permitting I'd pull over at some highway McDonald's and try to get through the *Confessions* of Rousseau. The books he had read as a child, said Rousseau, "gave me odd and romantic notions of human life, of which experiences and reflection have never wholly cured me." I resolved, also, never to be cured. I went to the parties we still threw that summer, melancholy keggers at which we told tales of our heroic college exploits, and got drunk, just as in college, and once in a while, to salve my wounded heart, the not-yet-graduated Amy Gould would let me kiss her behind a tree.

Then summer was over, and I returned to school for more of what I'd left. The couch, my old television, our *Simpsons* tape; my laptop in the library, the lectures at ten in the morning, the wind as I walked to them among a herd of faces, very few of whom were my friends. Ferdinand, for his part, only accelerated his activity. His groundwork had paid off. He had, as F. Scott Fitzgerald once said of his friend John Peale Bishop, "an insatiable penis," and by second semester sophomore year he was running a hotel room, as he liked to put it, out of Leverett J-12. No one knew this better than I, who as his bunk mate had to journey to the yellow common-room couch every time I heard an extra pair of footsteps accompany him through the door. Things got so busy that I suggested to Ben, who'd won the coin flip at the beginning of the year and thus his own room, that he give up his place to Ferdinand and move in with me. "No way," said Ben. "What about when I get laid?" There was a pause. "Look," he said, "a coin toss is a coin toss. Or isn't it?" It was, it was, and so I continued to make the trip, and to be honest I didn't mind. Ferdinand was not discriminating, not at all; he had a massive tolerance for giggliness or crudeness from attractive women, but just as often they were very impressive, the women, and increasingly so. The silhouettes of the daughters of our professors, and of hedge-fund presidents, junk-bond kings, and Hollywood impresarios, flickered through our hallways, whispered good-bye in the morning, walked quietly out. They were the sorts of women that, if you had a rule against sleepovers, for them you'd make an exception.

And then one day—it was a cold lazy Sunday in what was now our junior year, we had all, even me, gone out the night before and spent the day lying half ruined and miserable on the couch, watching football—Ferdinand came home with Lauren, whose father was Vice President of the United States. Four of us were there, in various states of recline, Ben and I and Nick and Sully, and we accepted her presence with a lordly calm. We were all here together at this college, after all, this just and classless place, all our destinies were set at zero, and anything was possible, was the idea. Anything was possible, but it was hard not to notice how much Lauren resembled her father—she was blond where he was dark, but otherwise they shared the same soft features, and the slight blurriness or sensual weakness in the mouth, and they were handsome in a similar way, and also a little regal and a little outsized. We acted casually enough, we thought, but it was hard not to feel that here, in our room, we were finally coming into contact with greater things.

Lauren began to come by in the evenings, and often she was drunk. Are the rich very different from you and me? Judge for yourself. She was drunk, and it was my role to sit in the room I shared with Ferdinand and try to work on my junior paper. "It's important that you do this," Ferdinand told me. "You need to be, like, the Scholar. It creates an atmosphere."

I didn't like this very much. "Why can't someone else be the Scholar?"

"Because," he answered, leaving, "you're our last best hope. And, anyway, you never go out."

"I do too!" I called after him. Immediately I put on my coat and walked out into the night. But Ferdinand was right, of course; I had become a shut-in, a recluse, and outside the room and outside my carrel I wasn't sure what to do. The libraries were closed now, and when I ducked behind big redbrick Leverett to walk along the Charles, the wind came off the river mixed with a hard dust. I went to the Grille finally and drank a four-dollar pitcher without talking to anyone—by this point I didn't know anyone—and then, defeated, I went back home. I had a paper to write. That semester I was working on Lincoln, and something of his tragedy had entered my bones, so that if I was noble I was noble like Lincoln, and if I was solemn I was solemn like Lincoln.

I was open to influence then, to any influence. I was ready to rearrange myself, if that's what it took. Because the plans that I'd had for myself had faltered, somewhere, and I could not tell why. Does he who fights douchebags become, inevitably, something of a douchebag? I don't know. Maybe.

I was lost.

One night as I worked on Lincoln, Lauren came into the bedroom to visit. Ferdinand had gone out for cigarettes, and it was just me.

"Whatcha doing?" she asked. She was a little drunk, she wore jeans and a loose light-blue cardigan over a white T-shirt, and she set herself down on the corner of my bed.

"Nothing," I said. "A little Lincoln." In fact I had an idea about Lincoln that I'd stolen from Edmund Wilson—that by his eloquence he had foisted his interpretation of the war on future generations—and I was now trying to so muddle this idea with quotations from various French theorists that it might come to seem my own. But I didn't feel like sharing all of this with Lauren.

Perhaps she sensed my disapproval, my remove, because immediately she tried to bridge it.

"Ferdinand says you're from Clarksville?"

"Yup."

"It's nice up there."

"It's up and down. We were in between."

"Oh, it doesn't matter," she said quickly. "I hate being rich. Don't you think money is so dumb?"

"I don't know," I said. Of course I did think it, but abstractly. My parents had done fine, financially, especially after my mother also became a computer programmer, but they never had the sense that they would do fine indefinitely. It was occasionally suggested during money-related arguments in our household that computers might get canceled. "I don't know," I repeated. "I guess there's no use being ashamed of it."

"I just wish I could be more like you," she said. "You know? Sort of serious and scholarly."

"And I wish," said I, "that I could be you."

"We could trade," she decided. She leaned over toward me in such a way that I could see down her shirt, but what struck me then was just her nearness, her girliness. "But you have to warn me first—why don't you like being you?"

"I don't know." I shrugged. Jesus, where to begin? "I just—" And here something happened to me that had happened to me once or twice before, always with women: a moment of unpremeditated screaming honesty, of saying out loud what had remained in my mind only a kind of vagueness, a foreboding, not even a thought. "I just don't understand what people want from me," I said. "I just don't really understand what I'm doing."

Her eyebrows went up, momentarily. She looked great doing it—I realized her features were so generous that her mouth and brow and jaw could absorb a great deal of emotion without actually seeming to move. A few years later, during the campaign and on her father's face, it would be called "stiffness." That's not what it was. "Yes," she said now. "I feel like that too. I see people looking at me and I don't know what they mean. Or what they see, you know?"

"But you get along with them."

"I'm not as grouchy as you," she said, shrugging. I liked it how she shrugged, and when she smiled at me I smiled back. I disapproved of her, disapproval was what I knew, but she seemed so young to me then, so changeable.

And so I pushed my luck and asked, "How are things with Ferdinand?"

"Ferdinand . . . ," lying back woozily on my bed. I wasn't a big bed-maker but on this day, miraculously, I'd made it, and cleared off my clothes to boot.

"Listen," I said, standing up, standing over her. "What do you see in him?"

"Ferdinand?" With some difficulty she propped herself up on an elbow. "I don't know. He's . . . fun. And I'm—" She lay back down, lounging. "You know, I'm just in college."

I looked at her—closely, closely. She resembled royalty, I tell you. She was practically the leader of the free world. Yet she lacked speech. I—on the other hand—standing in that little room, my fingertips still warm from the keyboard—I did not lack it!

"But that's just it!" I began. "I mean, we're in college. It's time to get serious! It's time to get to the bottom of things. The meaning of them. I mean—"

As I began to expound on this, I thought I saw her looking at me in a way I hadn't seen a woman look at me in a long time. Probably she wasn't, or she was just startled by all the words, but already in my mind, in my loins, I sensed a looming ethical dilemma. And I took a deep breath, a pause, because first I needed to tell her what I thought of things, and I needed to blow her mind. It wasn't Ferdinand himself that I wanted to dissuade her from, exactly, and not in favor of me, per se, but the idea of Ferdinand, and the idea of me: it was important that I arrange these properly in her mind. Because *fun*—I turned the word over in my mind. Did she mean sex? Boats? Ice cream? There was right action and wrong action. There was Kierkegaard. There was fun, and then there were those ten minutes before the Grille closed, the music turned off, the lights coming up to reveal the beer spilled on the floor, the plastic cups lying there, and people's coats had fallen off the little coat ledge in the corner, and you'd be going home alone. How was I going to explain all this to anyone? To Lauren, for example, poor privileged Lauren for whom no amount of grooming and training (and we were all getting it, in our way, the grooming and the training) would turn her into the person she actually wanted to be? To Lauren, who'd passed out on my bed?

This was all in 1997. It was before the scandals broke, one after the other, in a rising, crescendoing spiral of tawdriness, and before it became clear that though her father was innocent, he lacked the skill to distance himself in quite the right way—that even his innocence appeared somehow manipulative. For now, the economy was moving along, the Serbs were off the hills above Sarajevo, the party of the opposition was in confusion and disarray. Ferdinand discovered Diesel jeans and, walking around with Lauren, looked better than ever. I began to think that she was right, right about everything, and though we didn't talk much after that episode in my room—I wrote her a long e-mail, and she didn't write back—I suspect it was the happiest time of Lauren's life.

And then, about a month after the e-mail, things came to a head in Leverett J-12. I had been buried in the library, reading all of Lincoln's little notes and letters, all sixteen volumes, and finishing my great Lincoln paper, though admittedly much of my time was spent imagining what it would be like already to be the author of a great Lincoln paper. Would I grant interviews? But now things were getting tense, the deadline was nine in the morning, and I had to finish the Lincoln, for no one else would. When they stumbled in at around three I was already in bed, turning some final phrases over in my mind. When I heard them pause in the front hall and then paw each other for a while—transparent were the ways of Ferdinand to me—I knew I should get up. The trip to the couch was momentous, and though I wore a fairly new T-shirt and my best boxers I felt underdressed. I took my laptop along, and they smiled sheepishly at me, apologizing, as they walked past into the bedroom. And Lauren, happy and seeing me there on the ridiculous couch, my face illuminated in simulated concentration by the bright nimbus of the monitor, Lauren winked.

For the next two hours I sat at my laptop, that small and nimble machine, its purr doing little to muffle their sounds.

At first they wrestled, she giggled, he growled.

"My shirt's chafing me, man," I heard Ferdinand say, cracking up. "I'm taking it off."

A bit later I heard his shoes thud against the floor, separately. Hers followed, together and daintily, as if she'd not only taken them off simultaneously, but tried to lighten their fall. And presently, I thought I heard from the bedroom little wistful sounds, hesitating, like Ferdinand's laugh, as they rubbed against each other.

"My pants," he then said. "They're chafing me." They giggled and again there was a furious rustling. His ambition was like a little engine, his secretary said of Lincoln, that knew no rest.

What now? Was he sucking on her breasts? He'd explained to me once that if a girl has larger breasts, you can be rougher with them—was he being rougher? I suppose he massaged her inner thighs.

And then there was a silence, some quick rustling. "No," she said, regretfully but sharply. "You're drunk."

"I'm shit-faced," he agreed.

"Me too."

"Oh, man," he said after a while. "My pants were really chafing me."

She did a Mr. Burns imitation, thrumming her fingers to-gether diabolically and intoning, "Excellent." The moment had passed, and already they had settled into positions of sleep. I had listened to all this with profound attention, and now it was 5:00 a.m. I was just a paragraph away with my paper but this was rather a lot to take in. I was going to need a few more days for the Lincoln.

There is the event, which simply happens, and the interpretation, which never ends. After that night, fierce debates were held in the Leverett House dining hall over our strange mixed-together foods. Over heaping green salads, over General Chung's chicken, over sloppy Joes—I myself had taken to eating grilled ham and cheese sandwiches, the meal of conscientious objectors to the daily menu—we found Ferdinand uncharacteristically vague about what had gone on. "It was close," he said. "I'll tell you that much. But, you know . . ." He gestured with his hands. "It gets confus-ing down there." He shrugged and smiled.

Mayhem ensued. What did he mean? The collected sages were forced to speculate. Had he come prematurely? Had he entered partially? Had he merely, just, been in the neighborhood? We deliberated. What was sex? What was not-sex? "Penetration with-out ejaculation," I proposed, as a general rule, "that's not-sex." "But getting her to agree to penetration," countered Nick, a social studies major, a fierce debater, "that is most difficult." "So?" I said. "A lot of things are difficult. It's difficult to persuade a girl to take her underwear off, but you wouldn't claim that that's sex." "Is difficulty the prime consideration?" Nick switched his tack; he was on the defensive. "Like in gymnastics? Because that seems pretty reductive." There were murmurs of assent. It was a dirty debating trick: No one wanted sex to be like gymnastics. "I'm just seeking clarity," I said now. "Just as sex itself should be consensual, so should the definition of sex. What I think we all want is an act about which both people can say: That was *it*. That was the *deed*." Sully suggested: "Maybe we should ask some girls." We all looked at him for a moment, with a mixture of annoyance and surprise.

On the question of sex/not-sex, Ferdinand kept his own counsel. But this did not mean he could keep his hands to himself. Within two weeks of their night together, Lauren saw him leave the Grille with Stephanie Stevens, a short, perky soccer player who lived in distant Cabot House. I, in turn, heard them come in and, in a final burst of loyalty to Lauren, refused to sleep on the couch.

"Come on," said Ferdinand. "Don't be a douchebag."

"No," I told him. "I'm not leaving. You can go ahead and do your thing, but I'm staying here."

"You are a professional DB," concluded Ferdinand. "Come on," he said to Stephanie Stevens, "we'll take a cab to your place."

But the damage was done. Lauren was livid, if only briefly, because she must have known this was the nature of Ferdinand, and she'd signed up for it. And if she hadn't known, now she knew. In any case, we soon entered, all of us, a period of reaction, of retreat, of private humiliations and things said in public that should never be said at all. I never more had the privilege of ceding my bedroom to Lauren, in fact I never really saw her again, not as I'd seen her, for there was soon another woman in our lives, so silly and so much like us, and at night we dreamed of her softness, at night we dwelt on her details, her credulity. We were disgusted by our President but secretly we lamented only that he hadn't done enough.

I was disappointed that Ferdinand and Lauren did not stay together, but overall I was proud. I did not come to Harvard so that my roommate could sleep with, or almost-sleep with, the Vice President's daughter. In my secret dreams of Harvard, of what Harvard would mean for me, it was of course I who slept with, or almost-slept with—that would have been fine!—the Veep's handsome daughter. But to have a roommate who did—well that is also something. And to realize this, that it is something, may just be the beginning of wisdom—or almost-wisdom, as the case may have been. Sometimes you end up in bed, was the idea—but sometimes you're just the guy on the couch, writing your Lincoln paper, smiling at some of the things that have been said, and half hoping you'll fall asleep.

After that happened, anyway, things got a little easier for me. I think now that every life contains three, four, five lives, and at each one of mine I have been progressively more amazed. It was too late, this time around, to salvage college, but I did start studying a little less, and less desperately, and I began to look about me. My Lincoln paper, which I had thought so great, proved a disappointment to my adviser, who met me in his little postgrad office in the history building and said, wearily, "This is just aphorisms and jokes, jokes and aphorisms." So? He didn't like it. But I was soon launched on a new paper, on Henry Adams, and it was all education, as Adams liked to say.

Not long after, I ran into Jillian in the basement of the Harvard Book Store, where you could still buy old Anchor paperbacks for fifty cents. She had been in our entryway freshman year, a sweet and optimistic girl from Palo Alto with chestnut-brown hair who had run track in high school and was determined to study English, even though both her parents were doctors. Freshman year, at our many politically correct orientation meetings and at the freshman mixer at which we danced a slow grown-up dance (what a nice place college was, when you think about it), I'd not really noticed Jillian, even Jillian pressed against me: I was too intent on Ferdinand and my classes, I was too intent on my disappointment. Two and a half years later, running into her in the basement, I saw her as if for the first time. She was less optimistic now, and though she was still studying English, she had also begun to accumulate credits for the med school requirement. I proposed dinner in fashionable Adams House. She agreed, and that weekend we also went to a party her friends were throwing in nerdy Quincy House. What a nice place college was, I suddenly realized, even Harvard, if you let it be.

A year later, after graduation, I followed Jillian to Baltimore. She was going to med school, and I—I was going to write. We got a place in yuppie Mount Vernon—my father had just moved down to the Bay, so we got all the old Clarksville stuff—and while Jillian went off to her classes, I sat down and studied the political situation. It was 1998, the impeachment had passed but not without the special prosecutor's special little book, and the President for the next two years was as good as a lame duck, I thought. It was up to Lauren's father now—to begin the equitable redistribution of the new wealth, to fight for labor protection for the subjects of globalization, and, also, to save the earth. The administration had conceded a great deal to the Right, but I knew that Lauren's father would take it all back, if only he knew how many of us there were, there are, who were with him; if only, as I had sometimes felt with Lauren, he could convincingly be reassured. And as I began to submit articles to the liberal magazines in D.C. and New York, I tried, in every word I wrote, to reassure him.

I don't know if it worked—that is to say, obviously it didn't. But if he wasn't reading, others were. I had tapped some kind of vein, and editors responded to the things I sent. Quickly I found some of the bitterness of my Harvard years dissipating, and the rest of it going straight into my prose. Everything I wrote then had a kind of glow—from a spark that I had hoped but did not know was in me—and it returned to me in print, or online (I had so many ideas that I started a blog at one of the liberal magazines), with an alienated majesty. It was a time of online love affairs and paper billionaries—a space of some sort had opened up in the universe, a distortion—and with my belief in my own moral purity, and in the destiny of Lauren's father, I stepped right into it. I was big, for a while there—reading my e-mail each day was like watching a parade. People wrote e-mails of praise, e-mails with offers in them—people asked for advice, over e-mail. Oh, you should have seen my in-box!

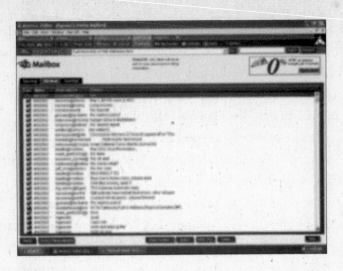

"I always knew this would happen," Jillian said over my shoulder one day as I typed excitedly into the void.

"You did?" I had spent a lot of time wondering. "Why didn't you tell me?"

"I didn't *know* know, I guess. Sorry."

She was very busy with school those first two years, but we still managed nearly every week to visit my father, lonely now in his quasi-beach house, and Jillian helped him furnish it. As for me, I started traveling here and there, especially as the campaign and my career heated up, to Philadelphia (by car) for the convention, to Los Angeles (by plane) for the other convention, and then for dinners, lectures, working lunches, to New York. And there were moments, in all these places, when I felt like maybe, just maybe, I was playing ball.

And as I had to go to these places fairly often, mostly by myself, there were conversations, flirtations, with women. I accepted them, as I accepted all those e-mails, as part of the largesse of the late Clinton years. And one night in New York I stepped out into a hallway—I would have liked to say, a balcony—and a woman, just a few years older than I was, but already established, and impressive, with long straight black hair and a way of dipping her head down when she smiled, looked at me and said, "You can have anything you want." Was she crazy? Maybe she was crazy. But sometimes you are young, and strong, and you believe that because of this you have a right to the things that others have—because look at the mess they've made, and look at how tired they are. The woman said, "You can have anything you want," and on the long drive back to Baltimore I wondered what she meant.

The night of the election Jillian and I stayed home and watched the results come in, and ate fancy pizza, and blogged away. When they called the election for Lauren's father, I asked Jillian to marry me—it was corny, it was psychologically obtuse, but I couldn't think of a better way—and she said, "Yes." She put on the ring I had bought her and added to her acceptance: "Especially now that we'll have an environmental President who'll assure a future for our children." I kissed her.

When they called the election back, we sat there together in disbelief. The diamond dangled on her finger like a fake. "Oh, sweetie," she said, as if I'd disappointed her but she forgave me, and put her arm around my shoulder. But I was in shock, I was aware suddenly of my body, how foreign to me it had become, and Jillian's, as well, now pressed awkwardly against mine, and I wondered what would happen to us. We had become a little strange, living together all by ourselves. Jillian had to get up early for classes; I had to stay up late to write. Perhaps there was another way, but we hadn't found it, and anyway it was easier for us, just then, to be more like siblings than lovers, though we loved each other a lot—and after things settled down we'd work it out, was the idea.

Now it was as if a flood of light had burst into the apartment on St. Paul Street and caught us out. I spent the rest of the night on the old Clarksville three-part couch in the big living room/kitchen area of our wonderful apartment, unable to move. When Jillian came over and told me that Lauren's father was within five hundred votes in Florida, that they had uncalled all the calls, I didn't believe it, and of course I was right. The next day, crowds of maniacs had materialized outside Lauren's house, yelling through loudspeakers for the Vice President to vacate the premises.

And, eventually, he did.

It was almost a full year later that I ran into Lauren and her father on the street, and things with Jillian, by then, were very bad. That night, as I went to some extremely expensive bar on the Upper East Side and drank a pile of beers before settling down, as I suspected I might, to sleep in my car, I wondered how much of everything Lauren still remembered, and whether she thought of it in those strange, distended seconds on Madison Avenue. I knew from Ferdinand that they no longer spoke, but though I had no way of knowing why, I did see at that moment that she was ashamed of me, and I—well, I was ashamed of us. Nothing had gone as we had hoped. We might still recover—I might still make a wonderful career in liberal punditry, she could still rejuvenate the Democratic Party—but the success we'd glimpsed, that we had smelled with our noses, in anticipation of which our hands had trembled, our throats made moaning noises, our hearts swelled, was denied us. We might still make it but it would not be for many years, and we would not be so beautiful as we were, and our teeth would not be so bright—and the country, by then, would be in serious world-historical shit. There was Lauren, who'd been our blond-haired, soft-faced conduit to history—there she was, with a man who would never be President. And there was I, once so serious and so unhappy, holding a cell phone in my hand like a failed investment banker. Life is of course very long, and as I said we all have several lives. But that doesn't make it one long party.

Right of Return

What Sam needed to do, he realized after much thought and much agony and some introspection, was write the great Zionist novel. He needed to disentangle the mess of confusion, misinformation, tribal emotionalism, and political opportunism that characterized the Jewish-American attitude toward Israel.

But first he had to check his e-mail.

No one—neither Jew nor Gentile—had written, and it was back to work.

What would be in the Zionist novel? Zionists, to begin with. Hardened, sun-drenched survivors of the European catastrophe, making the desert bloom. Occasionally firing rifles at the locals. "The bride is beautiful"—his grandmother used to love telling the story of the cable from the 1897 rabbinical delegation to Palestine—"but she is already married to another man!"

Guilt: though Sam's own private guilt would have no place in such a novel, it would hang over its writing like the broken shadow of the Temple Wall. And guilt not for past sins, either: he had enough of those, certainly, especially with regard to the women in his life, but they failed really to gnaw at him. Instead he was repentant for, he felt an intolerable anticipatory guilt in light of, the possibility of future sins. He was capable of great evil, and though he had never actually committed this evil, the very likelihood of his iniquity propelled him into an overbearing virtue. He was always making amends for things he might have considered doing: abandoning Israel was one of those things.

So Samuel Mitnick began his journey with Lomaski, the bad Jew, the race traitor, the author of an extended *anti*-Zionist epic in which the crimes of Israel since 1948 were placed on an enormous chart—845 pages of crimes, more crimes, crimes upon crimes, compounded by crimes. *A Chart for a Charter*, it was called, referring to the U.N. charter, which in Article 80 rubber-stamped the British policy then barreling toward a partition of Palestine into two deeply unviable states, one Arab, the other Jewish.

Lomaski in his office was sweaty, skinny, ill-preserved, drinking tea after tea so that his teeth seemed to yellow while Sam watched. Lomaski was originally a seismologist who'd made a few groundbreaking discoveries in his late twenties before moving on to the comparatively glorious task of protesting American involvement in Vietnam, and then the significantly less glorious task of protesting its involvement everywhere else. Throughout the seventies he had slipped slowly from the pages of prestigious magazines, like a thwarted slug sliding down the bathroom wall in the Mitnicks' summer house, until disappearing entirely into the floorboards in the aftermath of *Chart*. Regarding this malodorous coincidence one commentator remarked that attacking Israel was a poor career move "for those seeking to pursue the contemplative life." It was already widely believed, when Sam came to visit, that

Lomaski had gone mad, observing the humans from underfoot, and indeed like a madman he answered Sam's questions with an air of great amusement, as if Sam too would share a good laugh with him at the other side's expense.

"Israel says: 'We are making peace,'" Lomaski began, sotto voce. "'Look at us, we are signing treaties, secret treaties, open treaties, and we are a textual people, the People of the Book, we do not sign all these treaties lightly.'

"Meanwhile, settlements are being built, contingency plans—also textual, but with pictures, you understand, of Apache helicopters—drawn up, settlements augmented whose express purpose is to render *geographically unthinkable* the possibility of a Palestinian state.

"*Ergo*," summed up Lomaski, "we have something of a logical contradiction: on the one hand peace treaties, on the other hand settlements. Or is it a contradiction? What if you think it's your right to give peace, as well as to build? What if you think, in a vaguely theological way, that whatever happens within the auspices of your military dominion is part of your general plan? Then there's no logical contradiction. It makes perfect sense.

"The fact is," Lomaski concluded, "there almost never *is* a logical contradiction, given certain premises. You just have to find the premises."

"I do?" Sam asked.

He had grown a little lax, in his exercising, but sitting in Lomaski's office in jeans and an Abercrombie button-down that hung off his neck, Sam still resembled an athlete—for he had once been an athlete, a great Jewish athlete. Now he wondered whether this strange man, in his little lair, was giving him life advice.

Sam smiled politely. "I have to find them?" he asked, about the premises.

"No," said Lomaski. "*One* has to find them. We all do. Of course," he added, considering it, "I already have."

* * *

Sam left Lomaski's office and emerged, still young, into the Cambridge midday. The geniuses were at work—or the genii, as Orwell called them. He walked contemplatively for a while along the river as the cars sped past him on Memorial Drive. Across the way, a few gold cupolas sparkled on Beacon Hill. Perhaps if he wrote an epic, if he was paid for his epic, he and Talia could buy an apartment there. Is that what he wanted? A one-state solution, he sometimes thought, a Jewish-Arab democracy, was the only way. But owning an apartment would also be nice.

He wanted to write the great Zionist epic, full of Jewish women— why, he'd use the women he'd known, the women he'd loved, they would fill his epic with their laughter.

His friend Aron said to him: "You can't write this. You are not the man."

"Who is the man, then? Point him out."

"Well," said Aron, "for one thing, Leon Uris, for example"—he paused—"has already written a Zionist epic."

"He has?" Sam was crestfallen.

"It's not very good," Aron admitted.

"Really?"

"In fact it's cheap and sentimental," Aron went on.

"See?" Sam said, triumphant.

"See what?" Aron asked, but Sam could no longer hear him.

Others told him the Zionist epic was already under way.

"Every day that Israel thrives, that it exists, this is another chapter," Talia told him. She was Israeli. "There are over nineteen thousand chapters. It is a long book."

"Talia, darling, you don't understand publishing," Sam said. "New York is not Haifa. Such a book will never attract readers."

"It's already found six million readers. They read it every day they live there. It is a very popular book."

"You are giving me a headache with these metaphors."

Talia stood up. They were in the kitchen of Sam's apartment on Cambridge Street, in unlovely East Cambridge. Talia was in her coat, on her way out, when they'd begun this argument; Sam had been washing dishes while she prepared to go and stood now in his black NEWTON FREE PUBLIC LIBRARY apron. He used to walk Talia downstairs, but recently this seemed an excessive gesture, her spending so much time here, he couldn't just walk up and down the stairs all his life. Her coat was wool and pea-colored, a peacoat, and with her rich olive coloring, her dark black hair, her strong arms and hips underneath the coat, she looked fantastically *Israeli*, arguing with him. Maybe she was right about everything? She said, "Have you seen my yellow scarf?"

"I don't think so."

"I need it."

"OK," said Sam. He found it quickly, he had a knack for this sort of thing, underneath a hat on Talia's side of his little home office.

"Thank you," said Talia, wrapping the scarf around her neck, then stopping and turning back toward him from the doorway. "You do not love the *land* enough," she said. Her black hair shone in the pale hallway light. "You are not enough of a Zionist to write a Zionist epic."

He returned to the dishes; a minute later his phone rang. It was Talia calling from the bus stop across the street. "Anyway, Sam," she said. Her slight accent flattened the *a* in his name to make it more like *Sem*. He hated that. When they were getting along she used a pet name; when they fought, it was *Sem*. "Sem," she said now, "you can't even read Hebrew."

"I know," he admitted. "I feel terrible."

His parents had been radical secularists, followers of Lomaski, who'd neglected his religious and spiritual training. When Sam finally got around to Hebrew without them, the letters looked like Tetris pieces. They piled against one another as if asking for someone to collect them into the least possible space, to fit their protrusions into their cavities. He was happy to do this, of course, but it was not reading.

His ex-girlfriend Arielle was more generous. "Really?" she said when he told her. "*That's* ambitious."

All the women in Sam's life italicized things.

But then Arielle was his ex-girlfriend. She inspired complicated emotions in a way his current girlfriend did not. Talia was a long-term endeavor. They practically lived together, though they kept separate apartments, and they had merged their wardrobes if not yet their libraries. They did not say to each other, in the course of a day, fifty words. Talia was a strategic, a territorial, problem: where would Sam be when she was at Spot A; what was Talia's current liquidity, and did he need to withdraw cash; where was her silver hair clip? Talia had weaknesses, aspirations, well-mapped idiosyncrasies. He would, perhaps, spend the rest of his life with her; that is, if he played his cards correctly, and she also played correctly; there were complications, corrections, concessions.

But Arielle, his former girlfriend, was an existential question, an event of the heart. What was that feeling he experienced when he heard her voice? And was it wrong to see her? She was a separate woman being, whose fate and finances had diverged from his, whose problems were her own to resolve. Yet she had called him, after months of not-speaking, with accusations and recriminations.

"I cannot believe I ever loved anyone," she said, "who was so cruel.

"Everything you ever told me was a lie," she went on. "It was a line."

She repeated some of them now. They were good lines.

"Where are you?" Sam asked, for there was an echoing on the other end.

"Calvary-in-the-Fields."

"What's that?"

"A sanatorium."

He drove up the next afternoon. She had been very depressed and angry, she said, after the Republicans took the White House, but she'd finally checked herself in after breaking her television set during the inauguration. It was still early in the Bush years, and her health insurance was paying in full.

During the drive he considered casting his epic in the form of a dialogue/interview with the state of Israel.

Q: When did you first think you would become independent?

STATE OF ISRAEL: There was the Balfour Declaration, of course, and the compromise on the Mandate. But I didn't consider myself a true nation-state—and what independence can there be, Sam, if you're not a nation-state?—until we took back the Temple Mount in '67. That was something.

The sanatorium itself was charming, a group of cabins in the woods, a place for overworked urbanites to feel pleasantly melancholic. A slackertorium. Its chief promise, its chief premise, was a regimen of well-regulated sleep.

Pulling into the visitors' lot, the sharp angle of his space a neat contrast to the imminent clumsiness of his self-introduction to the receptionist, Sam wondered why he was still within acceptable phone range of a girl, a woman now, from whom he'd supposedly parted five years before. It was his own fault. He could never let things go. Forgetting, according to Nietzsche, was strength, and they lived in a country where amnesia was peddled like corn futures. Even the Israelis were becoming forgetful. It was the Palestinians who seemed to remember everything—the Palestinians and Sam. And now Arielle. Perhaps she'd begun to do excavation work in her mind when a big undigested clump had emerged, like a baby, looking just like him.

They had dinner at a small, upscale pizzeria down the road. You could tell it had been an ordinary pizza shop once, with the linoleum tabletops, until the rich people started going crazy, or sort of crazy, and arriving at the sanatorium nearby. Therefore Sam was confident, given the pizzeria's usual clientele, that the beautiful young waitress—there must have been a college nearby, in addition to a sanatorium—would be able to distinguish the civilian Sam from his crazy ex-girlfriend; nonetheless he couldn't help producing a series of gestures throughout dinner to indicate his companion's dubious state of mental health, just in case, with the unhappy result that the waitress avoided his side of the table entirely.

"They call it psychodrama?" Arielle was telling him about her therapy. "You beat on a pillow or like a padded tube and pretend that it's your father or your sister or whoever fucked you up."

"Or me?" Sam guessed.

"Yes! I've been beating you up in absentia for two weeks now.

And then I figured, why not get the man himself up here?" She smiled—she was a little tired, of course, but still straight-toothed and well-scrubbed and pretty. As promised, over lasagna, she maligned his past behavior. It wasn't nice—his past behavior—and he was sorry about it, but in the end, if he were to give a general summary, it mostly involved not returning enough phone calls. They both grew bored of this, finally, and that's when Sam told Arielle about the Zionist epic.

"Wow," she said. "But what about all the other things you wanted to do? Teaching? And organizing? Is this really what you want to be doing?"

To recap thus far:

- Current girlfriend: Where did you put the red umbrella?
- Ex-girlfriend: Who are you now? Whoever you are, are you happy?

Was he a small-souled coward, not simply to have two girlfriends?

"It just seems," she was saying, "so . . . endless. So serious. There's still so much fun to be had, after all."

Oh. Ah. That was the Arielle touch, her temptation. Her hair was back in a ponytail, and she wore faded blue jeans and a long wool sweater, the official uniform of the mildly insane. Even in her breakdown she was perfectly conventional, a lifetime of television compressed into a few perfect gestures, and nothing could have been more devastating for a man whose life was as strange and unlikely as Sam's, who had begun so badly to lose his way among the many desires he was supposed to desire. He loved conventional women, he loved Arielle, he loved that she knew he hated the word *fun* ("That's when I reach for my revolver," his friend

Mark used to say of the word *fun*), and used it to tease him and remind him that she knew. The waitress came over to refresh their wineglasses, describing as she did so a careful arc around crazy Sam, and, amazingly, *he did not care*. Would this have been the joy—what was the line?—he'd enjoy every day of his life?

"What fun?" he gasped. "The epic will be my martyrdom."

She smiled again, as if she might just ruffle his hair. "That's what you've always wanted, right?"

And with this the nostalgic wheels began to turn again, old facts remembered, a few perfunctory recriminations hurled. They laughed and drank. Part of it was that Sam had a certain relation to time, perhaps even a theory of history: he did not believe, theoretically or functionally, in deadlines or dates. For the author of a Zionist epic this was not without its problems; for a man, an ex-boyfriend, it was disastrous. His relationships and then his breakups were characterized by backsliding, second thoughts. He kept in touch with old girlfriends, former teachers, anyone whose e-mail address he'd figured out. He and Arielle drifted in an altered space that allowed them, occasionally, to come close enough that their lips grazed, their hands intertwined, and their tenderness settled on them with a pleasant buzz—to depart shortly thereafter, their inner beings only slightly unsettled. This was apparently another such time, for at the end of the evening they went back to her cabin and slept together.

Strange, then—was he growing older?—but upon returning home Sam found the experience with Arielle had misaligned his soul more than usual. A disturbance of some sort had taken place in the universe. He slept at his bare home for the next week, pleading tiredness and overwork to Talia and generally exercising caution in his physical movements. He wondered whether he had done right. Was it a trial of some sort, and had he failed? Was it part of the Zionist epic? Who knew? Not Sam. He knew so very little. He had forebodings and predictions, to be sure, and these often found, with an adjustment for spiritual inflation, factual confirmation in the future. He knew what was going to happen with Arielle, for example, and he knew that he would eventually tell Talia, and what would happen then. He knew that the landlord would add $150 to his rent in the fall without fixing the drip that was ruining his bedroom floor, and he knew that eventually one of the companies or schools for which he now performed part-time work would offer him a permanent place, and that eventually he would accept. And he knew as well that he was a child compared to these various forces, and would not have the tenacity to reckon with them—not because he lacked courage, really, but because he hadn't the certainty of his right. He didn't know Hebrew and he didn't, *really,* love Israel, *eretz y'Israel,* and though he loved the Jews, and he loved Arielle and Talia, perhaps there were people more qualified to love them? And better informed? He just wasn't quite sure, Sam was never quite sure, that he was doing as he ought.

And he lost arguments, lost them with regularity and consistency, found ten thousand ways to lose them the way a streaking baseball team will find, in the late autumn crunch, ten thousand ways to win. As the already much-rumored author of a Zionist epic, he was often called upon to argue; and, guilt-ridden as he was, he felt it necessary to oblige. More than that: at parties to which his Zionist reputation had failed to precede him, he was like a man stumbling violently about a bar just before closing time, looking for trouble. As soon as conversation inched however imperceptibly toward the Middle East, Sam would pounce.

And lose. Though skilled in debate, he reserved too much respect for his antagonists' moral fervor, for their loud-mouthed certainty. He felt invariably like a journalist, making the precise, well-mannered objections that would set his opponent off on tirades of great passion, and then into insults, interjections, aperçus. Also, despite numerous prep sessions with Talia, Sam was a little shaky on the facts.

"What about 1948?" he said to his friend Aron, like Talia an Israeli émigré.

"There was some violence," Aron admitted, small-voiced and careful, a graduate student in his tenth year, a doubter of his own doubts. "In some of the villages there was violence, and where the Irgun was operating there were massacres. In a few towns on the road between Tel Aviv and Jerusalem, Yitzhak Rabin himself evacuated people. But the U.N. partition plan was completely ridiculous, and these people had sworn to destroy Israel.

"In any case," Aron went on, "now we are proposing to give it back. Barak offered ninety-four percent of the West Bank and three percent in other places. He offered to divide Jerusalem. They refused. They demanded a right of 'return' for four million residents—not to their future homeland, but to Israel. They began to fire Kalashnikovs and detonate grenades. Why?"

"Because they've been under military occupation for thirty years? They're angry?"

"OK, OK, I understand. Look. If we're talking about Galilee, even a bit of the Negev, I say fine, have a slice here, have one there. Arab population, Arab land, I think that's fair. But not Jerusalem. You cannot divide Jerusalem. You cannot give them the Temple Mount, you cannot give them the Western Wall of the Second Temple after the plundering and vandalism that took place under the Jordanians. Jews were not allowed to pray there until we conquered it by force of arms! So if we're talking about the territories, please, you think we want them? But if it's Jerusalem they're after, then I say we must meet force with force. *If the Palestinians have embarked upon this war to see what they can get, they must emerge from it knowing that they will get nothing. If they want Jerusalem, then I say fight."*

With the suggestion, not altogether subtle, not altogether muffled, that Aron himself would fight. The same Aron who, rather than confront the student with whom he shared a library carrel for not arranging his books neatly, had requested a different carrel—this Aron would hire a taxi to the airport, board a plane, and emerge in Tel Aviv. What on earth could Sam say against that?

This was a week before he met Arielle for dinner at the Indian place in Inman Square, she having released herself from Calvary with a clean bill of health. "OK on the territories," he said when they also began to argue. "Let the Syrians place their guns on the Golan, let the Egyptians supply mortars to Gaza. But we can't give up Jerusalem."

"Not give up Jerusalem? To whom not give it up? To the people who live there? What on earth are you talking about?"

"Well, you know, the Old City. The Temple Mount."

"Al-Aqsa? Is that what you mean? You think that's just a cynical slogan, the 'al-Aqsa Intifada'? A brand name? Not as holy as our Wall is holy? You think they're not willing to die for their al-Aqsa? You better believe they are. And part of the reason for that, of course, is that they're desperate, that a brutal military occupation makes people fucking crazy."

She was furious with him, as if, here in the upstairs seating area of the Indian place in Inman, lawyers and students rushing in and out with their six-dollar dinners, he had finally unmasked himself—as if, having known him so long, having even, perhaps, loved him so long, she had never suspected what a shallow, despicable creature he would at last turn out to be.

Before her eyes could adjust to this new Sam, he called out: "All right, East Jerusalem, they can have East Jerusalem! So long," he added, though not so quickly that his concession would lose its force, "as the Temple Mount remains under an international mandate. A shared zone."

"Well, obviously. Of course."

"OK." He smiled—a pained, humiliated smile, a grimace. He had never even been to Israel; all his hypothetical concessions came from him as easily as water sliding off a rock. It was the hundredth time in the past month that he had given up East Jerusalem.

Arielle tore off a chunk of naan. She looked good.

"Talia," he said as they were getting into bed at her place, shortly before the prime ministerial election, "I think Sharon is dangerous."

"Do you?" she shot back. "I also think he's dangerous, actually. Dangerous to those who would threaten the security of our people. That's right, our people. Or have you stopped being Jewish, the better to look down from above for your *epic*?"

In the darkness, Sam clenched up.

"Because, you know, this is what I expect to hear from Arabs. It's not what I expect to hear, not what I ever expected to hear from one of my own people. Because they would kill you, you understand that? They would kill you without thinking twice about it, they would dip their hands in your Jewish blood and for them it would be a great orgasmic pleasure. Do you understand that?"

"A Jew can kill a Jew."

"But he won't do it because the other is a Jew! Look. Sem. We offered them the West Bank. We offered them Jerusalem. Jerusalem! They refused. Now they'll get something else from us, you understand? They'll get the fist. *And they will never have Jerusalem.*"

She turned over on her side and squeezed herself into a tiny ball.

"Whoever said anything"—Sam grumbled as he put on his clothes—"about Jerusalem?"

He made a great deal of noise leaving her apartment, but no one tried to stop him.

Frightened, angry, vengeful, the Israelis elected Sharon. Intifada II continued, however, and for all the Marx-quoting Sam liked to do, it was nothing like a farce. He soldiered on in the libraries and coffeehouses, beating forth ceaselessly, here and there, against the tide. After receiving, in the wake of many laudatory lunches, a small advance from a publisher to work on his epic, he quit his many jobs and made even less progress than before. One morning he spent two and a half hours searching for Talia's sunglasses—they had been, it turned out, in her purse.

That day, sitting in cave-like Cafe 1369, hunched with the other patrons over his notebook, all of them in the darkness like a poor-postured group of shtetl scholars, Sam gave up hope. Israel was too complicated; life was too complicated. If he had once believed he could bring his women to the bargaining table, get them to listen to reason, sign on to some kind of accord, it was increasingly clear that nothing of the sort would occur. Talia was fiery, brilliant—and from another country. She wanted to make a Jewish home, that is to say a secular Jewish home, with Sam, here in Cambridge; she wanted to make Jewish children with Sam. Whereas Arielle wanted more and wanted less: she wanted a life of excitement, witticisms, put-downs, quasi-psychoanalytic late-night discussions, then make-up sex—and no children. Children would slow her down. Meanwhile, politically—politically Talia was moving right and Arielle was moving left and, if you added it up, they were all moving toward disaster. *Al-naqba.* Sam straightened his back and looked around. Everyone in Cafe 1369 seemed to be writing poetry and having a lovely time. Even if in fact they worked on financial reports, initial public offerings, quarterly earnings statements, they enjoyed this, and what is more they had, unlike his medium black coffee, interesting drinks. Mocha chai lattes, caramel macchiatos, espresso con pannas. In any case, before launching his Zionist epic he would have to decide what he thought of the Holocaust.

What he thought? Well, it was a bad thing, naturally. A moral and spiritual catastrophe like nothing that had ever preceded it? Yup. A window into a realm so inhuman, with certain standard automated functions—trains, vans, showers, ovens—abused so hideously as to have brought the whole project of modernity into question? Certainly. An action so monstrous that, if it cannot be called religious, is nonetheless such in the precise degree to which the hand of God was absent? *You bet your ass!*

He looked around the cafe—no one was staring at him. He had not uttered anything aloud.

But beyond that? Was the awful scale of the killing, and the ethnic identity of its victims, part of the post-Holocaust world? Should it be remembered and invoked at all times, in all places— was it really paradigmatic in some profound way? A mile and a half from where Sam now sat they had constructed, in the center of historical Boston, a memorial to the millions dead. Of all the places to remember them; of all the Bostonian history to com- memorate at that spot. It made no sense unless you thought it was some kind of *justification.* For a hack like Uris (Sam had been reading up), the events of the forties flowed together like a Sab- bath meal: the Holocaust was cause, Israel effect; a mortal danger existed in the Diaspora, as evidenced by Auschwitz; and the six million Jews stood on a scale—or was it, more physically plausible, just their ashes?—on which scale's other half were weighed the fact of Israel and All That It Had to Do.

"Fuck that!" Sam cried, and now people looked. He gave them all a shrug and bent again over his notebook. So Sam was not with the Urisites; the Holocaust happened under unique and terrible historical conditions, no longer ours. The Polish branch of the Mitnick family had been entirely wiped out in it—in the Bialystok ghetto, in the Warsaw ghetto, at Majdanek. *But a lot of things had happened since then,* including several generations of Mitnicks—including, even, Sam.

He would have to formulate this, somehow, without pissing off the ADL. While trying to sell a Zionist epic, the last thing on earth you wanted was the ADL on your back.

Refreshed by his summation of the Holocaust, Sam decided to put the rest of his life in order. He felt the need to expand. Into Jordan, Lebanon, the Sinai. This body, this Boston, could not hold all of him, could not contain the bustling, bursting energies. He had two women, he loved them both, and he could not, would not, imagine it otherwise. He was just twenty-five years old; he had strength in him, and courage. At twenty-five Israel was invaded on the Day of Atonement, on Yom Kippur, from the east by Syria, from the west by Egypt. Caught off guard, it nonetheless repulsed the invaders and had crossed the Suez when the United Nations finally intervened. It was only at thirty-four that Israel invaded Lebanon, watched gloatingly as its nasty friends the Phalangists slaughtered the Palestinian refugees at Sabra and Shatila, and ceased forever to be a light unto the nations, though hundreds of thousands flooded the streets, Israelis the only people on the planet to protest in such number the massacre of their enemies.

So he would set in motion processes, gradual processes, of reconciliation. Tonight he would stay with dark-eyed Talia, tomorrow he would stay at home, and then the next night he would see Arielle. He called Arielle from the cafe to tell her about this.

"Why are you calling?" she wanted to know.

"I'd like to see you."

"OK," she said, as if it were a challenge. "Come over."

"No, not now. Friday."

"You said you wanted to see me."

"That's not what I meant."

"What *did* you mean?"

And he began to do the calculations, count the permutations. Her italics! Her sarcasm! But he could not tell her what he meant. What did he mean?

"Sam," she said, clearly exasperated. "We can't go on like this. We cannot! I will not play along anymore, I will not be the other woman in this."

"You make it sound so tawdry."

"It *is* tawdry. It's unbelievably tawdry and conventional."

"No," he said. "No." And he meant it. This was serious. If she hung up—if he lost this argument—that would be it. He would lose her, here on this telephone, in the back of Cafe 1369; he would be all alone.

"Look," he began again. "What you're saying is reasonable, I see the logic, but it's just not *true*. Look at Israel. I mean, we're supposed to be with one person, right, we're supposed to sit at home and believe in our tiny little life with that person, we're supposed to just stay within our boundaries. But look at Israel—it's the only country on earth whose borders are unrecognized by international law, whose borders are always changing."

"A lot of good it's done them."

"But at least they feel alive!"

There was a silence on the other end. The metaphor, like a cease-fire, had collapsed more quickly than he'd hoped.

"I'm telling Talia," she said finally.

"No," he laughed. "No, no. You can't do that."

"I'm going to do it. She's a right-wing loony but she deserves to know."

"No, but, you can't do that."

"I can't?" And she began to upbraid him. While he dutifully fed coins to the extortionary Massachusetts pay phone, Arielle read, Lomaski-like, from the great chronology of his crimes. It must have been hanging, in large block letters, somewhere near her phone. What a woman! She wanted a final settlement, and if she did not have it she would drive him into the sea. It was land for peace—he gave up his moral land, his settlements on the territories of her conscience, allowed her the last word on everything, and she, in theory, would absolve and release and not tell Talia. He could promise her this. That was the thing to do; that was what men did. They promised and promised, and when it emerged that they'd been building settlements and buying arms all the while, they made incredulous faces and promised some more. That was what men did! But Sam could not. The moment demanded large mendacious strokes—but he was a peacenik, it turned out. The Israelis had an unpleasant word for that, probably.

He picked up the thread of the list: he had failed to e-mail congratulations on her graduation; drunk, he had tried to kiss her at a party though he knew she had a serious boyfriend; they were only up to 1997! She was reducing him to rubble, and he was letting her.

"Sam," she said, serious now in a way that boded ill. "I cannot have this in my life. I can't have this uncertainty. I mean, when will it end? Where?"

"Why?" Sam asked, knowing before he did so that it was the wrong line. Helpless Sam. "Why does it have to end?"

And so it was over, again. He lay in bed for three days, tasting the residue of her voice in his throat as if, through some transference of force, he had spoken with it himself. He was getting to be a certain age, he thought. It was the age when his never-to-be-written masterpieces had begun to outweigh the masterpieces he was still going to write. The Zionist epic belonged in the latter category, certainly, but it was creeping, dangerously creeping, toward the former. He had already spent the advance a hundred times. And he could see the future. In the future, Arielle got married. Talia got married. Neither of them married Sam, who was left alone, with slightly less hair on top than when this story began, sitting in a small academic office, sweaty and tea-stained, galloping his mare at the *New York Times*.

When Israel declared statehood in 1948, precipitating thereby the first of five regional wars, Sam's grandmother sent a telegram from Moscow to the representative office of the Yishuv in Warsaw, the capital of her former country. Just months earlier the great Yiddish actor Solomon Mikhoels had been murdered by the NKVD, which ran a truck over him several times to make certain he was dead. "They killed him like a dog," Khrushchev would later say. The Mikhoels murder was Stalin's preface to a mass expulsion of the country's Jews into the deep Asian provinces (for their protection), and people were beginning to lose their jobs. Nonetheless, Sara Mitnick's telegram read: CONGRATULATIONS ON YOUR INDEPENDENCE. *L'SHANA HABA'A B'YERUSHALAYIM!* Next year in Jerusalem. She would later learn that she'd been the only private citizen in the Soviet Union to wire greetings. It took her many, many years to reach Jerusalem.

When Israelis elected Ehud Barak on a platform of peace in 1999, Sam had sent an e-mail from work to his cousin Witold, who lived in Jerusalem and was the brother of his other cousin, Walech, who lived in New Jersey. Despite the fact that all outgoing e-mails were monitored by his employer with the use of keyword surveillance technology, Sam wrote: DEAR WITOLD! HAIL TO THE PEACE! CONGRATULATIONS CONGRATULATIONS CONGRATULATIONS. And added: *L'SHANA HABA'A B'YERUSHALAYIM.*

On the day the World Trade Center was destroyed, Sam watched a lot of television. When television went into a loop, he resorted to the Internet. Another of his cousins, a well-known journalist, filed four different articles with four different journals of opinion, each of them describing his walk down a different New York street. There was an unseemly outpouring of poetry; the radio quoted a few lines about New York by the fascist poet Ezra Pound—though not ones in which he called it, as he often did, "Jew York." Talia, when she wasn't crying, could hardly be kept from gloating. "Now they'll know what it's like to live the way we live," she said. "They'll know what the Arabs are about."

Sure enough, that evening at www.JerusalemPost.com came the headline:

(17:55) Israel evacuates embassies, Palestinians celebrate

It is exactly a year after the breakdown of the Oslo Accords, just a little under a year after the beginning of the new Intifada. It is immediately assumed that some group with ties to the Palestinians—of blood, or politics, or sympathy—is involved. And the Palestinians go out into the streets, before the AP cameras, and cheer. Sam had to hand it to them—every time it appeared that the international community was beginning to lose patience with the interminable occupation of the West Bank, with the hopelessly stupid Israeli attempts at creating peace by waging war, with the tanks and the settlements and the prevarication, these folks went out into the streets and cheered the murder of people no less innocent than themselves. No, thought Sam, you really had to hand it to the Palestinians. In their ability to fuck up a late lead they were truly the equals of the Boston Red Sox.

Aron was on the phone. "How do you fight a country that isn't even a country?" he wondered of the Palestinians. "Maybe we should make them a country. That's what they want, right? Good, you're a country. Now we're going to bomb the shit out of you."

Next up was Sam's literary agent, who'd sold his epic for a modest sum. "Are you OK?" he began by asking. "Is it an OK time to call?"

"It's fine," said Sam. Already he could summon no enthusiasm for these national days of grief; if the business of America was business, it may as well be gotten on with.

"Then listen to this," his agent said, crinkling a copy of the liberal weekly *New American* in the background. "*We Americans no longer need any instructions in how it feels to be an Israeli. The murderers in the skies have taught us all too well. We are all Israelis now.* We are all Israelis now! He might as well have said we are all *Zionists* now. This really ratchets up the stakes here, man. We suddenly have three hundred million more readers. Three hundred million!"

They hung up. The television trundled on. "America is changed forever," the newscasters kept saying, the experts interviewed repeating it as if that was the price, these days, for getting on TV. Sam did not want to laugh but, a little bit, he laughed. Nothing ever changes, he thought. No one ever changes. Things are destroyed and things are created: people can die, they can disappear from your life forever, so that a horrible gaseous hole seems to have been burned in the place where they once stood; and it is even possible that an epic, a Zionist epic, might be written, might be finished. But change? Change does not happen. And next year in Jerusalem, or next year in New York, will always be an infinite distance away.

This is what Sam thought.

And just then Arielle rang the doorbell. His Arielle! And with tears in her eyes, shining, she hugged Sam, handsome Sam, and then Talia, lithe lovely Talia. And the three of them sat there, watching the television repeat itself—AMERICA UNDER ATTACK was the caption to the newscasts, and this caption was pierced by an eruption of bullets—their arms around one another until they grew tired, and then, sitting there, fell asleep. At some point Sam woke up and stumbled into the bedroom to sleep some more. He woke again later in the night, alone in the bed, hearing a familiar, sardonic voice on the television. "To pretend like we're surprised by this?" it said. "To pretend as if we haven't done worse? It's laughable. Three years ago we sent cruise missiles to destroy a medicine factory in the Sudan. The U.N. has been trying to investigate it, but the U.S. is intent on keeping—"

"Professor Lomaski, I'm afraid we're running out of time. Isn't it true that you once defended the murderous Khmer Rouge?"

"Are we really—"

"Thanks, Professor. That was Professor Lomaski, speaking to us from MIT, though frankly it could have been Mars for all I understood of what he said. You, Joe?"

"That's a fact, Jim. Didn't understand a word."

The TV was violently silenced. Dozing off again, Sam heard Talia and Arielle begin to argue the Zionist project, their voices rising and falling against his scattered bulk like the sirens out on Cambridge Street. Their meeting, their inevitable meeting, failed to stir him to fear. All they needed was to talk, to find common points of understanding, to rehearse the obvious—and while they talked Sam would sleep, tired Sam, our friend Sam, Sam of the passions, who only wanted to kiss the throats of women, and who only wanted peace.

But he could not fall asleep.

Isaac Babel

In the summer of 1996, after my sophomore year of college, I found myself back in Maryland, with no money in my pocket and no job to speak of. Around early May of that year it had emerged that all my friends were going off to make connections and fetch coffee at NASA and the NASDAQ, and that I was too late. So I returned to my father's house and moped around and signed up, finally, at the student employment agency at Johns Hopkins, which sent students out on odd jobs—mostly, as it turned out, moving furniture.

I was good at this. I was a natural geometrist, calculating the angles of couches and desks and mattresses against doors, stairs, and cars. I was still lifting weights despite no longer playing football, and had enormous forearms and no neck. That summer I could bench-press 285 pounds.

My father was often away then, on business, or with his new girlfriend, or maybe, just, who knows where, and also my house was in a less-nice part of Clarksville than most of my friends' houses, and so it became the house that if anyone happened to be around, it's where they would go. Dave and Josh Quigley, my best friends from high school, came in and out, though they had jobs that summer. Amy Gould, my sort-of ex-girlfriend, would come by, and so would her friend Amanda. But above all that summer there was Ali Dehestani, a big Iranian boy who'd played offensive tackle on our high school team, and his tyrannically strict curfew, the enforcement of which was entrusted by his parents to their killer dog. If he came home past ten, said Ali, the dog would simply tear his throat out—which was odd, after all the dog must have known Ali. But we didn't ask. The point was that he was often at my house past curfew, so he was forced to stay at my house, on the couch in the living room, an infamous three-part couch that slid apart as you lay on it, so that sometimes, when I came downstairs in the morning after a night of drinking, Ali would be sleeping on the floor, the couch in a terrible state beside him.

On the other hand he would often drive me into Baltimore and drop me off, so I wouldn't have to deal with the meters and could concentrate on my work. Ali himself was working for his uncle's rug-cleaning company and apparently his uncle wasn't too particular about his hours.

That summer I relocated lawyers from Mount Vernon to Fells Point; hippies from pretty Charles Village to boring Towson; a professor's desk from the graduate poli sci department to the undergraduate poli sci department across the street. I abetted gentrification, such as it was; the invisible hand of the market, redistributing the choicest properties as they became more choice and pushing those who couldn't hack it to the peripheries, was actually my hand, my two strong hands, carrying the antique armchairs of the upwardly mobile and the heavy fold-out couches of those who were falling behind. I moved a doctor couple to their new house in burgeoning—Clarksville! I moved a group of beautiful undergraduates, with long soft sleek hair, from an off-campus apartment on Calvert Street to one on St. Paul. We had some friends in common but somehow the conversation stalled; it was a hot day and I was sweating through my baseball hat and even through my weight belt, which I wore to protect my back while carrying people's stuff. At the end of such days I'd sneak into the Hopkins gym to work out and shower. Afterward I'd sit in the lobby and try to read the unread books that had piled up during the semester, as well as, more often, copies of the *New American* and *Debate*. It was a nice time, though the work was hard and the money was bad, and I had no idea, really no idea, what would become of me in the years ahead. My college career had been, so far, disappointing; I was still drinking too much and giving up on people too quickly; I kept waiting for someone to tell me what they thought I should do, should be, what particular fate I, in particular, was fated for. It was the last summer that I hung out with my high school friends, and it was the last time I'd ever feel that strange, expectant, hopeful, pleading way.

Halfway through the summer the girl from the employment office called to offer me a different job. A group of high school kids in Glenwood was preparing for the August SAT and needed a tutor. I'd done well on the test itself, really very well, and tutoring paid much better than moving, and I'd be able to drive there and park. "You'd mostly just sit there while they took practice tests," the girl told me. "It's a nice gig."

I turned her down. Even then, I knew: better to carry couches, sweat through my shirt, be dropped off by a hungover, unshaved Ali Dehestani (who was losing his hair), better to remove the doors from their hinges and see people's squalid, empty lives—emptied out of their apartments by me—than dress in khakis and tuck in my shirt and hang out with a bunch of snots. Even then, I knew.

A week later I had my reward. The student employment office asked me to move Morris Binkel.

Insofar as I had a hero, Morris Binkel was my hero. Until that semester I'd been a reader exclusively of books, though I knew that some kind of action, some kind of movement, was going on in the intellectual magazines. But there were so many! Toward the end of my sophomore year I'd begun to wander over to the periodicals section of Lamont Library to look. I made my way through the magazines blindly, knowing only their historic incarnations—Emerson and James had published in the *Atlantic*, Mark Twain in *Harper's*, Nabokov and Salinger and Cheever, of course, in the *New Yorker*.

Most of these places had declined or changed—they were not for me, just then—but Morris Binkel's articles in the *New American* were a different story. His mind was ablaze. It was his belief that American culture was corrupt; that it was filled with phonies, charlatans, morons, and rich people. Also their dupes. Binkel called for a renewal of an adversary culture—the young writers of today, said Binkel, were social climbers, timid and weak; they stood around at parties in New York waiting to be noticed, waiting to be liked. He reserved his especial scorn for his own people, for young Jewish writers, who had once been the bravest and the most outrageous, and now were the most timid, the most polished, kowtowing to their elders' ideas of orthodoxy and demeanor. (None of them, I read between the furious lines of Binkel, could lift a couch in a Mount Vernon apartment and toss it in the back of a U-Haul truck.) No one spoke anymore from the heart, said Binkel, and it was a shame.

Well. Now. *This* was it. Oh, it spoke to me. And it made me feel that should I ever meet Morris Binkel, he'd know right away how different I was. Every time I was faced with a decision, I had begun to think, quietly but nonetheless with some insistence, of what Binkel would say, whether he'd approve, whether he'd call me out. His byline that year said he was a visiting professor at Hopkins, and I sometimes wondered vaguely if I might run into him when I went home for the summer. Some of my professors at Harvard wrote for the *New American,* and I could probably have asked them for an introduction—but that wasn't the sort of thing I knew how to do as a young man, though I'd certainly read about it in books.

So when the beefy man who met me at his apartment in Hampden Village, taller than me, with a wry smile on his face, introduced himself as Morris Binkel, I blurted, surprised at my vehemence: "I'm your biggest fan!"

"Then it's a pleasure to meet you," said Binkel, and, smiling, shook my hand.

He had a big pockmarked but lively, intelligent face, with small eyes, and he had big hands, and he wore a sport coat, like a grownup. When he smiled I saw his small, poor teeth, but he was, any way you looked at it, an impressive figure, an imposing guy, and not the sort I'd been used to moving all summer. His apartment was filled with books. Binkel's books: I ran my eyes over them. They were all the books I'd been having trouble getting at the library, even Hilles Library, which usually had all the books—he had Foucault, Bourdieu, Gramsci; he had Jameson. I'd never seen such a thing, in someone's actual house. My parents had many, many books—the first argument I ever saw between them was over whether to take more books to America. My mother said yes, my father said no, they fought bitterly and she won. (The second big fight was about moving to Maryland; my father took that one.) They brought the complete works of Dostoyevsky, and Tolstoy, and Pushkin, Chekhov, Gorky, everyone. They even brought the world classics in Russian translation—Balzac, Stendhal, Sir

Walter Scott. These books were on shelves in the hallway, in my father's office, in my room, in the small upstairs hallway, in the basement. But they were all in Russian, a language that I could read only very slowly. They were mostly in my way, those books.

Whereas Morris's books—not only were they in English, they weren't even originally in English. They'd been *translated* into it. Pink, green, black, red—they were beautiful books.

Morris watched me study them. He asked me where I went to school, asked about my major, and when he learned I knew Russian, he grew excited.

"Keith?" he said.

"It's Kostya, actually. Konstantin. My parents thought it sounded too Russian."

"Ah."

He was moving back to New York, he told me, to work on a short biography of the writer Isaac Babel. He would need someone to look over some Russian text for him. "It's either that or learn Russian. And I'm not Edmund Wilson." I smiled—I caught the allusion to Wilson's voracious reading in many languages in his composition of *To the Finland Station*; it was the last allusion I would catch from Morris—and said I'd be happy to help.

"Then you can help me with something else, too," said Morris, "since you're my biggest fan. I'm moving this weekend, and your agency probably takes—how much do they pay you an hour for this?"

"Eight dollars."

"Right, and they charge me twenty. Ideally I need someone for an entire weekend—forty-eight hours, more or less. So how about let's split the difference—I'll pay you five hundred dollars and your train fare back, you make all the arrangements, pick up a U-Haul on Friday, we move my stuff into it, drive it up to New York, unload it into my apartment, you return it, go to Penn Station, end of game. What do you think?"

"What about the agency?"

"Screw the agency."

"Wow," I said. "You're my hero."

Morris laughed and we shook on it.

That night I invested some of my future earnings into a keg party at my house. Ali Dehestani got drunk and we wrestled in the backyard; he had four inches and forty pounds on me, but I was stronger. It was an even match. Jen Cohen got so drunk she passed out on Ali's couch. Amy Gould for her part got so drunk, and so angry, when she saw me (briefly) kissing her friend Amanda that she kissed Ravi Winikoff, which was a surprise to everyone involved. And from my father's lovely ivy-bestrewn porch I made a speech about Isaac Babel: "They didn't let him finish!" I cried. "Don't let them not let you finish! Finish! Finish while you can!"

My speech made no sense. Everyone cheered.

Two days later I picked up a smallish U-Haul, pulled it up to Morris's place, and very quickly with Morris lugged his boxes of books, and then his heavy wooden futon and his cherrywood writing desk into the truck, and then drove us to New York in three and a half hours.

On the way Morris talked to me about literature, politics, the movies. Henry Adams, when he met Swinburne, thought it would take him a hundred years to catch up to the poet's erudition, his learning, his reading. I felt a little like that with Morris, but I thought—I was young—that I could make up the difference in ten years. He was twelve years older than I was. I had two years to spare.

Also, Morris talked about publishing. What a bunch of miserable careerists his contemporaries were.

"John Globus is a joke. It's a mystery he still gets published.

This is what is known as publishing inertia. They publish your next book because they don't want people to think that publishing your previous book was a mistake.

"Joanne Simkin is actually Alfred Simkin's granddaughter, did you know that? One thing you learn in New York is that if it sounds like a relative, it's a damn relative.

"Harold Phillips," Morris concluded. "How many times can you confess in print that you're a middle-aged mediocrity who is envious of his friends? Jesus. Don't read him."

I never had read him. In fact, I'd never heard of him, or any of the others—mediocrities, as it turned out, and careerists, careerists, careerists, every one. It was news to me. I dealt then exclusively with the great dead—and with Morris, who carried them all like a bright banner into the present.

But I sat there—or, rather, I sat at the wheel—and nodded. I was sure there was a good reason to beat up on these jokers, and after all here I was so serendipitously with Morris Binkel, and I did not want to seem like a fool.

"Judith Hestermann is a miserable excuse for a television critic. Her idea of greatness is the NBC Thursday-night lineup."

Morris shook his head and looked out at the woods of suburban New Jersey as we drove through them, alternating between the enormous shopping malls and the New Jersey state police. "Jesus, it's the chain mall archipelago," said Morris. "It's all malls and state troopers. These people on their death marches. You step outside J.Crew and they shoot you." He shook his head but also smiled—it was a good line.

Morris's apartment was a small, handsome one-and-a-half-bedroom on Riverside Drive. It looked out over the Hudson and on into New Jersey. Aside from the office, which we now repeopled with Morris's books, it looked surprisingly lived-in for an apartment he'd been gone from for a year. We moved him in and I took the U-Haul down to 23rd Street.

Walking over to the subway—Morris told me to take a cab but I wanted to ride the subway—I passed through Chelsea. I had never seen so many beautiful people. I was sweating, tired, gruesome, and these people had left their houses looking like movie stars—perhaps they were movie stars? One fell behind on such things in college, or anyway I did—and, oh God, what would it take to live in such a place? What reserves of strength? What reserves of cash? And yet I thought that I could do it. These people looked soft, for all their movie-star hard bodies. They looked like they were unsure of what they wanted in life but that they suspected they'd gotten it. They hoped anyway that this was it.

By the time I got back Morris had set up shop and he'd even photocopied some Babel stories for me. I showered—his shower was clean, his towels were reasonably new.

"It's nice here," Morris called out from the living room as I got dressed.

"Yes," I agreed, when I walked out.

"My wife just left me," he said. "Did I mention that? I had a lovely wife and she's gone." I didn't say anything to that.

"My going to Hopkins for a year was the last straw. She decided I was sleeping with all the grad students."

I could not understand, at the time, the allure of grad students.

Morris stood with his big hands in his pants pockets by the big window that looked out to New Jersey, over the Hudson, the sky now beginning to dim and the lights like little candles beginning to burn on the other side. "Should we go to a party?" he said.

So we did.

*　*　*

What did I want from Morris Binkel? The man was practically a sociopath. He had been in New York so long, had ingested there so many values that he at heart despised, that he knew to be false and cruel, that, in angrily rejecting them, he felt also the extent to which he was beholden to them, and grew angrier still. He could no longer read five pages of anything without losing his temper, without clutching his chair in rage. Surely he'd be dead by forty. And yet the great ones were like this. And Morris, I think, had greatness in him, even if he squandered it. His anger at his era rose like vomit to his throat.

I was twenty years old. When you are twenty years old, and twenty-one, and twenty-two, and twenty-three, and twenty-four, what you want from people is that they tell you about you. When you are twenty, and twenty-one, twenty-two, twenty-three, you watch the world for the way it watches you. Do people laugh when you make a joke, do they kiss you when you lean into them at a party? Yes? Aha—so that's who you are. But these people themselves, laughing and not-laughing, kissing and not-kissing, they themselves are young, and so then you begin to think, if you're twenty or twenty-one, when you are young, that these people are not to be trusted, your contemporaries, your screwed-up friends and girlfriends—that it's not because of you that they kissed you, but because of *them*, something about them, those narcissists, whereas you were asking about you, what did they think of you? Now you have no idea. This is why it's so important to meet your heroes while you are young, so they can tell you. When I met Morris Binkel I wanted merely for him to say: Yes. I see it in you. You can do with it what you will, but you've got it. You can be like me, if that's what you want.

We went to the party, which was in Brooklyn. For a long time we rode the train as Morris explained various things to me about the world of literature, by which it turned out Morris meant the world of publishing. He rarely discussed actual literary works; he knew all the writers personally, so he just gave me the straight dope.

We'd drunk a bottle of wine from Morris's cabinet and when we arrived at last the party was well under way, and everyone greeted Morris with a mixture of regard and something like relief—I don't know—or fear. As we stood getting acclimated, people would come up to him and welcome him back to New York, and then comment on his latest broadside in the *New American.* "What you did to Phillips, my God," said one kindly-looking man who seemed about Morris's age (most of the others were slightly younger), identified to me by Morris later as a socialist history professor.

"Oh, I didn't really—" Morris protested demurely.

"No, he had it coming," said the man, then turned to me: "Morris is like American foreign policy. The only thing he knows how to do is bomb people. But sometimes the people he bombs really deserve it."

Morris laughed happily.

At some point Morris went outside for a cigarette, leaving me on my own. Naturally I went to the kitchen to fetch another beer. I had been drinking heavily now for several years, and I'd had only five beers this evening so far, not very much for me at the time, but Morris and I had forgotten, somehow, to eat, so I was reason-ably drunk, and when I found a woman—a fairly stunning woman, maybe just a few years older than I was but a whole world away from me, with blue eyes in a round, pretty face, and long curly black hair spilling over her back, in jeans, in a kind of low-cut black short-sleeve shirt with ruffles along the hem—this was not how girls dressed at Harvard—and several bracelets, bangles they're called, on her wrists and hoop earrings in her ears—a real woman, in other words, which I was not used to—when I saw her standing before the refrigerator, I felt stymied, and I blushed. I was wearing a polo shirt from the Harvard Coop and jeans while everyone around wore a sport coat, and this woman was looking at me with amusement in her eyes.

"Hi," I said, looking down at the floor.

"You're Morris's friend," she said.

I looked back up. "Well, sort of."

"That's an intriguing response!" she said, laughing. Her earrings and her hair jangled when she talked. Her eyes laughed differently from how her mouth laughed.

"Thank you," I said.

"And?"

"I moved Morris up here. I was working at the agency. Uh. Instead of tutoring SATs."

She nodded encouragingly. I told the rest of the story a bit more coherently.

"So he owes you money," she concluded.

I hadn't thought of it that way. This girl was way out of my league.

"Join the club," she added.

And I certainly hadn't thought of that. But then this sudden revelation—that Morris was not good with money, or not to be trusted, and that this woman and I were bound together by this—emboldened me.

"I'm Keith," I said.

"Hi, Keith," she said. "You'd like to get a beer, wouldn't you?"

"Yeah," I admitted.

She stepped aside. As I reached in, I thought of something. I said, "Would you like one?"

"Yes."

I took out two and opened them carefully with the Miller Genuine Draft bottle opener on my key chain.

"Nifty," said the woman, accepting her beer. "I'm Emily," she now said, proffering her hand.

So I said, again, "Hi."

"So you go to Harvard?" she said, and when I nodded, she went on: "Does it suck?"

"Kind of."

"Yeah. I went to Swarthmore and we were always pretty sure Harvard sucked."

"Yeah. Kind of."

When she told me what school she'd gone to, it gave me some assurance. Not the school, but just the fact that she'd gone to a school, at one time.

"We always thought there was something wrong with everyone who went there," she went on. "Just—something weird."

I thought about this a moment. "That's true," I said. "But it raises a kind of epistemological problem. Because I can tell you what's wrong with everyone else—but what's wrong with me?"

She laughed. "Ah," she said. "That's the thing."

I was immensely pleased. I was holding a conversation with a real woman, and I had made her laugh. Wait till—but who could I tell who would understand? Not Ali Dehestani. And Amy Gould would only get angry. As I pondered this problem Morris materialized beside us. Emily's countenance changed. He leaned over and hugged her more intimately than seemed appropriate with me standing there. She knew him well. But—I half stutteringly thought to myself—he'd been married until recently! And he was such a jerk! Emily! Hey!

Then again, I did not begrudge Morris this beautiful woman with her sharp tongue and her simple grown-up jewelry. He had published so much more than I had.

***

That was the turning point in the evening. Pretty soon Morris took both me and Emily home in a cab, and they set me up nicely on the couch, and they did not make too much noise in Morris's room, which was considerate, and in the morning they made me eggs, and I sight-translated some passages from Babel's story "Guy de Maupassant," about a young man, like me a little, who helps a rich man's beautiful wife translate some stories by Maupassant and then seduces her. I had not seduced anyone, but I had seen something, or I had begun to see something, there was a glimmer that I saw, of how things worked—and that was what the story was about. I explained this to Morris and Emily, though leaving myself out of it, of course, and they were pleased, Emily especially. "Keith's a lot smarter than I was when I was twenty," she said. It had turned out that Emily was closer to thirty than to twenty. "Is he smarter than you were, Morris?"

Morris smiled, and held the smile a beat too long. "Nadezhda Mandelstam once wrote about her husband at the beginning of the Terror," he said, going back to pouring coffee and divvying up the remains of some crumb cake. "He looks out the window of their Moscow apartment at all the people going about their business—it's 1936 or so—and says: 'They think everything's fine, just because the trams keep running.'" He put the coffeepot in the sink. "There's this thing about guys from Harvard. They think everything's fine, just because they went to Harvard. And for them, you know, it is. Even the most mediocre mediocrity can make a nice life for himself in New York if only he went to Harvard."

Emily blushed—I saw it, I still see it now—and I looked at Morris, looked at him anew. Because the whole thing seemed to be directed at Emily, not at me: This is how brutal I am, Morris seemed to be saying, this is how much of a dick I can be. Any promises I made you are null and void and not to be believed.

He turned now to me and added quickly, "I'm not saying you're a mediocrity. I'm just outlining the sociology of the thing. You might be a genius, for all I know."

I nodded gratefully, and that was that. In between sips of coffee Morris had concluded that I was a mediocrity—or a genius. I happened to know already that I was neither—that if I applied myself, I'd be fine, more than fine, and if I didn't, I would probably fall through the cracks. I knew that. What I hadn't known was something else. Looking at Morris looking out the window across the Hudson, I suddenly wanted very badly to cry. Not for myself, for the first time, maybe, in my life—I had managed just by sitting here quietly to get the better of Morris, to cause him to falter into rudeness—but for myself in ten years, because the other thing I suddenly knew was that Morris's life was a very likely life, the sort of life one could end up having, if one was not very careful, and I knew, already, in addition to knowing that I was neither mediocrity nor genius, that I was not very careful at all.

"When you are young," Morris said now, looking out his window, his back to us, "and you're on your way, and you have everything before you and everyone with you—you don't know anyone else—and you look at all the others with their screwed-up lives and you know you'll do things differently, you know you will, and you do. You are kinder, gentler, you are smarter. And then one day you look up and you've done all the things you said you were going to do but somehow you forgot something, something happened along the way and everyone's gone, everything's different, and looking around you see you have the same screwed-up life as all those other idiots. And there—you are."

He turned back to us and bravely smiled.

*　　*　　*

Ten years later, when I stood in a room in Brooklyn—a slightly younger room than the one Morris had taken me to, then, though that may have been an optical illusion, and there were women in the room who looked at me, now, the way Emily had looked at Morris then, sort of, because like Morris I had won a place for myself among them, among them and above them, and also because I had made a mess of my life in the way that Morris, in his time, had made a mess of his—and, standing in this room, I suddenly apropos of nothing heard someone make an unkind remark about Morris, and then look up at me, for approval, not knowing what I thought—what did I think? Well, I thought that if you have made a career of denouncing careerism, eventually someone's going to call you a nasty name. Someone had called Morris Binkel a nasty name and I did not speak up in his defense. In fact I agreed. And I thought of the train ride home from New York that weekend, with $500 in my pocket after all, and still high on the things I had seen, wanting to tell people on the train about them, share this with them somehow, knowing that Ali and Ravi and Amy would not really understand, sensing already that they would not be interested in what I'd learned in New York, in fact no one would be interested—despite Morris's remark, which by then I had dismissed, I shone on that train and glowed, and I launched, self-important, into Morris's first chapter—it was the only chapter he'd ever write—of his book on Isaac Babel.

Babel had moved to Petersburg when he was nineteen years old. He met Maxim Gorky, who told him that his stories were good, but his writing was too pretty. He should learn something about life.

Babel was in Petersburg when the Bolsheviks seized power. Later on, he claimed to have been an officer of the Cheka—most likely, he had run some errands for them. Then he went off as a journalist with a Cossack division invading Poland. This experience formed the basis for his classic book of stories, *Red Cavalry*.

Red Cavalry made Babel famous. It was the first great Soviet book. Gorky protected him, and he was beloved.

Then Stalin came and Babel stopped writing. He claimed to have become a "master of silence," but it was clear to everyone that he was simply a sensitive instrument; under conditions of total fear, it was impossible to write.

In 1936 Gorky died. "No one will protect me now," Babel told his wife. Three years later, he was arrested, interrogated, tortured, and shot. He was forty years old.

I still remember—how well I remember—looking out the window of that train. We were blazing down the final stretch of rail before Baltimore, toward the roads and multitudinous lacrosse fields and the late-night ice cream shop of my youth; Ali was going to meet me at the train station in exchange for a six-pack of beer. No one would ever arrest me at my house, take me to the basement of Lubyanka, and shoot me in the back of the head. Nonetheless I knew what Morris's book was telling me, what the book he never finished was telling me. In that train, on those rails, some premonition of the truth brushed against my side.

II

His Google

Something in reference to a man who subscribes to an agency for "clippings," to send him everything "that appears about him"—and finds that nothing ever appears. That he never receives anything.

—Henry James, *Notebooks*

His Google was shrinking. It was part of a larger failing, maybe, certainly, but to see it quantified . . . to see it numerically confirmed . . . it was cruel. It wasn't nice. Sam considered the alternatives: he knew people with no Google at all, zero hits, and he even knew people like Mark, Mark Grossman, who had never published, who had kept silent, but whose name drew up the hits of other Mark Grossmans, the urologist Grossman and the banker Grossman and Grossmans who had completed ten-kilometer runs. But Sam wondered—the afternoon was young and there was time for it—whether Mark might not be better off. He would finish his dissertation eventually; it would receive a listing in an electronic catalog. There, he would finally say when that moment came, I too am Grossman.

Sam: not Grossman. Sam: not even the size of Sam of old, Sam of last year, Sam of two weeks ago. After he'd failed to produce the great Zionist epic he'd been contracted to produce, after he'd stopped writing the occasional online opinion piece on the Second Intifada, after Talia had returned, angrily, to Tel Aviv, and Arielle had moved, icily, to New York, and he'd resumed his temp job to begin paying back his advance, there was, in the world, increasingly less Sam. He backed away from the computer, into the dark heavy tapestry that split his living room in two and made of this pathetic little desk and shelf, with its mass of undigested papers, its pile of battered books—a tax-deductible home office. Occasionally he photographed it, this consolation, this small triumph over the masters of his fate. His Google too had been a consolation once: if in those heady days, a book deal in his pocket, a girlfriend of complex cosmetic habits in his bedroom, his little AOL mailbox was momentarily silent and unmoving, he simply strolled over to Google to confirm that he still existed. Did he ever! Three hundred some odd pages of Samuel Mitnick on the World Wide Web, accessible to people everywhere, at any time. Want some Sam? Here you go. Some more? Click, click. Even absolutist states, even China, had Google—and there were a lot of people, he'd thought then, in China.

But not enough, apparently, or maybe they just weren't clicking through . . . for here he was. He wasn't due at Fidelity until four, it was barely one, and he needed to get out. Tomorrow night his date with Katie Riesling, author of sex advice, he should really stay and clean up, clean himself up, but this apartment was more than he could bear. And, in any case, if Katie hadn't seen the signs by now, she'd never see them. His unreliable car; his jeans with a hole in them just above the ankle. From what? He had no idea. They would have dinner, dinner at Jae's, the place where people saw you in the window when they walked by. He looked too shoddy to leave the house but he left the house. Out there: no Google; in here: Google; on Google: no Sam.

Or almost no Sam. Twenty-two. He was at twenty-two and plunging.

He patted his pocket for keys and moved out the door. Sam had other problems, maybe, or anyway the world did. Enter MISERY or ILLNESS or PLAGUE and what you saw was pages upon pages. PALESTINE. SHARON-ARAFAT. OCCUPATION. U.N. RESOLUTION 242. Put things in quotes and you narrowed the search, and even then "INSTRUCTIONS FOR MAKING A BOMB TO KILL JEWS WITH" or "DIRECTIONS TO THE NEAREST VILLAGE WHERE I CAN SHOOT ARABS"—very popular searches, page after virtual page of results. Sam would never have so many hits.

He headed to the 1369 on foot. There were sufficient humiliations in his life that he didn't need also to drive down to Inman Square and fail to find a parking spot.

The important part, in terms of your Google, was not to die. An initial spike from the obituaries, the memorial blog entries ("unfulfilled promise," "so much promise," "he never quite filled out his promise"), but in the long term a catastrophe. Yet what would be the opposite of dying, Google-wise? What would be the anti-death? He wondered this as he bought his Ethiopian coffee to-stay and sat down in the gloom of Cafe 1369. He arranged himself at one of the tiny tables and began his work hour by staring with disbelief at the praise lavished on the book he'd brought with him. The living writers of the world were Sam's enemies, Sam's nemeses. Sam was once a living writer himself, even better than a living writer, a future writer—there'd been a picture of Sam in one of the publisher's catalogs.

Fame—fame was the anti-death. But it seemed to slither from his grasp, seemed to giggle and retreat, seemed to hide behind a huge oak tree and make fake farting sounds with its hands. He unfolded his notebook. Inside, his notes toward greatness. Though he seldom read them over, the thought of losing the notebook troubled him. Consider Emerson: where would we be without his notebooks? Sam had recently photocopied the entire thing, just in case.

Yesterday's work was a list:

Melissa
Jenna
Sally S.
the girl in Brooklyn
the other girl in Brooklyn

It went on in that vein a little longer. He smiled, remembering. Something of a poem, here. Some poetry in it. A little vulgar, sure, but why not? Hadn't Sam been polite long enough? Hadn't he lowered the toilet seat, alone in his home, only Sam and his tiny Google in that apartment, courteously lowering the seat, raising the seat, lowering it again like an idiot? So he had earned a little list, he thought, he had earned that right.

Yesterday's was not actually The List. That venerable document could be found earlier in the notebook. Since its composition a few weeks before in a moment of sheer quiet desperation, Sam had compiled a number of suggestive permutations. Women he'd seen naked. Jewish women. Women he'd kissed. By height. By age. Political affiliation.

He was profoundly influenced, in his list work, by the baseball stat revisionists. These were the men who'd thought up the slugging percentage and then went on to invent further and more elaborate indices. They secretly hoped thereby to demonstrate that Ted Williams was the greatest hitter of all time, and of course Sam wished them well. But no matter how much they fiddled with the numbers, asserted that the most meaningful statistic in baseball, baseball's very essence, was slugging plus on-base percentage minus the average of the two hitters on either side of you divided by the league average—procedures that did in fact move the 1946 Williams ahead of Ty Cobb and Stan Musial and Barry Bonds—they could never, with any conceivable rearrangement of the statistical heavens, push Williams beyond Babe Ruth. It just wasn't possible. Sam found similarly that no matter how much he recalculated and recalibrated, took circumstances into account and multiplied by three, there simply was no avoiding the fact that he hadn't, in his life, received enough blow jobs.

He was also, he had to admit, influenced by the Holocaust revisionists. Had he really, in his excitement, ejaculated uselessly onto Lori Miller's thigh that night at Miles Fishbach's house? Had he *really*? And had he actually been so flaccid with Rachel Simkin that he never even penetrated? Says who—Rachel? Rachel was drunk, barely-human drunk, as was he. And Toby, to whom he'd confessed the next day? But Toby hadn't been there, and in any case witness testimony is culturally constructed, possibly a case of mass psychosis. Sam traced a thick, triumphant arrow from Rachel's name in the almost-slept list to the bottom of The List itself. Then he crossed it out.

What was it about this list-making? Was Sam a total degenerate, a sexual accountant, an Excel-chart pervert? Or was it a crisis: did he think he'd never sleep with anyone ever again? Or almost-sleep? So may as well draw up the career totals, send them off to the Hall for consideration? And did he really think he would never kiss or fondle the breasts of another girl?—for there were those to explain as well.

No, no, that wasn't it, exactly. It was more as if life, the life he'd known, had begun to seem so slippery to him. Who could say what had happened and what it had meant? There'd been so much drinking! He had been close to people—but not quite close enough; and he had given himself to people, but not quite, ever, quite the full of him. So there was a consolation to be had in these lists, he now thought, when he thought about it. With Talia he had been kind, and with Arielle he'd been dashing, and with Lori he'd been eager, and with Rachel Simkin, that time, he'd been an utter failure. And if you put them on a list, was the idea, if you added them up: there he was, finally, a human being.

Sam boarded the Red Line train at Harvard Square. Some people woke up before noon, and what did it get them? A good seat on the inbound 8:45, maybe. Maybe it got them that seat. But at 3:30 every seat was good, and there were plenty to go around. Perhaps this is why Sam worked the late shift at Fidelity. It also meant less interaction with the bankers themselves, some of whom were Sam's former classmates—some of whom, in that former life, he had asked out on dates. In certain parts of the temp world his mastery of Excel still held cachet, still commanded attention; but less so, increasingly less so, in the five-year alumni report he kept buried, but constantly updated, deep inside his heart.

The Google had helped, once. His poor little Google! Was there nothing to be done?

Arriving at work five minutes late, Sam ducked into the bathroom and changed into his work clothes, a pair of khakis and his tie, hopping around on one foot while he tried to keep from stepping on the bathroom floor with the other. The toilet with its scan-flusher kept flushing and flushing behind him as he hopped.

"Are you OK in there?" someone asked when he was almost

done, causing him to trip into the door, the right side of his face momentarily keeping the rest of him from falling.

When Sam finally entered the cavernous main hall of Fidelity's Creative Services, where a thousand monkeys clacked away at a thousand PowerPoint presentations, he tried to keep his head up proudly. He had once quit this place so that he could write his epic, and when he returned, some of his coworkers ... made fun of him. They resented his ambition, and even more they resented his failure. The Creative Services department at Fidelity was like a small town in an American movie from which everyone dreamed of escaping. It was the end of the line—and to return, at the end of the line, to the end of the line, was not what Sam had planned for himself.

He punched in at his workstation, stowing his backpack in the deep bottom drawer. His apartment was a horrific mess but at work he'd arranged things nicely. He still had, if he recalled correctly, half a roast beef sub in the mini-drawer fridge the company had installed at each quasi-cubicle—and he took it out now. The job queue was empty and so Sam checked his e-mail: nothing. Then his internal e-mail: nothing. Happily he clicked to Slip.com and read Katie's latest sex advice column, on what to do if your girlfriend is a virgin. As always, very sensible. They had met when he was still an up-and-coming Zionist novelist and seriously dating Talia. Katie was a bright and pretty girl and working for the *Phoenix*, when the alt-weeklies were still a proud institution, and they were at a party full of what few journalists and nonuniversity scholars could be mustered on a Cambridge weekend night. Talia wasn't there, for some reason, while Katie's boyfriend was. He was a management consultant, or a lawyer, tall and pasty, and Katie was visibly annoyed by him. That's what you got, Sam thought at the time, if you hung out in Boston. They had stayed intermittently in touch by e-mail—e-mail too was once a proud institution—and now, at last, they were single, and were going on a date! Except Sam wasn't the man he'd been when they'd first met. He looked around briefly and Googled himself. Fifteen!

On the screen, a job appeared—apparently they knew Sam's schedule, knew when to send down their Excel spreadsheets. This one was easy, almost offensively easy, but Sam took his time. He clicked, he dragged, he checked his e-mail again, then finally he dropped. He glanced at the request form—John Laizer. Sam recognized the name from college, though beyond the inexplicable (except statistically, except statistically) conviction that Laizer was a jerk, he couldn't remember him. He sped up production anyway, forestalling the possibility of Laizer hovering behind him, making nervous hurry-up noises and obnoxious cell phone calls. The resulting chart looked a little goofy, Sam would admit, but rules were rules and he was following them. Besides, he was the only Excel man at Fidelity. He sent the job off and decided to avail himself of the company's long-distance plan.

"Hello," a deliberately bored male voice answered on the other end. "Google."

"Hi," said Sam. "Could I speak with Max Sobel, please?"

"Who's calling?"

"My name is Sam. He might not know me. I'm a writer."

"Whom do you write for?"

"Not anywhere in particular. I'm sort of freelance."

"Well, Max is out today. Why don't I take your number and he'll call you."

"I really need to talk to him," said Sam. For all he knew this *was* Max. It was a small operation, still, maybe just Max doing Google in different voices.

"I said he'd call you."

Sam checked the faces of the nearby PowerPoint hipsters. He really had freelanced a bit along the way, that much was true, and he'd interviewed people for his Zionist epic. But now he lowered his voice.

"Look," he said. "My Google is shrinking."

"Excuse me?"

"My Google. I Google myself and every time it gets lower."

"Right. Pages often go off-line and then they no longer show up on searches."

"Yes, I understand that, but this is getting out of hand. I was in the mid–three hundreds before. Now I'm at, like, forty," Sam lied.

"I'm afraid there's nothing we can do about that, sir. Maybe, if you don't mind my saying, you need to do something notable. Write something. Start a blog."

"Look, I tried that, don't you think I tried that? I'm calling because I thought maybe you could shift the algorithm a little."

"Oh, no, we couldn't do that."

"You couldn't just up my count a little until I get back on my feet?"

The man laughed an uneasy laugh. You couldn't do anything in this country anymore, thought Sam, without someone thinking you were a creep. When the man spoke again it was with a forbidding formality.

"Sir, there's nothing we can do. I can only suggest writing more. Distinguishing yourself somehow. Google is a fair search engine."

"It's a search engine run by Jews!" Sam suddenly cried, a little louder than he'd meant to.

Everyone turned to look, and though Sam raised his palm and curled down his mouth in an expression meant to assure them of his abiding control, the man had hung up.

* * *

He sent his next job over to technical services to print. He needed to speak with Toby.

Toby was a good friend to have, and Sam's only one. They were brother losers, kindred spirits—a computer genius, an animations specialist, Toby had refused to cash in on the Internet boom just as Sam had somehow refused to cash in on the post-9/11 fascination with the Middle East.

"I guess you don't want to be on *Talk of the Nation*" was how Jay, his former agent, had put it.

"Of course I do," Sam had replied. "More than anything in the world."

"You got an advance for this book," said Jay. "You realize you'll have to give it back?"

"I realize," said Sam. "I realize."

Toby was his only friend, and as Sam made his way over to tech services, he wondered about the others. It used to be, when Sam was still with Talia, that he couldn't get them to stop calling, he had to juggle and sort and combine visits, just to fit them all in. And then—well, would it be banal to admit that, when Sam's epic was going well, he'd traded them in for better friends? Friends like Jay, who lived in lofts, who lived in Brooklyn? And that when his epic collapsed he'd gradually felt this new company sour, himself out of place? That, unable to match them book party for book party, he began to decline their perfectly friendly invitations—so that eventually he was left with no one, or rather with Toby? Would this be banal, too much like a movie, would it be not quite the way life was? And yet it was exactly the way life was.

So therefore Toby, who had been working for several years on a novel about his hometown of Milwaukee. . . . At least, Sam realized as he raised his hand in greeting, that's what he assumed it was about. Toby had given him a printout of the first two hundred pages a few weeks ago, and Sam hadn't yet gotten around to looking at them.

"What brings you to the lair of the technically damned?" said Toby in greeting.

Sam winked. "Accidentally sent my job over here."

"Listen," said Toby. "I've been meaning to tell you. If you haven't looked at my manuscript yet, will you wait? I've made some changes."

"OK," Sam said, trying to sound disappointed. In fact he was relieved—and grateful to gentle Toby for his forbearance. Still, he had to tell him about his Google problem, and so he did.

"Look," he concluded. "Couldn't you make my name appear places, kind of invisibly?"

"Heh." Toby chuckled. "Why not just write something? That would be easier."

Toby nodded to the printer, which had long ago emitted Sam's three Excel pages.

Sam took them in his hand. "You see that happening, Toby?" With the Excel pages he gestured in the direction of the Power-Pointers; he hinted broadly, with the sheets, of his enslavement. "Do you?"

They stood in silence for a while, and Sam must have looked bad because eventually Toby relented. "OK," he said. "Theoretically it's possible to write a program that would trick the Googlebot into remembering all the pages you used to be on, almost reposting them, sort of, assuming they've gone off-line, and restoring them within the domain of your own personal private Google search."

"That sounds great!" cried Sam.

"But we can't do it. It wouldn't even be that hard, to be honest. But if the Google people caught me, they'd break my fingers."

"Let me worry about the fingers."

Toby snorted. "They're *my* fingers!"

"And it's *my* Google."

"Right."

"Right."

An impasse. They stood facing each other. Toby was a little taller, but Sam was more full of ire and life, and he had more hair; after Talia broke up with him, Sam had met Semra, an attractive photographer friend of Toby's, and Toby had proceeded to warn her, properly perhaps but still, thought Sam, unnecessarily, against him. She stopped returning his calls. "So you won't do this for me?" said Sam. "There's an injustice being perpetrated, right now, against your old friend, and you won't help him. That's what you're saying."

Toby shrugged helplessly.

"I see," said Sam. "You know," he went on—something in the back of his head burning now, not quite knowing yet what he was about to say, but knowing that it would not be something he could take back—"I always suspected that when the shit hit the fan, you'd be too much of a pussy to help me out."

Toby did look taken aback by this. "This is the shit hitting the fan?" he said. "This is an injustice?"

"For me it is. Yeah. They're trying to disappear me!"

"I'm sorry," said Toby. "That is just crazy. I just—sorry. I don't get it."

"No, you don't. You don't get it. You're going to sit up here with your computers and your so-called fucking novel. Good luck with that. And they are going to eat you up when they're done with me! They are going to fucking disappear you." Sam was sticking his finger in Toby's face. "Well, I'm not going to be here to watch."

And with this he gathered up his printouts in disgust and walked off to his workstation, his friend count down to zero.

And at his station he found John Laizer waving Excel sheets angrily in the air. He gestured broadly with them at Sam's incompetence, his carelessness, his indifference to the team, the play of the team, playing as a team. Sam recognized him now—they'd thrown up together over the side of the boat at the sophomore year Owl Club Booze Cruise, except that actually they hadn't. Sam threw up, he was a big thrower-upper then, while Laizer just made some throw-up noises in the spirit of team throwing-up. "You didn't throw up," Sam had said. "I kind of did," said Laizer, and then gave him a look that beseeched Sam not to tell the Owl Club members, not to ruin his chances. Sam didn't, and now Laizer pretended not to recognize him. Maybe he'd truly forgotten. Laizer demanded to know where Sam had been, and demanded to know why his columns looked so funny, and demanded all sorts of things before, finally, his cell phone rang, and he left Sam to fix up a chart that really was, now he mentioned it, pretty terrible looking.

* * *

The next night he had dinner with Katie. Somehow he'd managed, through the wreck of his male friendships, to continue seeing women. Perhaps because they didn't notice how sad a spectacle he now was (they weren't Googling him), or perhaps because his demands on them were so trivial, and he always paid for drinks. As for Katie, she was, like many of the girls Sam knew,

- pretty,
- Jewish,
- a Brown graduate,
- a reader of the *Times* Sunday book review,

with

- short black hair fashionably cut,
- a pierced navel,
- and a tight black semi-turtleneck thing that hugged her breasts,

and as dinner progressed Sam realized he didn't have a chance. He must have been quite formidable when they first met, a man with an agent and a book deal, the audacious self-appointed laureate of American Jewish anxiety over Israel. Did he cut a dashing figure? No, not exactly, probably not, but in retrospect, as he sat before her thus diminished a year later, he thought maybe he'd once exercised a certain pull.

But that was then. Now she told him about how early she had to rise the next morning, a flight to New York for a sex-advice panel sponsored by the MLA, and if Sam was any sort of semiotician, this was not a good sign.

After two beers, however, he didn't care. "My Google," he told Katie. "It's shrinking."

"That's awful. Can't you see a doctor?"

"Funny."

"Well, so what? The important thing is to smell nice. And be good to others."

"But I'm not any of those things! And anyway, what do you know? *Your* Google is massive. You have like a thousand hits."

"I don't think I do," said Katie very sternly.

"You do, you do. You're more famous than Jesus."

"That can't be," she said, looking at him to know whether she should laugh.

"No, you're right. Jesus has the most hits, actually."

"More than Britney?"

"More."

"More than Osama?"

"More."

"Well, good for him," she said, smiling for punctuation. She had bright, beautiful teeth. Sam didn't have a chance.

Sam didn't have a chance. It had taken courage—not talent, not wit, and certainly not foresight—to refuse a regular job after school, to do nothing but read about Israel and worry and argue while his classmates found work at Fidelity or HyperCapital or joined rock bands or traveled the world. Sam knew he had more courage—they were taller, more attractive, they had better table manners and better skin, but he'd gotten all the balls.

It took balls to do what he did because if he failed—and he had failed—he'd end up where he was. He hadn't accomplished the things of which he'd dreamed, and now he couldn't even get done the very basic things that most adults did—like pay his bills, for example (a most unpleasant form letter—and purple—was lying on his cluttered desk, somewhere, from Commonwealth Gas), or alphabetize his books. And when he tried, when he took the books off the shelves in order to put them back in alphabetical order, he became so discouraged at the impossibility of categorizing them properly that he just left them lying there, heaped upon the floor. He worked out a lot but he didn't apply moisturizer to his skin at night, and he seldom flossed. And then there was the Google. . . . Whereas Katie, Katie was the sort of girl who, when she replied to e-mails, spliced her responses into segments, in which she answered specific points, which were set off from the margin by little arrows. This just wasn't something Sam could do. He was always writing people back about other things.

And yet Katie seemed willing to sit there. Was she dumb?

*   *   *

"Do you get many e-mails from creeps?" Sam asked.

"Yeah, sometimes someone who doesn't read the magazine will stumble onto the site and write something nasty."

"It *is* a real bourgeois genre, you know."

"I don't think that's what they're objecting to."

"Who knows? It's like those late-Victorian conduct manuals, so that the barbarians could behave themselves in polite society."

"So it's egalitarian. And as far as women are concerned, you know, it's nice when even barbarians know how to behave themselves in bed."

This thought of the barbarians troubled Sam. Sex columns and deodorant, also the Gap: these were the forces allowing them into the bedrooms of attractive women who'd studied at Brown.

"You realize how bad the working class used to smell?" Sam wanted to know, launching into a cultural history of bathing. He believed that the olfactory element in social interactions had been unfairly neglected in the historical literature. "Orwell has a whole chapter on this in one of his books. He said the Left needed to face facts. Or smell them."

Katie thought Sam was being funny. She studied his face to make sure. Sam tried to look serious. Dinner had ended at some point while he talked, and he had paid, though he couldn't recall how, and they had wandered, almost automatically, into the Irish bar near the intersection of Cambridge and Beacon. Dinner, a bar, conversations about the sex ritual, and a thirty-minute monologue on deodorant—if Sam was any sort of semiotician. . . . But he wasn't sure. Katie was so perfectly composed, and so much better dressed than he, it was hard to tell. They'd kissed once, on a porch in Jamaica Plain, having stepped outside a party for a smoke. They'd kissed and then she'd reminded Sam that she had a boyfriend and, more pointedly still, that he had a girlfriend, and, with autumn in their hearts, they'd stepped back inside. And then he'd failed to call. And then they'd seen each other a few times for coffee and not-kissed. So it was hard to say what exactly was going to happen, but for the moment, while they stood there at the bar, Sam knew he wanted nothing else.

"Look," he said after ordering a gin and tonic for her and a beer for himself. "What's the official Slip position on candles?"

"We're all for." She laughed again.

"OK, how many?"

"We believe"—she cleared her throat—"we believe that anything more than three begins to feel a little spooky. Like human sacrifice, basically."

"So, three. That's your official position."

"Three's good."

"Right. I just can't get over how programmed it all feels. It's like right now"—Sam looked at his watch, it was almost midnight, any minute now Katie would announce that she had an early flight; he needed to suggest that they go home, but he couldn't figure out how!—"all across America, diligent men who've been studying your sex columns are lighting three candles in their little bedrooms and demanding of women, 'Does this feel good?' 'Does this?' 'Does that?' It's like three candles and twenty questions."

"So what you're saying is"—Katie looked up and her eyes flashed at him—"you don't want to take me home?"

"Oh," said Sam, losing his cool, "I do. So much. You have no idea."

They were leaning against the bar. The place was just crowded enough that they were pressed together but not so crowded that anyone would elbow Katie, forcing Sam to kill him. They had been locked for some time in a de facto embrace, and yet there was drama, there was drama and anticipation, when he crossed over and kissed her. He had no idea what would happen, until she kissed him back.

"OK," he allowed afterward. "I'll take you home. But no twenty questions."

"No questions is fine with me," she said.

And then they were walking down the street, down interminable Beacon Street, to her house. Because of course they couldn't go to Sam's, it was too messy, and of course his car hadn't started that evening, and of course, of course. They hadn't been able to find a cab—they had begun to walk, thinking a cab would come, but it never came, it never came—and though it was a warm April evening, and though they occasionally stopped to make out against some fence, the walk was so long that he was beginning to lose his buzz. Why, he'd lost it. Two in the morning, a night of drinking behind him, six hours of it, $140, that would be $25 an hour, almost, more than he made at Fidelity, gone, all gone. He recalled now, nostalgically, the moments during the evening when he'd been pleasantly drunk—after the first two quick beers, before eating, his face already flushing and his voice animated with indignation about his Google, and then again in the bar, oh the bar, where he'd gone to the bathroom after their kiss and returned to find her there, *still at the bar.* For a man who'd been to as many bars as Sam, had been to them alone and left alone, this was no small thing. He kissed her neck, then, in the bar. He kissed her lips, sloppily. Conscious of the stares, he had broken it off, had taken her hand, as if to say: We cannot be here any longer. Another minute and we'll be tearing our clothes off. We might get arrested. Let's go home and fuck.

But that was forever ago. Before the Long March down Beacon. Now it was two, it was past two, and soon it would be dawn and his penis would turn into a pumpkin, and all was lost, all was darkness and loathsomeness, his buzz gone, his erection gone, and we are all so alone, surrounded by people so powerfully unlike us, and then she was kissing him again, and they were on her doorstep, they were on the little porch in front of her house, they were kissing-stumbling into her room, all was darkness, loathsomeness, but they were kissing and their lips described ovals around each other's, their tongues came out, bit by bit, they eased themselves into a kiss, standing next to her bed, and suddenly he wanted to kiss her shoulder, her arm, to press himself against her, and her throat, and then, kissing that throat as she threw back her head, he remembered her belly button and descended, felt the cool of her silver studs, the futuristic metallic taste of them against his tongue, as if he were making out with a female robot, and who wouldn't want that?

He considered her sex column. Would this be featured? Sex with the former future author of a Zionist epic? At the conference tomorrow—was he anecdotal material?

They had fallen into bed, her room was tidy but filled with knick-knacks, things would have been knocked over, damage done, and so they were in bed, and taking off their clothes, and suddenly Sam realized with a start that he wasn't hard. He was betrayed! Full of lustful thoughts, although also many other kinds of thoughts, but lacking lustful deeds. Saint Augustine had written of this—impotence, rather than sinful passion, was the crowning argument in his proof that lust was evil, that it was not subject to the human will. And now behold poor Sam: It was one thing to go out with a woman and possibly sleep with her, knowing all the while that she would eventually tell her friends about Sam's various idiosyncrasies—that is to say, this was already bad enough—but to not-sleep with a woman who had access to a Web-based media outlet? That was a terrible idea! And it wouldn't even raise his Google, because obviously she'd use another name.

Here's how it was, in short: if in the next five minutes Sam failed to produce an erection robust enough to last while he located his jeans and extracted a condom from his right front pocket—tens of thousands of readers would know about it before the week was out.

Just then she said, as if to seal the contract of his humiliation: "Relax."

An hour later, it was over. There had been a few false starts, but Katie turned out to be an exquisite machine. It did not mean, as Sam had often thought it meant, a knowledge of sexual arcana, but rather a sensitivity, an efficiency. Katie's body was, as Henry James would have said, one upon which nothing was lost. And Sam himself had been here and there, had certain interests, pro-clivities, higher math. In short, an hour after his panic they lay, pleasantly out of breath, and she had placed her head on his shoulder, trapping him underneath her.

"You know," she said, sighing, "I think Brown gave me an unrealistic idea of what life would be like."

"Hmm?" Sam perked up. He was always anxious about sex, about the physical mechanics of sex—poor Saint Augustine!—but he loved talking after sex, sometimes he wondered how people talked at any other time. "What did you think it was going to be like?"

"I thought it was going to be, you know, Marx on Tuesday, naked copulation on Thursday, and then on the weekends I'd go out with guys kind of like you."

"Like me?"

"Maybe not you exactly. But, you know, idealistic. Maybe a little crazy."

"Ah."

"I think you're sweet," she concluded, and dozed off.

He lay there half trapped underneath her, the words ringing in his ears. Oh, Sam. You idiot. Katie was a sex advice columnist but she didn't sleep with you because she wanted advice on sex. She slept with you because you represented something, or the idea of something, even if it was just one of those gooey ideas they fed kids in the semiotics program at Brown: for all your problems you still read books, you were still a thumb in the eye of the way things were. You still thought, despite what you told Toby, that you had something new to say. Why should Sam of all people be famous, why should his words be disseminated via his Google count across the earth? Did he think Israel would pull out of the West Bank because of him? Did he think the Palestinians would finally relax? No, not exactly, but also, well—who knew? Secretly, quietly, he still believed this, and apparently so did Katie; believed that Sam wasn't like the guys she knew, the pretty boys with online movie reviews, big-Googled hipsters still showing up at the 1369 to read the first thirty pages of *Infinite Jest*. Not enough books in their apartments to cause a clutter if they'd combined them all together and thrown them in the doorway.

Katie was different. She had books on shelves, lots of books, and books on her windowsill, neatly pressed together as if the windowsill were a shelf. This was surprising. There was some art on the walls, some photographs; the only thing Sam had on the wall was a PEACE NOW map of Israeli settlements of the West Bank and Gaza. Katie's apartment was less tidy than it at first appeared, it was pleasantly cluttered, a pile of DVDs lay next to the television in the corner—her mind was at work, by the looks of it, her mind was engaged. And her activity seemed suddenly to speak to his own lack of activity. What was he doing here? He should be working! All at once he felt the guilt descend, as it almost always did, the desire to be back in his apartment, to be out of this girl's life, which was not his life, and back into his own. He had a wish, an insane wish, to update his lists, to move Katie from the kissing to the sleeping column, he saw it in his mind as an Excel operation, the dragging of a cell.

His notebook was in the back pocket of his jeans, which lay in a puddle atop what seemed to be Katie's travel case, and now he slipped gently out of bed and picked them up—only to find, as in a mystery novel (was it the bit of moonlight beginning to slice through the window?), that something had caught his eye. Underneath the jeans, atop the suitcase, was a little red book, the kind sold at fancy airport stationery shops, the gift you typically give to people you don't know, and now it was, just as typically, oh Katie, a diary.

It went back an entire year. And what a canny, savvy young lady this Katie turned out to be! For all her sex advice and Brown, for all her books and semiotics, there was a lot of career in here, and more career—Should she pitch this magazine? Should she e-mail this editor? Should she take a job in publishing? Sam was a little puzzled. He flipped through for the graphic sex descriptions, but they were absent. Maybe she kept them for the sex column. Maybe Sam would be featured, after all.

At last he found some Sam in the diary. *I've been interested in him for a while,* said Katie, *but I don't know if he's good for me. He's a little crazy and I'm just finally getting back on track with things. I wonder why he couldn't finish that book, though, or hold on to Talia. She was cute.*

He went through the rest, looking for himself. A little sex here, more career, more editors, some clippings. No Sam. Then, two days ago, this: *I think I'll sleep with Sam this time, I think there's a good chance. I don't expect too much, but it might be nice. He's funny. And he has such beautiful eyebrows, I want to kiss them. I promise you this, though: if he starts talking about Israel, I'm out. It's over. A peck on the cheek and a see you later.*

Oh?

Really?

He set the journal down—he was sitting on the orange bean-bag in the corner of her room—and looked at Katie. She slept soundly, one thin sheet draped diagonally across her back, a thin long arm stretching out from beneath it. A beatific scene, and the anger that had flared up over the Israel comment subsided. So she didn't want to hear about the depredations of the IDF; and so she worried a bit more about her career than was strictly proper. So? Didn't he have enough integrity and self-denial for two people, for five, for all the good it did him, and enough Israel talk? And that bit about his eyebrows—how interesting, how strange. And wasn't she pretty, there, and sweet? And weren't they two very human people, on long lonely Beacon Street in Somerville, wasn't this all they ever wanted, really, wasn't it enough?

Meanwhile the journal had fallen open to its very last page. On the inside of the back cover, writing—in Katie's slightly loopy hand, in different-colored pens, at different times—a list. First names and initials.

Katie's List!

Sam glanced up nervously to make sure she was still sleeping. She was. So he counted. And counted. And counted.

It was longer than his by six.

And what was worse, after all that money spent, all that charm expended, all that panic and anxiety, he hadn't even gained on her.

He was still holding his jeans in his hand, poised in case she awoke and he needed them to cover the journal, and now he extracted his pen from its little niche in the rings of his own notebook. This practice of keeping the pen in the ring binding of his little note-pads was bad for the notepads but it was good for the pen—his beautiful pen, the translucent Gel Ink Roller G7. He unsheathed it now and as the moonlight crept into the room, as it touched his bare back, a swimmer's butterfly back, and as it kissed his gel-point pen, he flung himself defiantly in the face of all the Katie Rieslings in all the world. When he'd finished, he returned the diary to the suitcase, dressed, and let himself out of the house. It would be waiting for her next time she opened it, he thought as he inhaled the cool April predawn air, perhaps on the morning's Delta Shuttle, or perhaps on the way back from New York. Perhaps with another notch in her belt. It would be waiting for her in his best, his square and manly hand. "Samuel Mitnick," he said it aloud as if it mattered, *Samuel Mitnick,* as he made his way back home.

Sometimes Like Liebknecht

Just after the civil war in Russia, and just before Stalin started starving the peasants, there was NEP. NEP was nice, people liked NEP. But then Lenin died, and there was the struggle for power, and Stalin moved to consolidate his control of the Party. In response, Trotsky tried to organize a resistance. He gathered some of the old gang again ("We're getting the band back together!" "The band?" "To overthrow the government!"), and just as before they met in cramped apartments, agitated secretly among the workers, wrote intelligent analyses of the situation. But it was 1925 now, and things had changed: they were fighting their former comrades this time, and the working class was exhausted. Some of their number defected, some gave up, one of their friends committed suicide. A follower wondered aloud what would become of them. Even Trotsky had to admit he didn't know. "Sometimes you end up like Lenin," he said. "And sometimes like Liebknecht." Karl Liebknecht was the German communist murdered in prison alongside Rosa Luxemburg after their bid for power failed in 1919.

So why was Mark *always* ending up like Liebknecht? There was something about him—in his vicinity, women seemed constantly to decide to exercise their virtue, to try it on. They always emerged from relationships for whose moral shortcomings and sexual frenzy they wished to compensate, somehow, with Mark. "Every guy I've dated since I got here turned out to be a major asshole," Leslie Devendorf told him just the other day as they drove home from a history department potluck, with Mark, fairly drunk, wondering if he should try to kiss her. "Just fucking, fucking, fucking," Leslie went on, of the guys. "But that's over now." She smiled sweetly at him. Mark shook his head, amazed, and did not try to kiss her.

Half man, half Liebknecht, he drove home and called Celeste. It was still early. Maybe she'd invite him to New York?

"I cheated on my last boyfriend," said Celeste, who now had a different boyfriend, "and that turned out badly."

"I'm not asking you to cheat on him," said Mark, desperately. "I'm asking you to leave him."

"Mark," said Celeste. "Seriously. You live in Syracuse. What would we do, meet up on weekends in Scranton?"

This was painful to hear. "I have a car," Mark said with dignity. "I have a fast car and I can drive it to New York."

"Marky, you're sweet. I'm tired."

"Next weekend," said Mark. "Let me come down next weekend. Let me spend the night."

"Oh," said Celeste kindly. "Let me think about it, OK? Just let me think about it a little."

"OK," he said, and they hung up.

* * *

That was a week ago, and now he stood in his apartment, his and Sasha's old apartment, waiting for Celeste to call.

It was a little over a year since Sasha left. Or maybe he had asked her to. Or perhaps they'd decided it together. It was a little hard to piece together now. In any case, why'd they do it? They loved one another, were true to one another, even after moving up from New York they'd had a nice time together, more or less, driving to Skaneateles, going to bookstores, camping in the national parks. But his dissertation was taking too long, and really Syracuse was killing them. "If I have to spend another week in this fucking town," she had said, in English, "I will go fucking crazy." Usually she spoke Russian, but there were certain expressions she preferred in English, and to be fair they'd spent three years in this fucking town.

"Well," said Mark, coughing a bit, and choking, and making a face—and though this was an important moment, a really crucial situation, Mark saw an opening, a joke, and he was powerless not to take it. Sasha—his wife—*was already fucking crazy,* was the joke, and that's what his face said, and his cough, and his second cough, when he said, "Well."

"*Merzavets,*" she hissed, and she meant it. She'd never called him that before. They made up after that but they did not make up, they fought again and it got worse, and in the end it was typical Liebknecht on his part to have let her go. Yes, he had a dissertation to write on the Mensheviks, and yes, it was important that he write it. He was married to the Mensheviks, say, like all those socialists were married to the Revolution. But, with the notable exception of Liebknecht, they were also married to their wives. Liebknecht was not married to his wife. Liebknecht had a hole in the head.

105

It was early afternoon, an early Friday afternoon, but that made it early Friday evening in New York—that is, by the time he got there—so time was running out. Mark paced his apartment, what was left of his actually very attractive Syracuse apartment, and wondered what else he could do.

History was a science, according to the old revolutionaries; its laws could be studied. Mark had spent a year mourning for Sasha—yes, mourning, though it might not always have looked like mourning. He played hockey, he went to Tap's and got drunk, and gradually he began to relearn some of the movements he'd forgotten, some of the expressions his face needed to make to communicate with people who weren't Sasha. In the realm of women, in the realm of talking to women, it was particularly hard to tell what they thought. And it was hard to tell what *he* thought, what Mark thought. When he'd been married, all non-Sasha women seemed equally very attractive. Now he had to make some distinctions.

In that first year of his mourning, then, Mark studied the Internet. He found some very disturbing things. He found a site, for example, that showed the filmed adventures of a group of men who drove around in a van, or a small bus—technically speaking it was a van, though they called it a bus, the Buck Fuck Bus—and picked up young women, college girls possibly, on the street, and paid them a dollar for filmed sex. "Fuck yeah it's real," claimed the site, anticipating Mark's objections. For he did have objections. He could not believe that one could simply drive around in a van and pick up women—good-looking women—and get them to have sex with you, in your ratty little van.

What if Mark were to purchase a van?

The Buck Fuck Bus disturbed Mark's equilibrium. It wasn't

that he wanted to operate his own porn site, exactly; he was fairly certain that was not why he'd let Sasha go. And the anonymity of the filmed and very graphic sex did not appeal to him—it was the only site to which he ever subscribed, and he'd quickly canceled his subscription. Really it was the principle of the thing. If there were men Mark's age driving around in a ratty van, having sex with women, with complete strangers, and paying them a dollar for the pleasure—even if the women were their friends, or aspiring porn stars, or were being paid a lot more than a dollar—still, even then, *what was Mark doing in the library?* "I have spent," he had said the other day to Celeste, "most of my life in libraries." This was not quite true: he had spent most of his life in hockey rinks and gyms. And the time he spent in libraries these days was mainly spent looking at naked people on the Internet. But he'd not spent—this was the point—a single minute on the Buck Fuck Bus. Now he watched the wasted hours drift away, all those hours he had spent with Sasha, those warm gentle hours, gone forever with their marriage's collapse. Mark was like those stunned post-Soviet Russians during the draconian free market reforms, watching their ten-thousand-ruble lifetime savings, still active in their memories, turn overnight into fifty dollars. The Devaluation, it was called. And it hurt.

So in the second year of Mark's mourning he endured humiliations. He went to bars. He tried to talk to women. It was horrible. He was almost thirty years old! In a college town like Syracuse, they had a name for people like Mark, and it wasn't "graduate student in the department of history." It was *creep*. He bought girls drinks, as if he could afford to buy drinks; he asked them to dance, as if he knew how to dance; and then, alone, he stumbled home, or stumbled to his car, in which case he and the car stumbled home together.

One night, driving-stumbling home through the empty Syracusean streets after a wasted night in the bars of Armory Square, he saw a girl on a street corner near the horrific highway underpass, crying. The girl looked like she'd fallen through the space-time continuum, out of a dance club in Manhattan into the scariest part of Syracuse, so scary there wasn't even a gas station in sight; it was so scary that even drunken, careless Mark had rolled up his windows and turned down his radio, just in case. In addition to the usual horrors, the *Syracuse Post-Standard* had been filled that week with the arrest of a man who for nearly a decade had been kidnapping teenage girls on the street and keeping them in a kind of dungeon he'd built under a shed in his backyard. Eventually he'd blindfold them, drive back to where he found them, and leave them there, and when they went to the police, unable to say where they'd been and who had done this, the police didn't believe them. Now Mark was not a teenage girl, but the crying teenage girl was a teenage girl, and so he pulled his car over in an especially nonthreatening manner and asked, before the girl could become frightened, if she was all right.

"I lost my friends!" the girl said, and burst spectacularly into tears. "I was walking and then I lost them and I kept walking. Oh!"

"Hey," said Mark, trying to sound educated and adult as he stepped out of his car. American English was such a flattened tongue by now that it might have been hard to tell—from a few monosyllables—that Mark had once been considered a very promising scholar, in his field. The best he could do was sound grown-up. He moved away from the car a step and left the door open so that the light lit up the car's interior, empty as it was of bandits and fiends. "I can drive you, if you'd like," said Mark.

The girl hesitated, sobbed, and then, after peering into the empty car, nodded her head OK and sobbed once more. She was a sophomore at the nearby teachers' college, she told Mark; she had long brown hair and a tube top—she was perhaps twenty years old. The girl's breasts pressed forward against the fabric of her top, which pressed back and dented them slightly, you could see, on the side, just below her shoulder. Mark's stomach clenched. He drove her to her campus. If he were still a man married to Sasha, this would have been an odd situation, nothing more. But things had changed—and Mark, apparently, had changed. He began to wonder if the girl might like him; she seemed to lean toward him a little in the car. What is more, she had stopped crying, and she had gone out of her way, Mark thought, to tell him that she and her boyfriend had broken up just the other day, which is why she had got so drunk with her friends, and then they'd become separated, oh!, and Mark for his part was also reasonably drunk, though he'd sobered up somewhat, and finally, the point is, when Mark dropped her off at her dorm, which she looked at and pointed out as they pulled up, then turned to thank him—there was Mark's face, trying to kiss her! The girl jumped back in her seat, turned her head to the side, so that Mark kissed her clumsily on the cheek. Almost immediately she began to cry again. "I'm sorry," she said, apologizing for it wasn't clear what, and getting out of the car. "I'm not feeling well. Thank you for driving me." And walked briskly up to her dorm.

In Mark's entire life—a life of embarrassment, awkwardness, sexual fumbling, occasional drunken throwing up on people's couches, a really stupid major penalty in his senior-year game against Deerfield, and other assorted Liebknecht-isms—he had never felt more ashamed. He was a monster! And a loser! But first and foremost a monster! If Jeff, his saintly dissertation adviser, could see him now. Mark was disgusting. He went home and had another beer and tried to masturbate to some pornographic photos on the Internet—but they were too small, or partly obscured, because Mark was too cheap and too embarrassed to pay the four dollars a month, or whatever it was, to have them normally displayed.

The third period of Mark's mourning was even worse—more expensive, more humiliating, more emotionally damaging all around. It consisted of dating. This, Mark knew from watching television, was the prime historical movement of his time: it was the biggest industry, the most potent narrative device. It was bigger than sex, bigger than pornography. *Dating*, builder of cities. And Mark, of course, wanted to be current, he wanted to be historical, to participate in the truth regime as it was now constituted: to date, in other words, with maximum anonymity, without the safety nets of parental and social networks, potluck dinners, and work parties. It was the only way to find out, for sure, who Mark was.

So Mark dated. At home after his few duties at the university, he would log on to the Internet dating sites and send out a dozen personal messages to a dozen different women; he also, to widen his search, set up a profile that indicated he was in New York City. It was the way of the times, and Mark believed in the times. Unfortunately there were limits, certain formal parameters he had to observe. He could not post a photo along with his profile, for example, for fear that Sasha would be checking in on him, and in fact every message he ever exchanged with a girl—there weren't very many—was vetted by a subcommission Mark set up, inside his head, to make sure it wasn't actually Sasha in disguise. If he couldn't be sure, he didn't write back, and in this way his already tiny pool of willing women grew tinier still.

Nonetheless, for all the good it did him, he managed to secure some dates. J., one of his three New York dates (the only one that did not end with him sleeping in the 4Runner), lived in a tiny studio on 80th and Amsterdam, the nicest neighborhood in the city, decorated with posters of Al Pacino movies from the early 1980s, so anonymous, so casually everyone's favorite movies, that a desolation spread over Mark. He was drunk. S., from Ithaca, took him to her capacious sunny first-floor 2-BR, with wood everything and perfect place settings and fifteen books, total, on the shelf. D., who lived in a strange housing complex, with a little fake pond, somewhere between Ithaca and Syracuse, occupied a third-floor apartment with worn brown carpeting and toddler noisemakers for—what? a little girl? She hadn't mentioned that to Mark at the bar.

"It's OK," D. assured him. "She's spending the night with my ex."

Ex-husband, that is, with whom she'd had a child. Mark was stunned; D. was his age exactly.

And it wasn't as if, once in their rooms, things had gone so well for Mark. In New York, J. passed out on her twin bed. Mark lay next to her for a while, calling her name, "J.? J.? J.?," and finally went to the couch to sleep. In Ithaca, S. suddenly froze as they entered her bedroom. "I just can't," she said. "I just can't." "OK," said Mark, "we don't have to now." "I mean I don't know if I'll be able to later, either," she answered. S. was kind of strange; she'd held a long argument with the waiter at dinner about the wine. "OK," said Mark. S. began crying, and motioning for him to go, and he went, stopping at the all-night gas station on the edge of town to pick up a big black coffee that churned his insides out for the whole hour's drive back to Syracuse. D., whose little daughter was staying with her ex, was the only one willing to live up to the dating bargain. And Mark was also willing! But in truth he had gone home with D. largely out of principle—the photo she'd e-mailed him was at least five years old—and now he found to his dismay that he could not do what he had come to do. D. was kind and understanding, and let him stay the night. In the morning he saw that pulling up to the building he'd neglected to put his car into first—a forgetful man under any circumstances, Mark used first gear as his parking brake—and while he had ignominiously failed in D.'s cheap rooms his 4Runner had rolled backward across the small parking lot, off-roaded it over the little lawn, and landed in the fake pond behind the housing complex. The SUV stood now in the middle of the little lake, and the waves as they rose didn't even lap its muffler, and its alarm had failed to sound. Mark took off his shoes, it was summer, and rolled up his jeans and walked out to the car.

Still, for all his failures, he had heard so many things. "New York is a tough place," said J. "You might be the best-looking person in a room, but there will be someone smarter, or you might be the smartest but there will be someone better looking." Then she passed out. "I just find the guys at work so mean and hurtful," S. told him at dinner. She worked in the administration at Cornell. "My ex broke the mirror in the bathroom last week because he saw I had an Internet profile," said D. "But if I get a restraining order now, how are we going to share custody?"

And Mark, who was so used to Sasha, who was so used to being kind to Sasha, wanted to say to them: No, no, you are splendid. You are the best-looking and smartest girl in New York; your coworkers are idiots; your ex doesn't deserve you and you should get him out of your life. And to make sure of that I will stay here and repeat this daily. There is no one like you.

But he'd done that once before and now, un-Liebknecht-like, he refrained. You couldn't just go around saying that to people.

Celeste was not calling. The afternoon, the Friday afternoon, moved and waned, but Celeste did not call. Mark was in his apartment, staring at a phone that had become—after eight weeks of

Celeste's streaky calling practices—a kind of techno–death trap for the phone calls of Celeste. At first he'd simply used *69 whenever he got home, but that was expensive, and so he'd ordered unlimited *69. Unlimited *69 was good—sometimes he'd dial it just for fun—but it was not enough, because it only recorded the last call, and the trace of Celeste, he realized, could be obliterated by a Sasha call, or a call from Papa Grossman—and so finally Mark ordered flat-out Caller ID, and received, in the mail, a little Caller ID box, for which he bought batteries separately. This was enough, this was basically enough—and yet he worried, now, on this lonely Friday, that Celeste could simply block her number, clever Celeste, and that the cordless's ring was too weak, and he was playing his stereo too loud (all the hip-hop he'd missed, while married, now played on a continuous loop from the overlarge speakers—"Y'all can't *floss* on my level," Mark might have sung along now, if he'd been in a better mood), and also his hearing wasn't so great to begin with, truth be told, and so, in short, at long last, he simply thrust the receiver down his pants. "There!" he said to the empty apartment. "When the phone call comes, I will feel it like a man."

But it was not coming. He was in the fourth and terminal period of his mourning for Sasha. He had stopped looking to the Internet for dates—you spent eight hours on the computer, an hour in the car, and at the end of it was, well, another human being, who'd have been easier to meet in more human environments. He was still, it must be said, painfully awkward around grown-up and non-grown-up women, but he had met Celeste at a party in New York, and she had responded to him. By her education, her wit—she was a reporter for one of the big newsweeklies, and her tongue was sharp—and by her style, she was a category higher than everyone Mark had been out with since Sasha. That she had a boyfriend only proved it. Now events had reached a crisis. On Tuesday, they

113

had talked about his coming down; on Wednesday he had pressed the issue; on Thursday, they didn't talk, and Mark bravely refused to call, and went to sleep early to avoid temptation. Now it was Friday, and here we were.

More than that, it was four o'clock on Friday; outside, the people of Syracuse were gathering provisions for the long weekend, their cheap wines and jugs of rum and frozen pizzas and romantic comedies. In Syracuse it was better to stay drunk and drugged, and the Syracuseans knew it. On the news it was emerging that the man with the dungeon in his backyard had forced the captured girls to read to him from the Bible, before raping them. Nonetheless the city authorities were still planning to build an enormous mall, the biggest mall in America, on the outskirts of town.

If Celeste did not call soon, Mark would have no choice but to attend the history department potluck that night. He would have to get drunk; he would have to snort pharmaceuticals up his nose; and he might find himself in a situation with Leslie, and then what? He didn't think Leslie was very nice, for one thing, and for another, once out with someone in your department that was it; you were under strict surveillance from then on, at least in Syracuse. Whereas Mark loved Celeste. She came to him from the great world, from which he'd been shut out so long; she represented the possibility of *conversation*, of banter, which he'd never really had; and most of all, above all, most incredibly of all, she lived in New York. He loved New York.

Celeste was not calling because she had a boyfriend. This did not trouble Mark, very much: all women had boyfriends. The great Ulinsky once said that the Bolsheviks did not seize power—it was lying in the street, they merely picked it up. Mark was not a Bolshevik, however; he did not expect to find a presentable woman of anti-imperialist views lying on First Avenue, or East Genessee.

Indeed he would have been suspicious. Women did not leave their men for nothing—they left them for other men. And Mark himself, though he did not leave Sasha for another woman, did leave her for the *idea* of other women—all the non-Sashas out there, he saw them daily at the Starbucks, at the library, wearing fitted sweats, wearing hundred-dollar sunglasses, promising and promising. And who knew?

So it wasn't her boyfriend that troubled him; it was the position he was in now, and the looming danger of his ridiculousness. Just three days earlier, they'd been flirting on the phone. She was going to Detroit for the nation's biggest auto convention—she was the magazine's correspondent for odd stories, which were often odd criminal stories, and off she often went.

"Come by Syracuse on the way back from Detroit," Mark had offered.

"What's in Syracuse?"

"Misery. Depopulation. College kids getting mugged."

"That's not really national news."

"It will be eventually when the nation is all colleges and ghettos, colleges and ghettos. You should see this place."

"I would, Marky-poo, but it's not like I can just go where I please. Plus where would I stay?"

"You could stay with me. I'd sleep on the futon."

"No you wouldn't."

"You're right. My futon's covered with books about the Russian Revolution."

"No it's not!" said Celeste, and laughed. He could almost see it through the phone, the most glamorous laugh, he'd noticed it the first time they'd met at the party on East 11th Street, her mouth opening wide, and her head tilting back. She'd held out her hand, as if for balance.

No, Mark was not a Bolshevik. He found their tactics—and their rhetoric, their dogmatism, their secret police—appalling. But one thing he had learned from the Bolsheviks: history helps those who help themselves. *Yest' takaya partiya!*—Lenin's battle cry in 1917. We are that party, baby. Mark couldn't get over what a bunch of fuckers the Bolsheviks were. They yelled "Fire" in a crowded room, as Ulinsky once put it, and then took over.

Well, Mark was a fucker too.

"I'll come to New York then," he said. "We'll have a date."

"I can't have a date, Mark."

"Sure you can have a date. Tell your boyfriend you're going to dinner with someone from work. And I'll concoct a similar tale for *my* girlfriend. It'll be like eighth grade."

"You don't have a girlfriend."

"You're my girlfriend."

"Marky-poo," she said sternly, then sighed. It wasn't at all clear to Mark, not at all, why Celeste even talked to him—he was, to put it most plainly, *a divorced fifth-year graduate student who lived in Syracuse and masturbated to simulations of online pornography that he refused to pay for*—but who knows the secrets of the human heart? "You shouldn't talk like that, Marky-poo," Celeste had said, on Tuesday. "Though I admit I like it when you do."

Some theses, then, on the philosophy of history:

- All women have boyfriends.
- Mark was reasonably certain he could beat this boyfriend up.

It was four-thirty. Somehow the afternoon had slipped, the afternoon had scurried. Darkness began now definitively to fall on lonely Syracuse. Mark found that he was staring, the phone down his pants, at the bare white patches, like water stains, left on the wall by the framed photographs he'd taken down and sent to

116

Sasha. No one called, no one ever seemed to call. The apartment was in decline—Mark cleaned, occasionally, when there was some chance of visitors, but increasingly he made excuses (it would be dark by the time of the visitors). Over the years Sasha had set up a lovely little home for them, and Mark now resembled those peasants who took over the mansions of St. Petersburg after October and began burning the Venetian furniture for heat.

He gathered some books, some notebooks, some scattered pages of his dissertation, and walked out the door. He lived at the Roosevelt, on Genessee, and even in the middle of the day the parking lot behind the building looked desolate and dangerous. It was in fact strange that anyone ever used it, given that there was so much parking on the street. Maybe it was less dangerous than the street. When he and Sasha had lived for a year, that glorious year, in Queens, he'd woken every few days at 8:30 so as to move the 4Runner across the street; in Syracuse he could have parked five school buses in front of his building, and not moved any of them for months. So he didn't want to go back into the parking lot, in short; on the other hand, walking up Genessee, empty, downtrodden Genessee, was too depressing, and cutting through the park could get you killed. Celeste would respect him more, perhaps, if he chose the danger of the park—but then being murdered with a tire iron by a gang of roving teenagers would play straight into her boyfriend's hands. Her boyfriend wrote chatty lifestyle pieces for glossy magazines. He was a jackass. Mark exploded out the back door of the Roosevelt and jumped three steps later into his car.

And, arriving at the campus, failed to park. A mile south, on the other side of the highway, there was desolation, there was emptiness, there were parking spaces; even less than that, even just back at Mark's place, there were spaces, there were openings; but here the people massed and then, by the time Mark came, drove around and around. And Mark followed them. It was remarkable, the number of people in the world who had cars, specifically Ford Explorers, even in Syracuse, and how many of them sought parking.

He finally found a spot a few hundred feet into the park—barely more than halfway from his house, and it had taken him half an hour to reach it. In the library there would be sanctuary, there would be the accumulated weight of thousands of years of scholarship, and Mark adding his tiny little contribution, his tiny rock for the gravestone of human knowledge. Perhaps he could forget, momentarily, about Celeste.

Except he had a handful of quarters in his pocket and there were pay phones in the library, even now, even this late in history, and he could get up and check his messages anytime he wished. On the desk in front of him he placed the first volume of the exhaustive account, newly published in Russian, with a bright yellow cover, of the Menshevik Party from 1903 until 1931. He had reached approximately 1904. Those were the days: Switzerland, exile, the battles with Lenin. Had Lenin slept with Inessa Armand? Mark couldn't concentrate.

It was years ago now that Mark first entered this rather grim and unimpressive library. "We have," the great Ulinsky had told Mark when he came up for his interview, "a lot of work to do." The professor handed him a syllabus—Abramovich, Deutscher, Serge, Ulinsky—and Mark went into the library that very day to begin. When he returned to Syracuse in the fall, having read perhaps a fifth of what had been assigned, his head was a-blur with ideas, interpretations, interpolations. Two weeks later Ulinsky was dead of a stroke, and five years on Mark continued to explain that he had come to study with Ulinsky, and stayed for—the quiet.

He saw two of his fellow students on the first floor, checking their e-mail. They made no motions of greeting for Mark. While Sasha was around he'd simply laughed them all off; he'd had no time for them. They hung about in clusters and deliberated on departmental gossip, on the drugs they'd tasted, on the nicknames they considered assigning to one another. Mark avoided them because he was a Menshevik—from *menshinstvo*, the minority. A *menshinstvo* of Mark. Perhaps there was an arrogance to this, a sense of his own moral superiority. In any case now he was left to his own devices, in this business of waiting for Celeste to call him back.

It was past five already and the undergraduates in the library were on the phone, making their plans. It was always warm in the library and the girls seemed to think this gave them license to take off their clothes. Well, what could Mark do? These were the new conditions, the new late-capitalist conditions, and they were hard on Mark.

He shook his head, as if clearing it of cobwebs. Lenin was always accusing the Mensheviks of being revolutionaries in theory only—"professors of revolution," as someone else had put it—and in much the same way Mark was a scholar in theory only—he loved to talk about studying, but when he was in the actual library, he didn't get a whole lot done. Now he walked over to the pay phone, put in a quarter, and checked his messages. There was nothing; there was nothing at all.

It was not as if he'd never studied. His head was filled with Ulinsky's tales of 1917, and in fact he'd recited one such tale the one time he met with Celeste in the city. He was there for a conference at NYU, and busy Celeste came downtown to have lunch. She wore a smart gray suit and though naturally he had built her up unreasonably in his mind, she was still very impressive: compact, her black slightly curly hair short and expensively cut, her skirt straight but short as well. Upon saying hello, she tilted her head a little and looked at him. He was embarrassed by his jeans and his old dress shirt, but other than that he was OK. "Let's go down to the Vesuvio Bakery and sit outside," said Celeste. "How's that?"

It was fantastic, though the names and descriptions of the sandwiches confused Mark, so that he ended up ordering one with a lot of lettuce and some red peppers. But Celeste laughed at his jokes, and listened to him talk about the conference. As they sat on the benches in the little concrete park at the corner of Sixth and Prince, he told her the story of the unarmed Mensheviks.

It was a few months after the Bolsheviks took power, and the Mensheviks organized a large anti-Bolshevik rally—but asked the soldiers and sailors to come unarmed.

The sailors were incredulous. "Are you making fun of us, comrades?" they said. "And what about the Bolsheviks—are they little children? You think they won't shoot?"

But the Mensheviks insisted that the rally be unarmed. And the next day, the Bolsheviks fired into the crowd, and the rally was dispersed.

"That's hilarious," said Celeste. It was loud in their little park, so they huddled close and ate their sandwiches and talked. Mark was not expecting much, but he was very happy to be here.

"It's our first date," he said.

"Yes," said Celeste, looking at him again with a kind of appraisal in mind. "Thank you for taking me."

Mark had paid sixteen dollars for the sandwiches.

"And now I need to run!" She suddenly jumped up, remembering something. "This was very nice." She put a hand on Mark's cheek and leaned over to kiss him on the other. "You'll finish my sandwich," she said. "I'll talk to you this week."

And she was off.

As Mark ate Celeste's much more filling sandwich, he wondered that this attractive young woman could be interested in him. But then Sasha was also attractive. Mark just needed a pep talk. He considered the Mensheviks. They were wonderful people. Deeply schooled, thoughtful, chary, ironic, they told wry jokes and wrote intelligent books. After the Bolsheviks took power, they were scattered to Berlin, Paris, New York—also to the camps.

This was not encouraging. He was going to the gym.

Mark was a selfish person, perpetually imbibing information, sometimes alcohol, also food, and rarely giving anything back; his sole exports were theories and sweat. On the StairMaster, especially, he produced a prodigious amount of sweat and, looking out over the roiling cauldron of undergraduate flesh, a fair number of theories. He felt bad for the kids. Now Mark, Mark at this point was mostly in competition with death—he worked out a little, benched and StairMastered and sat up a little, and then death and decrepitude made him sag a little, and then he StairMastered a little, and so on. It was noble and dignified, his death and his exercise. Whereas the kids were battling only themselves: they spent an hour on the elliptical machines, another hour with the Nautilus contraptions, and then went out to the bars and drank eight beers. The next day they returned. He recalled his high school football buddy Willy Flint, who'd once declared, while taking a leak and sipping on his beer simultaneously, that he was enacting the "chain of being." Where'd he get that?

Mark pounded the StairMaster. You competed against yourself, in this life, and also against the people you went to college with. Those were the parameters. So was it cool to be stealing Celeste from her boyfriend, whom Mark had actually known, a tiny bit, in college? He considered this. It was cool. No doubt her boyfriend was a nice enough guy, but then why did he write such stupid articles? What's more, Celeste didn't really like him. And if it came to it, Mark could *wreck* him. You want some more? Mother-fucker? You want some more of this?

"Mark!" a woman's voice appeared next to his elbow.

He nearly fell off the StairMaster. Not only was he sweating so much that his T-shirt stuck to his torso and revealed the incredible hairiness of his chest, but in his frenzy over Celeste's gossip-mongering boyfriend he had begun to make inept shadowboxing motions with his arms.

"Leslie," he wheezed.

They hadn't talked since the other night, now a week ago, and Leslie looked at him neutrally, guardedly. It was unclear whether she was angry, but it was definitely clear that she expected some form of approach from him.

Mark couldn't do it. She had joined the program after Ulinsky was dead and two other real historians had defected to Columbia. Her seminar comments were filled with jargon imported from the English department—and not even Marxist jargon, at that! She was part of the new barbarian horde that liked

- cultural analyses of tiny objects,
- prescription medicines,
- elliptical machines.

"Pretty old-school," she said of Mark's StairMaster.

"I don't trust the ellipticals," he managed, even as his interval training took him into the higher exertion brackets. "I haven't seen the studies. It's like the number of peasant deaths during collectivization." He tried to take a breath. "No reliable statistics."

"And the treadmills?"

"The treadmills are a menace! You're not doing anything, you're just lifting your feet up. It's a big lie."

"I see," she said, not laughing. "How's your work coming?"

"Oh," said Mark. "I don't know. I've been thinking a lot about Lenin. I should be thinking more about my Mensheviks."

Leslie nodded. No one in Mark's department ever knew what he was talking about. "Are you going to the potluck tonight?" she asked. It was all up to Celeste, thought Mark. He told Leslie he was considering it. "I have this thing I have to do," he said, "but I'll try." Leslie gave him a skeptical look—what sort of thing could he possibly have to do, on a Friday night, in Syracuse?—and they spoke for a moment longer before she walked away. Why shouldn't she? Mark had been distant and even a little rude. He felt it. But what else was there to do? He had escaped from peril the other night, truth be told.

By the time he got off the StairMaster, Leslie was gone. Mark toddled on weary legs to the floor mats, placing a towel underneath him, and wiping around himself every time he stopped to rest. No one wanted to see a man this sweaty, and this old, leaving stains all over the equipment.

He thought about Lenin. It was not healthy to think this much about Lenin. But he'd really done it, was the thing. Lenin, not Hitler, was the Napoleon of the twentieth century. He had ideas. He was a scholar, a student. He seized power by willing it, by planning it; the world was a certain way, had been that way for two hundred years, for three hundred years, but Lenin didn't like it. The audacity of such an idea, in the Russian provinces, in the 1890s—remarkable. To be fair, it was also audacious for a twenty-eight-year-old man to sweat so profusely all over the sit-up mats.

Above all, of course, Lenin was an analyst of situations. This is what set him above the others. Right now Mark lived in a time of increasing consolidation of resources that may or may not lead to worldwide perpetual war; a time of truly rapid industrial development that may or may not, but mostly likely would, lead to a global climate catastrophe; and a time of political reaction that was exacerbating both of the above. Or anyway that's what it looked like. But what if in fact this period would be remembered as something else—as a period of progress, when America liberated the Middle East from a generation of tyrants? And a period of exponential scientific innovation that would save, rather than destroy, the earth? Who could tell? Who could say?

Lenin would be able to tell. Lenin would have been able to say. Mark lay on his towel and looked up at the distant, faraway gym ceiling. His brain had wandered back, willy-nilly, to the decline of him and Sasha. The trouble was—well, it wasn't like Mark was ignorant of the details, the minute details, the procession of events. But the subdetails, the archaeology of what happened—that was more complicated. Mostly it was money that had done them in. Money and Mark's ambitions, Mark's regrets. But mostly money. It wore you down: the worry, and the arguments, and the guilt, no longer a nebulous middle-class guilt but a specific guilt before a specific person; the disputes with the sorts of landlords you got when you tried to save on landlords; the nice car, a wedding gift from his father, that they couldn't maintain. They sent money to her family in Russia, a little bit of money, but it affected the way they counted what they had. And they had begun to grow old, was how it felt; whenever Mark met up with friends from college in the city he saw that his life no longer resembled theirs in any meaningful way. They dropped a hundred dollars on drinks; they took calls on their cell phones in the middle of conversations; and as they did so Mark calculated in his head the cost of the drinks on the table, counted the money he'd spent that day, and worried about Sasha's teeth, which they had to fix.

Back in the Syracuse gym Mark had stopped doing sit-ups and

was just lying there, motionless, taking up valuable floor-mat space. After all the trouble with Sasha he had now found Celeste. And it was not as if Celeste was rich or easygoing; in fact she seemed capricious like Sasha and morbidly sensitive like Sasha and often unpredictable, and her family had no money, just like Sasha's. Leslie was more like the anti-Sasha, he supposed, very broadly speaking. And he wasn't interested in Leslie. That was the thing.

Mark felt very comfortable on the floor mat.

"Professor Grossman?" A young man's voice startled him from above. Mark opened his eyes. Two shapes loomed there, blocking out the huge overhead lamps. One of the shapes said, "Are you all right?"

Mark shook his head yes. Had he fallen asleep? He smiled. "I'm good." He decided that the best move now would be to remain prone for the duration of the conversation; looking up again he saw the outlines of two students, a boy and a girl, from his European history section. One of them was named—Brad? The other was Gwyn. What was she doing with Brad? Gwyn was a beautiful girl with a square clefted jaw and thick, sensual lips; she looked like the Mona Lisa. He wondered that the other students could listen to him in section instead of staring at her; maybe they couldn't. As for Mark, the sweat that had poured so prodigiously from him while he flailed on the StairMaster was now caked onto his torso and arms and legs, possibly forever. He smiled up at Brad and Gwyn, whose genial concerned expressions, looming over him, he appreciated. "Good thing you woke me," he said, stretching. "I've got a big night out ahead."

"OK, Professor Grossman," said Gwyn. He thought he detected a slight edge of irony in her voice. "We just—sorry to bother you."

And, very respectfully, kind of nodding and bowing, the students retreated. Mark for his part sat up slowly, and then made his old-man's dignified way to the dressing room.

On Wednesday evening, Celeste had called for the last time. "Hey," she said.

"Hi," said Mark.

"I'm a little drunk," she said. "I shouldn't be calling."

"You should always call when you're drunk."

"I was out with the girls, then I came home."

"Where's your boyfriend?"

"He had some thing. Some event. He didn't invite me. And now it's lonely here."

"Lonely?" he echoed. "Lonely and cold?"

"A little cold."

"You're probably not wearing much."

"Not too much. How did you know?"

"I've been sitting here imagining you."

She laughed her laugh. "Are you trying to talk dirty to me, Mark Grossman?"

"Sort of."

"Don't you have a dissertation to write?"

He smiled. They'd grown more comfortable together on the phone, almost to the point where the space between them did not always need to be filled with sounds.

"Listen," she said. "What about if we had lunch this weekend? Can you come down for that?"

"Are you making fun of me, Celeste?" They had spoken so much of the logistics of their future sex life that this seemed unfair. "Are we little children?"

"No," she agreed. "We're not. I just don't know how this is going to work. You live so far away."

"Whereas he has an apartment in Chelsea."

"Yes, he does."

It was true. Silence and cunning were grand, but the exile might kill you. Still, he made his case. "Celeste," he began. "Listen to me. I beseech you. I feel like—I feel like we only have one chance at this, you know? And speaking strictly for myself, I've already done so many things that I didn't actually want to do. You know? I've succumbed to the prejudices of my class. I've embodied only the most pathetic cultural contradictions of my time, our time, and none of the really exciting ones. I guess what I'm trying to say is that I really like you, Celeste, and this is important."

There was a pause, naturally, and then Celeste said, "I like you too. . . ." With that ellipsis at the end, an extension of the sound, a sort of pleading.

"You're so *tragic*," she went on. "I mean, I like that, I do, but I also like to have fun."

"Fun? Are you kidding?" Mark had been indescribably moved, as sometimes happens, by his own soliloquy, and now there were tears in his voice as he said, "I love fun! There's a whole chapter on fun in my dissertation!"

"I can't tell if you're joking."

"I'm joking. Yes. I'm joking."

"I'm drunk."

"Can we go out this weekend? Can we have a date?"

"When?"

"Friday night."

"I don't know. Mark. This is really hard for me. Let me see, OK?"

"OK. But—this is it. I can't really—I need to know, OK? Will you let me know?"

"Yes," she had said, "I think that's fair," and that was the last time they'd spoken.

And now here he was, on Friday night, putting his clothes back on after his shower, as some remaining male undergraduates shouted at each other over his head about their evening's plans.

He left the gym at last, though not before checking his messages from a pay phone in the lobby. There was nothing, but this didn't mean much: Celeste might have called and failed to leave a message. He would have to go home and check his Caller ID. As he listened to his nonmessage, Brad and Gwyn walked by on their way out; he smiled at them and they looked back, a little pityingly. Had he put on his clothes funny? And then he remembered: one had to be a very strange man indeed these days not to have a cell phone. And Mark was already pretty strange.

Walking out, he found the campus already deserted, the girls in their dormitories putting on next to nothing for the bars—Leslie once told him about teaching a section late on a Friday afternoon, so that half the class was already dressed for going out, the girls crossing and uncrossing their legs under the little writing tables—and the boys in their frat houses, where they would begin drinking and plotting and playing beer pong, a truly stupid game. His car had a ten-dollar parking ticket on it, which Mark would never pay. "I've never paid a parking ticket," wrote the rapper. "It's twenty dollars now, and three hundred then. / You want your money, then come and get it. / *But you better bring two hundred guns and a hundred men.*" Rap music was the music of the lonely, thought Mark.

It was dark when he got home and learned, from his little Caller ID box, that there had been no calls, not a single one, and while trying to decide about the potluck he once again placed the phone in its waiting position. Ten minutes later—he was developing a lengthy, intricate analogy between the potluck and the pathetic first congress of Russian social-democrats in Stockholm in 1898—there was an explosion near his testicles. He knew it! If you waited and waited—like those revolutionaries had patiently waited—you would be rewarded in this life.

"Mufka?"

It was Sasha. Oh it was. And his heart filled with tears.

She called much less often now. She used to call at night, or whenever anything bad happened. "Mark"—unhappily—"I think there's a spider in my room." "Mufka"—at two in the morning—"I had a dream. It was awful." "Mufka, I hurt my finger." "How?" "I singed it. On the stupid pot without a handle." She'd taken the pot without a handle and refused to buy another.

"Mufka?" she said now. This meant "little fly."

"Sushok," he said. This meant "little bagel."

"What are you doing?" she asked sharply. He'd fumbled the phone in the process of taking it out of his pants, causing some commotion.

"I'm—nothing. Nothing much, Sushok."

She accepted this. "Mufka," she said. "I'm sad."

"I know, Sushok. I'm sad too."

"Mufka, listen." She could always turn, so quickly. "Today I learned that Canadians think John Irving is a great American novelist. Isn't that funny?"

"Don't be a snob, Sushok."

"Oh, all right. I really like Canadians, actually. They're very polite."

"Polite is good. Polite is a start."

"Mufka, will you visit me?"

"Of course I'll visit you."

"It's not far. And the border's not like the Belarusian border at all, they let you right through."

"I know, Sushok."

"Oh, Mufka," she said, and suddenly burst into tears. "Why did we do this?"

"We had to, Sushok," said Mark. "We were sad."

"We're sad now."

"That's true."

She cried some more. Mark listened. There was a time when her tears received, automatically, his tears in return. Now, standing in their old living room, he respectfully hoped that Celeste didn't call while he was on the line with Sushok. She stopped crying.

"Listen, Mufka." She turned on a dime, his Sasha. "Don't cry, OK? Don't you cry too. It'll be all right. Everything will work out. We're not even that old. I have a friend here, her name is Susan, she's even older than we are. So don't be sad, Mufka. I'll talk to you later."

And that was it. This phone, this aging, cordless Syracuse phone—such amazing things came over the line through it.

Oh, they had split up because they had to, they had to, he knew in his bones that they had to; and now, awkwardly and ridiculously, he was making a new life. Disoriented after her call, as he always was, he was beginning with a kind of resignation to put the phone back into his pants when it rang again. It was Sasha, he thought, forgetting to tell him something.

"Mark?"

But it was Leslie.

"Oh, hey." Mark gathered himself. He heard some noise in the background. "Are you already there?"

"Yeah. I got bored sitting at home. So, listen, I don't know if you're coming, but if you do come, you should bring some beer. There's a beer deficit."

Mark agreed to bring some beer.

It was night now, in dilapidated Syracuse, the cars crawling ominously down Genessee, with occasionally a snatch of hiphop crashing through Mark's window. He would give Celeste ten more minutes, and then he would go. But he did not return the phone to his underwear this time—what if his father called? P. Grossman was a reasonable man, to be sure, a man who enjoyed the pleasures of life, and although he was chagrined at the loss of

Sasha he quietly encouraged Mark's pursuit of further women. He would not think it blasphemous to care for Celeste, or to have chased after girls, even on the Internet. Wasn't it the case that fathers of his generation mostly feared that their sons would turn out a little funny, a little . . . gay? So P. Grossman would have been pleased, in general, with the new Mark. Which is not to say he wanted to hear about the phone receiver down Mark's pants.

Ten minutes passed, and then fifteen, and then half an hour passed, and finally there was nothing to do. He had pushed Celeste too far; he had tried to mask his desperation, but she had felt it. So it went—he was Liebknecht, after all. He put on a clean pair of jeans and went out, looking both ways before crossing the parking lot. He drove the near-empty streets of Syracuse to Peter's, where Brooklyn beer was sold for $5.99 a six-pack, and bought two packs. Then on to the house on Fellows, where they had these things always, where there was enough room for people to get drunk and fall over and no one to bother them.

Oh, what a sad place was Syracuse, what a sad place was graduate school! And on Friday nights these attempts at human togetherness. And yet, with the collapse of the discipline of history into *Antiques Roadshow,* history of social trends, history of the spoon, these department potlucks were pretty much all they had.

"Hey!" He was greeted in the front room by Troy, short and goateed, student of the cultural history of the coffee mug. "Mark, man, just the man we wanted! Mark, what do you think of B-2-phen?"

"What?"

"B-2-phenobetymide."

"Oh. I don't think I've ever—what, injected it?"

"No, it's a pill."

"Sorry. Swallowed it."

"You snort them," Troy said, contemptuously, and turned back to the conversation as Mark headed for the kitchen. The apartment occupied the first floor of an old, handsome Victorian triple-decker, the kind of apartment that didn't exist in New York but would cost $2,500 a month if it did. In Syracuse it cost $600. Mark had noticed that when things cost this little, people tended to get depressed, though as a historian he knew that this might not be a direct causal relation; there might be an intermediate or prior step.

In the kitchen, Mark met Leslie. She looked glum, in the kitchen, all by herself, with too much makeup on. The boys hadn't put a cover over the fluorescent ceiling light.

"Hi," said Mark. "You're in here all by yourself."

"Troy was going on about the pills," she explained, sighing. "I got annoyed."

"Yes, I understand that," said Mark. "All those pills and herbs. What's wrong with beer?"

"Yeah," said Leslie, a little warily.

"Beer and the Russian Revolution!" Mark cheered.

"Uh, right."

Leslie wasn't as nice as she could have been. Mark decided to take the high road. "I'm sorry about today in the gym," he said. "I was rude."

"It's OK," she said. "I was probably weird in there. I get self-conscious. The undergrads walk around practically naked. It's disgusting."

"Well," said Mark. He took umbrage at this insult to the naked undergraduates, but he kept his mouth shut. Instead he said, "Bottoms up," and he chugged one of the beers he'd brought. Then he scanned the counter behind Leslie and located a bottle of rum. He did not love rum, but he didn't mind it, and then, standing in the kitchen, under the bare fluorescent light, after a very bad week, a week during which his hopes of Celeste evaporated, during which his dissertation, while not stalling exactly, certainly did not progress, and in fact began to seem slightly ridiculous—during which the entire project, the sometimes utopian project, of Mark's life began to look like it was going simply to fail—well, Mark made a kind of decision. He said to Leslie: "Shot?"

"OK," she answered, still a little glumly.

But Mark was undeterred. He poured two shots into plastic cups and then, as Leslie put her hand out, quickly drank them both. "Ha-ha!" said Mark. "Psych."

"Hey!" she said.

"Sorry." He poured the shots again and now handed one to Leslie. He chased this third shot with some more beer. They were still alone in that kitchen; you could already tell, if you'd had any doubt about it, that this wasn't going to be much of a party.

In the months to come Mark would have occasion—he would have many occasions—to wonder just how drunk he was, and just how culpable he was, just how conscious he was, when he kissed Leslie briefly in the kitchen and then walked out with her to her car—she insisted they take her car, and Mark agreed to this so long as he was the one who drove. There was only one person Mark trusted to drive a car this drunk, and that person was Mark.

Leslie occupied the top floor of a two-story house just down the street from him on East Genessee. That was another thing about Syracuse, in addition to the fact that everyone was drunk: everyone had a nice apartment in which to sit wretched and alone. Some apartments were nicer than others. Leslie's had a little kitchen table with some plastic flowers on it, and posters from popular films, ironically posted; a little green rug in the center of the main room in front of the television; and on the coffee table a gigantic volume of Fernand Braudel's *The Structures of Everyday Life*. One thing you could say about grad students—"Excuse me a moment," said Leslie, and ducked into the bathroom—they might be philistines—in fact Mark now scanned the two bookshelves and they were exclusively populated by books from Leslie's field of study—but you'd never get bored by their libraries, unless you had something against the new trend in microhistories, in which case eventually you would.

There was still time to run. He didn't really want to be here; even in his current state he knew this. He could walk down the street and be home. And—but here was Leslie. She'd put on some lipstick, for some reason; she'd done something to her hair. Immediately she was next to him, and they were locked in an embrace. She wore perfume. He was a little dizzy. So this was it, then—this was going to be his new life in Syracuse. There were hands involved now, and some tugging. Mark supposed it could be worse. And soon—they were grown-ups, after all—they were on her full-size bed, big enough it seemed at the time—and tugging off their clothes. Mark didn't know if this is what he wanted to do, but events had a clear and simple logic, at this point, and he followed the logic. Then, suddenly, Leslie pulled up.

"I can't do this," she said.

"Why not?"

"Because I can't. I'm not going to do any more one-night stands. I told you that."

"OK," said Mark.

"I've just been taken advantage of, a lot, I think," said Leslie. "And we're in the same department, and that would just be weird."

"I guess so," said Mark.

"I mean, if we just hooked up. I guess it wouldn't be weird if we were like a couple."

"Right," said Mark thoughtfully. Then he tried to kiss her again, and she let him. After a while, once again, she stopped them.

"Do you want to be a couple?" she said.

"OK," said Mark. He sort of mumbled it.

"You're going to love me? And tell me you love me? And go on weekend trips to Skaneateles?"

Mark had often gone to Skaneateles with Sasha. Did Leslie know this? He rolled over and lay on his back, looking at the ceiling. Was he prepared to do this? What if in a couple of weeks he was no longer prepared? It might take more than a couple of weeks to get out of this. It might take a couple of months. But if he knew that now, shouldn't he stop? Shouldn't he let them both off the hook right away? At the same time, Mark had not been with a woman in many months. What would Lenin have done? Lenin would have called Mark's hesitation a social-democratic scruple. It's pretty clear what Lenin would have done. And so Mark did it, too.

"OK," said Mark. "Let's do it. That's what I want."

Leslie was as surprised as he was to hear him say this.

"Really?" she said, getting used to it.

"Really," said Mark.

Now it was her turn to say "OK," and she did. She slid down next to him and kissed him. He kissed her in return. This was what he wanted, even if it didn't feel like what he wanted. It was, in any case, the best he was going to do in this terrible town. Lenin always made the best of a bad situation, and so would Mark.

Awkwardly, after some false starts, partly attributable to drunkenness, they made love, and then they lay, like strangers, on her full-size bed, now one size too small. Mark felt sick at heart and so, he suspected, did she. Or not. It was hard to tell. He wanted desperately to leave, but he knew he could not leave, not after what he'd said. They lay there and eventually, without saying anything, they fell asleep. In the morning, like zombies, they drove to the Blind Eye Diner just off the highway and ate some eggs. Mark clutched the *Syracuse Post-Standard* to his chest: new revelations were emerging about the man who kept girls in his dungeon; plans for America's largest mall proceeded apace. From the side all this newspaper reading might have looked like intimacy. Mark felt queasy, after all the rum last night. Deliberately, after their breakfast-lunch, she drove him—Mark sat in the passenger seat now, like a little boy—through a gray drizzle to his car, parked outside the house on Fellows Avenue. So everyone had seen it there when they left; so everyone knew. She leaned over for a kiss and told him to call her soon.

It was past three o'clock, on a Saturday, when he finally got home to his apartment. How different it now looked! Cozy, messy, comfortable—if only he'd just stayed here all night.

He wandered over, somewhat idly, to his phone. Perhaps . . . Mark did not have time to finish the thought. There were eight calls on his Caller ID. Eight calls? He flipped through them: Celeste's cell phone from an hour ago; before that, a bunch of calls from the Syracuse Sheraton. Had something happened at the Sheraton? And if something had happened at the Sheraton—an emergency, say—why would they call Mark?

The first message was from nine o'clock the night before—just minutes after he left for the party. "Marky-Mark," said Celeste, Celeste herself. "Where are you? It's the weekend, you know. No time to be at the library." Mark had convinced her that he spent all his time at the library; it was his most romantic image of himself. "Maybe I'll call there and have them page you. You won't believe this—but I'm in Syracuse! Isn't that crazy? I'm supposed to write about that psycho who was keeping girls in his basement. Did you know him, by any chance? I'm at the Sheraton near the university. But it's a one-night-only engagement, Marky-poo, so call me."

That was last night.

Message 2, 9:30: "Marky-poo! I'm sorry I didn't call before, they told me very last-minute and then I wanted to surprise you! Call me!"

Message 3, 11:00: "Mark. You're out at some party with your brilliant grad school friends. I'm sitting here at the Sheraton in a bath towel, all by myself. I have to get up early and talk to a bunch of cops and be on a plane in the afternoon. Call me!"

Message 4 was received just half an hour ago: "Mark, I don't know where you went, but apparently—whatever. I'm on my way to the airport. You don't need to call me when you get this, I am going to be crazy with things the next week. I'll call you when it's over. Bye, Mark."

Oh, God. The anger in her voice, the frustration, was not feigned. He stood in his apartment, his messy, sweet, his stupid apartment, freighted with all the stupidities he'd committed in it, all the lies he'd told. And until last night they'd all been lies of omission, of not telling the people he loved how much he loved them, with how much agony of love. And now, what a grave miscalculation. He'd thought he was being like Lenin. He'd thought it was October 1917, a time for action, for decisive steps.

Except he was wrong. It was not October 1917 but January 1919, and not in Russia but in Germany, when the Spartacists, led by Luxemburg and Liebknecht, called the workers out onto the streets of Berlin—and the government, the social-democratic so-called government, called out its Bavarian peasants, its demobilized soldiers, who beat the workers to death, and then murdered, while the government looked away, both Liebknecht and Luxemburg. Oh.

The phone rang now in Mark's apartment.

"Hey." It was Leslie. "What are you doing?" she said.

Uncle Misha

Before I finally escaped from Baltimore in the spring of 2003 I spent several months driving up I-83 and I-78 to New York. It had been a point of great contention, between my father and my uncle Misha, whether it was faster to take I-95 all the way up, as my uncle and most other people would have it, or whether, as my father fervently believed, I-95 was so heavily trafficked, so miserable, so corrupt, especially in its Delaware portion, that one should take the long way—up to Harrisburg and then across the great state of Pennsylvania at top speed. Keep moving, was the gist of my father's directive. Keep moving. And I followed it.

I did this in a Nissan Maxima—which was after all a graduation gift from my father—a sleek black machine on its last few journeys in this life. It was a car about which my father's Russian mechanics now spoke in the most melancholy reproachful tones, as if to say, If only you hadn't taught Jillian to drive stick on it, oh, it might have lived a hundred years.

I too had my regrets. The car had started eating cassette tapes sometime in the late nineties, and we never replaced the thing with a CD player. The precariousness of our life together in the run-up to the election had come to infect everything, so that I often felt like, with us possibly breaking up, it probably wasn't worthwhile to replace our deteriorating earthly goods. Of course this made no sense—the goods would remain, even if we didn't—and now, in the case of the CD player, it really was too late—the car was dying, and though I had saved $150, I had paid for it a hundred times. Here I was on the way up to New York and I was forced to place a boom box on the passenger seat beside me and try to keep things steady, because the boom box had no tolerance at all for bumps and jolts, and the disc, if the car shook, would simply reset, in which case I'd have to fiddle with it, and this is how car accidents happen, at least to me. Luckily the long stretch of 78-22 across the Mennonite state of Pennsylvania, and 81 before it, was a good straight road—for I was speeding down it at ninety miles an hour, because I was free, again, and because I wanted to prove that my father's way was the fastest way, and so if I'd crashed into a tree, in short, because I'd been fiddling with the CD in the boom box, I'd have died in a burst of flames.

I was free. I was free, and having received my freedom I immediately reached for all the things I'd been so put-upon to do without. So I would leave our apartment and go moshing, sort of, at the Ottobar on North Howard; in our apartment I would leave my clothes on the floor, I'd go jogging at all hours of the day, at all hours of the night. I looked at pornography on the Internet, an activity about which I'd heard so much; I even tried, very briefly, to meet girls online, though I soon learned that this was mostly a way of meeting closeted gay men from Chevy Chase. And most important I would sometimes give up a hard-won parking spot to drive to New York to see a girl named Arielle whom I had met during the 2000 campaign. We had e-mailed a bit since then, and I had called her soon after Jillian left for California. "Oh, hi," she said, ambiguously, after I'd explained who I was. We had kissed one time in Los Angeles, after cops on horseback had chased us away from the Democratic convention at the Staples Center, which we were protesting, and it's possible that the kiss had meant more to me than it did to her. And it had been a while. But I persisted, and we'd begun to see each other, if it can be called that.

I was twenty-seven years old. Looking back now I see there were things I did not know about life. For example, that if a woman doesn't sleep with you right away, she might stay inclined not to—the pleasure of resisting has become too keen, or maybe she doesn't like you. At the time it seemed I was just messing up, showing up too late or too early; too aggressively or too demurely. I didn't know what the trouble was, exactly, but I thought it could be figured out.

Arielle was in New York for law school, and part of the trouble was that she lived with two other law students who disapproved of my visits, chaste though they were. "I can't *tell* them that," she protested, when I pointed this out. "I can't tell them anything. They're so weird!" She paused mournfully. "When I was searching for the room they posted it as being in the Gramercy area, but this is Murray Hill. That should have been a clue."

"You could move?"

"I signed a lease. And it's cheap here. And I can almost walk to school."

"But you have these terrible roommates."

"I have a terribly inconsiderate suitor, that's what *I* have."

Because the other part of the trouble was that she had a boyfriend. "In Boston I was involved in a situation where the boy had two girlfriends, so I don't see why I shouldn't have two of you," she'd said initially, but sometimes she had second thoughts. As for me, I didn't really mind. I loved my freedom, of course, in those first few months after Jillian left ("Tell me again why?" she had said on the last day. "Because I don't feel what I know I should feel," I said, lamely, and she nodded, generously, studiously, my studious Jillian)—but I also felt as if the thread of my life had snapped, and though my history with Arielle was a brief history, it was history enough. Even inconclusive wrestling on her bed meant something to me, for now. Also, I thought she was funny.

And now—on the night I'd driven up, a Friday, at top speed on 78, through the Holland Tunnel, straight up the gut of Manhatten on Sixth and across at 34th, and finally found a parking spot not far from Arielle's and valid, what is more, until Tuesday—she finally decided that my visits were too much. "We can't do this in my apartment anymore," she announced.

I froze. What did this mean? And my parking spot! Very warily I said, "All right."

"I asked my cousin if we could use hers," she offered.

"You did?" I was surprised. "I didn't even know you had a cousin."

"We're not very close. I see her about once a year, at like Passover."

"And you asked to use her apartment for sex."

"Not in so many words. And *sex* is putting it a bit strongly, don't you think? But yes, in effect. They're never even *here* past Friday at six."

"I'm touched."

"I asked if I could house-sit on weekends. And she said why not come up to Vermont with them. Skiing."

"And?"

"And now I have to go to Vermont. But no house-sitting."

"Right."

"And I'm not doing this here anymore, I repeat."

"Right," I also repeated. I would bluff my way through. I said, "I'll get a hotel room when I come up."

"And?"

"And—we can spend time there, when we're not out on the town having fun!"

"Hotels are slimy."

"Not the clean ones!"

She turned her head to look at me, her big blue eyes and thin mouth turned down in an expression of fine sarcasm. We were lying on her bed in a state of partial undress. She was a thin girl, and pale, her jeans hung loosely on her like a boy's, and it was a source of endless amazement to me that I was so fixated on her—and yet I was, I was! We'd meet up, have a few drinks, then a few more, and then go home and wrestle. "The rape game," Arielle called it. "I don't think that's funny," I'd say, and she'd say, "Yes you do." I'd wrestle her out of some clothes, then myself, then she'd say "Stop," then we'd wrestle some more, then she'd say, "Really, stop," and then we'd negotiate. Right now we were in a negotiation. I had managed to get my shirt off but not hers. Then we'd had the fight about the hotels. She said: "Please don't become hysterical."

"I'm not becoming hysterical," I said. "What do you propose?"

"Don't you have an uncle in the city?"

"No. Not really. We're not on speaking terms."

"You should get on speaking terms. And in the meantime get out."

"What?"

"Out. Now. Have you put on weight? My bed's too small."

"It's two in the morning. It's cold out."

She was sitting up against two pillows, like a queen, miles away from me.

I said: "I have a great parking space, I have it until Tuesday."

"That's all right, there's plenty of parking in Baltimore."

"But it's dangerous!"

"I'm serious," she said. "Go."

It was late by then, too late to ask someone if I could stay over, and anyway I didn't want to. Ferdinand lived with his girl-friend and now disapproved of anyone who didn't; Nick would start a long argument with me about the failures of the Left. I had momentarily lost my taste for New York. I walked, frozen and unhappy, to my car—so elegantly parked on 38th Street—and wondered at all the apartments that were not my apartment, and all the people living in them. Such warmth inside them! Such injustice! And there in the distance Grand Central Station looming like a cathedral. "Back then," someone had written of the old Penn Station, "one entered New York like a God." It was true now of Grand Central, and earlier in the evening I too had entered like a God (through the Holland Tunnel). Now I pulled out, defeated and still a little drunk, enough so that I didn't trust myself on scary, speedy 34th and crawled instead on side streets and marginal avenues until I reached the warmth of the tunnel again, almost empty at this hour, and went in.

Driving back through Pennsylvania on 78, nearly falling asleep, it was just too dangerous to fiddle with the CD player, the thing kept skipping and resetting, skipping and resetting, and before I pulled over at a truck stop near Harrisburg to finally change it I listened over and over to the first song of an album called *American Water*. "I asked the painter," it went, "why the roads are colored black. / He said, 'Man, it's because people leaving / know no high-way will bring them back.'" My life, I thought then, as I briefly considered taking 496 down and reconnecting with 95 on the other side of Philadelphia, before reconsidering—"You don't know anything about 95! You don't know anything about anything!" my father had yelled at my uncle the time they'd had a blowup over the route—my life was not very rock and roll. In a rock and roll life, you forgot everything and just moved on. Whereas I, if you asked, could still list all the people I'd ever been friends with, and all the people I'd ever loved, and all the things we did, and what they'd said. What is more I had a fellowship at a Washington think tank to write a postmortem on the 2000 election—what had gone wrong? I was looking into it. I'm still looking into it.

Uncle Misha had an apartment in Washington Heights. I even happened to know that he was usually out of town on weekends. But things had been said by him, years ago, that could not be unsaid, and not just about highways.

He'd arrived in bucolic, isolated Clarksville when I was fifteen years old. My mother, whose brother he was, had recently been diagnosed with cancer, and for a long time I thought that Misha had come because he'd heard the news. Later on I realized that, as with certain hurried weddings, the dates did not add up. But how else to explain it? He had no business there. He was thirty-five, he had a degree in American literature from Moscow University, a fairly dubious degree even in Moscow, and a just plain ludicrous degree for a Russian immigrant in the States. Before emigrating he'd had an exciting, or anyway a reasonably interesting, life in Moscow. He had girlfriends, he had briefly been married: an educated nonalcoholic with most of his teeth intact, he was considered something of a prize. But he had accomplished little of actual substance, and perhaps he began to feel—I begin to feel it with him, or rather I begin to feel it too—that what he needed was a new place, a new city, he needed to see the world anew so that it could see him that way, too.

In the meantime my father was keeping up a steady campaign

on behalf of the States. He was like Radio Free Europe, my father, except he wrote letters instead of producing radio broadcasts, and he wasn't directly funded by the CIA. We had a nice house by then, and two cars, in a prestigious town where there were almost no Russian immigrants, even if our part of it was not as prestigious as some others. So maybe it was just vanity on my father's part, the wish to make people see what he had done. Misha would later think so, certainly. But also it was just his belief—his beautiful belief. Halfway through life my father found himself in a place where he'd been spit on almost daily and insulted—and he left! He fucking left, and halfway through his life he went halfway across the world and found the capacity, inside himself, to believe that this new place was cardinally, was essentially and deeply different. This required courage as well as naïveté; and it required strength, too.

But all beliefs have their victims, and Misha was my father's. He made some brave forays into the world upon arriving in America—he went to the libraries, the mall, he went to movies and even some bars, though he couldn't afford those, and then he stopped. Eventually he settled in, to the partial annoyance of my father, who thought he was turning down good job opportunities, in the room next to mine and at the dinner table, feeling trapped. He spent all his time feeling trapped and fooled, and he believed it was my father who had fooled him.

"You're like the Bolsheviks," Misha said one day. It had come to him, he said, as he drove through the old Protestant section of Clarksville, past the big churches, the grand mansions set way back from the streets with lawns stretching to them like golf courses—all the places Misha knew by now he'd never be able to afford. "You keep talking about this bright luminous future, meanwhile we're all living in shit and you don't care. You just keep talking about it and feeling great."

"Are you talking about this house?" my mother said. She was going through chemo and had lost her hair and wore a little cloth on her head, to cover it up. "You consider it shit?"

"It's a nice house. But you think that means the people around here like you. They hate you! Haven't you noticed? There are fucking swastikas at Pimple-Face's school!"

"Bozhe moi," said my mother, at the vulgarity.

"I'm sorry if I express myself too strongly." Misha suddenly became poisonous. "You used to be a believer in strong expression."

"Misha, *polno,"* my mother said. Enough.

"What do we care if some kid draws a swastika in the bathroom?" my father thundered over them. "GET A JOB!"

My mother had been offended by Misha, but it was the sound of my father's terrible voice that caused her to break down and weep—at the table, in her little do-rag, in her dentures, and all for nothing, as it turned out, all that medicine and all for nothing. It was she who had suffered in this place; it was she who abandoned her books to become a computer programmer, learn to drive, learn about American mass culture, and now she had a pimply jock son who was forgetting Russian . . . and attending a school where, in fact, there had been a couple of swastikas on the bathroom wall. They were innocent swastikas, at least as far as we were concerned—people were suspicious of us for being Russian, but no one knew or cared that we were also Jewish, and in any case the only ethnicity people in our part of Maryland could ever really hate was blacks—but that wasn't the point. Misha was right, is the point, and though my mother hated him for saying it, she hated my father for yelling, for she herself had thought all these things too—had thought them and stifled them, the way mothers during the war would stifle their little babies, strangle them to death if necessary, if a baby by its crying was going to reveal a hiding place and get everyone without exception killed.

Misha must have thought that our house, our life, our two cars would insulate us against the whining of a thirty-five-year-old man with no money, no prospect of earning any money, no social position, and with bad smoke-ruined teeth and skin. He had not yet moved to New York, reconstructed his life; for now, in Maryland, he was nothing, worse than nothing. And as my mother ran from the kitchen weeping, Misha sat there with a look of deep perplexity upon his face. He must have thought, I thought, that we wouldn't care.

Which is just to say that I drove and drove. My father's route added sixty miles; I don't think even he would have prescribed it at night. But it was a way of seeing the world, I suppose. At around four in the morning, as I was getting onto 83, my cell phone rang. It was Arielle.

"Where are you?" she said.

"I'm coming up on York, home of the forty-five-pound steel plate."

"In Pennsylvania?"

"Yes. You can drive a lot faster on 78 than 95."

"In the middle of the night?"

"Look, it's how we do things."

"Why didn't you just call your uncle?"

"Because I didn't. And I won't. He—he didn't vote in the last election. He abstained."

"He did?"

"Yup. He said it made no difference who was President."

"He did?" Arielle was momentarily speechless. "Well," she recovered, "we'll avenge ourselves by doing terrible things in his apartment he wouldn't approve of."

"He's from the Soviet Union, Arielle. They were atheists. He doesn't disapprove of anything except money."

"We'll order expensive takeout."

"In Washington Heights?"

"We'll throw money in the fireplace."

"I'm not calling him."

"Ugh," said Arielle.

I loved the way she said it. "Do that again," I said. "Make that noise again."

"No," said Arielle, and returned me to the road and myself.

We tried to forgive Uncle Misha, and he us. Or maybe we didn't try, exactly—we just assumed it would happen. No one had really done anything. Money had not been expropriated, wills not contested—my grandmother had an apartment in Moscow, and it would be Misha's, no problem. We thought things would just work themselves out and instead they grew worse.

I finally got back to my neighborhood at six in the morning.

I drove up St. Paul, past our place, and there was nothing. I went over to Calvert and nothing. There was "Area 28" parking and meter parking, but I was not going to take a spot and then get up two hours later to move again. This was Baltimore! It's practically impossible to rack up parking tickets in Baltimore and yet I'd managed to do it, in no small part because my father had insisted I register the car in his new town, to save on insurance, and so I was not a member of Area 28. I wasn't a member of anything. I was a man in my late twenties who had accomplished next to nothing, had loved, properly, no one, and who was driving a dying car around a city in whose suburbs he'd grown up, but which remained to him, as he to it, a stranger. I drove up to the monument now, to the big obelisk honoring our nation's founding father, and then all the way down to Biddle, which really was as far as I was willing to go. Still nothing. I got back on St. Paul, and then made a quick left onto Eager, almost involuntarily, onto that crazy little on-ramp, and suddenly I was back on the highway, and a few turns later, I was actually on 95. I headed south. We no longer lived in Clarksville, we lived now on the water, near the naval academy, but I kept driving, and before I knew it I was getting off 95 again—it was actually a pretty nice road, between Baltimore and D.C.—and onto 108. Hello, River Hill HS. The football stadium, if it could be called that. I had once run the ball thirty yards downfield in that stadium before some guy accidentally stuck his helmet into it and caused it to pop in the air like a flying fish. And then, on weekend evenings, drawn there by some mysterious force, we returned to get drunk behind the tennis courts. I pulled into the lot now, tired and smelly and nearly thirty years old. It was empty, the entire lot was empty. I pulled the lever to the side of my seat, fell backward, and immediately passed out.

I woke up to someone tapping on the window. I had left it open a crack, so as not to suffocate, and now, awake, I found I was shivering. The person knocking wore a dark heavy coat; the person knocking was a cop.

"Good morning!" he said when he saw I'd woken up.

"Hi," I said, squinting up at him and very slowly and deliberately lifting myself up toward a sitting position. "Sorry about this."

"You can't be here."

"Yes." I explained that I'd been driving home and became sleepy and this was the only place I could think of to stop.

"Were you drinking at all?"

"No, Officer. I was driving from New York, there's a kind of complicated situation there, and I just became very drowsy. I'm going to move on now."

I could see him trying to think of some way to keep me under his dominion, for just another minute. But I was too old, I was too confident, even as a total derelict, sleeping in my car, I was still not really in any danger from him and he knew it.

Things do change. They change, but sometimes it's hard to tell the reasons why or what it means. We had spent so many nights running from the cops in this very place: before we figured out where to buy beer, we used to make bizarre drinks from our parents' liquor cabinets and sit on the baseball field behind the courts with the alcohol, and the cops, sensing us there with their special cop sense, would shine a spotlight on the field as they drove by. We'd hide. Occasionally they got out of their car and we ran.

Now I could sleep in the parking lot and still nothing would happen. I'd aged out of the bracket of hooligans; I'd consolidated the family's class status; my car was dying, but unless you felt the clutch stick under your foot every time you went into third, you wouldn't really know it. And for me, as the cop helplessly let me go, this suddenly took some of the flavor out of life. I left the lot and went back down Tridelph and then out of perverse curiosity to Columbia, to see which chain stores had replaced the chain stores I'd grown up with, and, feeling my useless freedom in my lap like a cup of coffee growing stale there, I drove down to Annapolis Junction, and then beyond, all the way to the coast.

My father's house is set back from the road, and the bulk of it lies on a downward slope from the driveway, so that pulling up you see only the front hall and my father's office, the rest of the house hiding behind them like a secret reservoir of wealth.

When I pulled up on this morning my father was out—running errands, I later learned, for my sister, who lived abroad and often needed things from the States, the world's convenience store. My father had not yet remarried and so, briefly, I had the house to myself. It had once been a barn, as you could still tell from the windows in the small upstairs vestibule, and now it sprawled down from its former barn self, down and out into the downstairs rooms, one of which was mine, and the downstairs bathroom, and there was even a Ping-Pong table down there, the dream of all young men who were too humble or too chaste or too dumb to dream of fucking girls on the billiard table in their basement. I was all three.

Now it had become so important to me that I sleep with Arielle! In retrospect it's hard to explain, but in that period after my breakup with Jillian, sex was all I could think about. It seemed there was a truth in sex that I needed to have about myself, and Arielle would be the one to tell it to me. And I was prepared to do anything, to drive down all the highways and byways of Pennsylvania and Maryland, to get her into bed. I was almost prepared to call Uncle Misha. But I was not prepared.

My father, my optimistic father, had spent too much on this house. Or rather, he was in the process of borrowing against it dangerously and putting the money in places where it was not as safe as one would have liked. The effects of this came later, but they were on their way now, even as I stood there, though I did not know it yet; they were an undercurrent in the house, a kind of premonition. That is another story. On this day, when I drove from Arielle's in Murray Hill, away from my Uncle Misha's in Washington Heights, and then to Harrisburg and past my apartment, where I couldn't find parking, out to my high school, where I could, all the way to the Bay—my father's troubles, which would shadow a good portion of my thirties, that is to say, are shadowing me now—were still very far away, or anyhow I had no inkling of them. I was still trying to piece my own life together. Because it had fallen apart.

Things fall apart. My father wanted nothing more to do with their old house, their old things, after my mother died. He sold the house, left the firm he was working for, and moved here; the furniture and dishes he gave to Jillian and me. When we moved to Baltimore after college we were able to drive down practically every weekend, almost, and while I followed political developments on the all-day cable news channels from the one old Clarksville leather chair, Jillian put away her textbooks and helped my father furnish the house. They studied the furniture catalogs, they made the rounds of the furniture stores, new and antique, they argued interminably about fabrics for the curtains and throw pillows. In general there was a lot of talk about the fabrics. My father was nominally in charge, as the bearer of the purse, but Jillian made all the final calls. Uncle Misha, the one time his opinion was solicited with regard to the fabrics, quite perceptibly sneered.

My dear Jillian. A year had passed since she'd last set foot in this house, possibly more, and it was likely that she'd never set foot in it again. Gradually my father was picking up knickknacks here and there, and lamps were breaking, and people brought him gifts, sometimes, which he had to display, and so little by little the colors and chairs and paintings Jillian had chosen were being diluted or occluded or replaced. Eventually there'd be nothing left here of her but the big plaid armchair in the library. Of course, even before then other things would happen, involving the movement of international capital and the hiking of the interest rate. But this was happening, too.

I sat down on the couch and turned on the television. My father had a thousand channels—eight HBOs, six Showtimes, and then

Cinemaxes, Movie Channels, multiple ESPNs. On either side of the television stood two sets of sliding glass doors leading onto the woods and the pond below, and so watching television you could pretend you were merely looking out the window.

Suddenly Jillian called. I had dialed her number at some point during the night, but she hadn't picked up.

"Hi," she said, a little warily. We didn't talk much anymore.

"Hi," I said.

"I saw that you called. Is everything OK?"

"Yes. I'm sorry about that. I was just driving to the Bay, actually, and I thought of you. Sorry."

"Oh, sweetie," she said.

"Hi."

"Where are you now?"

"I'm here."

"How's your dad?"

"I haven't seen him yet. How are you?"

"I'm OK. I've had a lot of work. I was going to call actually: I'm coming to a thing at Hopkins next month. We could get dinner, if you wanted."

I said I did want to, though the prospect filled me with a kind of dread. We'd sit across the table from each other, looking sad, looking lonely—and there wasn't anything for it, in the end. You can't go back to things, I was learning. And neither did I want to go back, truth be told.

We hung up. I hadn't checked my e-mail since leaving my apartment the day before, nearly twenty-four hours of no e-mail, but I didn't care. I got up and walked into the little library off the main living room, filled with my mother's old books on Russian literature, most of them put out by the émigré presses—Ardis, L'Age d'Homme, YMCA-Presse. Like everyone else, she'd been forced into programming, Russians like some poorly dressed

154

gang of programming mercenaries, but her old books from her old life had stayed, and occasionally I would look into them. The arguments no longer made much sense—over and over that Lenin was Stalin, that Brezhnev was Stalin, that if you didn't think so, you were Stalin—but the type, so clumsy and cheap, not mass produced and thin, like the Soviet books on the shelves, but as if an individual had gone into the DNA of every letter and somehow made it look awkward on the page, each letter in a different way— the type spoke of a world in which publishing these words and getting them to readers was the most important thing imaginable. I did not long for that world; I knew very well how much it cost; and I did not feel rebuked by it. But having been lived in once, by people I knew, and in these books—the world remained.

Here was this library, transported from Moscow to Clarksville and finally down I-97 to the water. It was like the legal discovery process that Arielle had told me about, where a suite of lawyers tramps into an office and seizes all the property to photocopy it. "The lawyers, meaning me," said Arielle, her big blue eyes lighting up at the hilarity of it, "we take the most detailed imaginable notes on where everything is, so we can reconstruct it exactly as it was—second file cabinet, third drawer, fifth file from front—and then off it goes in a truck."

"It must be strange to get it back," I'd said, considering it. We were sharing a final beer after a number of other beers and drinks.

"It must be *so* strange," she answered, laughing. "Is it still the same stuff? You'll never know."

I'd leaned across the table to kiss her and she batted me back.

My father finally pulled up. Immediately I wondered, standing in the library, whether I was doing anything wrong.

The door opened. "*A-oo!*" my father called in, having seen my car out front, still living.

I walked toward the front door. *"A-oo,"* I called back, more softly.

We shook hands.

"Kakimi sud'bami?" he said. By what fate? He was happy to see me. This enormous house, despite all the new furnishings, still filled with so many of the old things.

He made us lunch. It was too cold to eat outside on the porch, but the early-afternoon light flooded onto the big rectangular wooden table at which we sat. In the past twenty-four hours I had slept just that one hour in the parking lot; I must have looked bad; I felt horrible. My father made a grilled cheese sandwich with bacon—an old specialty of the house, prepared by placing two generously cheesed and baconed slices of bread into the toaster oven and waiting for the whole thing to melt down.

"I haven't made one of these in a long time," my father admitted.

"But you have bacon?" I said.

"Sometimes," said my father, "I fry eggs on it."

"Aha." I took in the thought of him, in all his father-being, developing his own habits, independent of my mother or myself, just kind of cast adrift into the world.

We spoke Russian. He told me his news. There wasn't much of it. The city works department had managed to burst a pipe under his lawn; the grass out front still wasn't growing. And yet he looked great, my father; he was getting younger, though in a Russian way—he had shaved the beard he'd worn as long as I'd been alive, it had grown too gray for him, and his features had become sharper, almost aquiline, though his large nose, his smile, his great eyebrows remained intact. My father.

He asked me how I was. I didn't tell him about Arielle; I felt he might still be obscurely loyal to Jillian. I told him a little about work, though not so much that we'd get into an argument.

I did tell him I'd been going to New York a lot.

"Your uncle Misha lives there now, you know," he said suddenly.

I nodded. "What's he doing?"

"Who knows. Your grandmother said he was working for one of the Russian papers, but I haven't seen his name in it, so."

I was sitting and my father was both standing as he worked in the kitchen and sitting with me at the remarkable long wood table he and Jillian had once picked out, an ingenious table that connected the kitchenette to the large living room on the other side of it. Watching my father then, moving between the toaster and the dishes and the refrigerator, I thought of the men in New York and Washington who were his age, and had his looks and education: They ran television networks and glossy magazines and restaurants and congressional committees. They had everything he had except his accent. And as I thought of this, of my father's accent, my father's accent here among the old Maryland WASPs and retired naval officers from Annapolis, my optimistic father surrounded by people who thought they had something on him because of it—I became angry, with a white-hot anger, which blazed out in my mind and torched everything it found there, even Arielle, even Jillian.

"Meanwhile," said my father, "an incredible saga has recently unfolded in the *Bay Courier*."

Since moving out there, my father—perhaps in this he was like all fathers—had taken an inordinate interest in the local news. He had also, through some zoning issues on his land, run into trouble with the local conservation board. And now the head of the board, my father's nemesis, was embroiled in scandal.

As my father told it, the conservationist had learned that a well-preserved nineteenth-century farmhouse was slated for destruction on the other side of the bar. Appalled, the conservationist immediately bought the house and arranged for its transportation to his own property.

"But the house was big and heavy," said my father, "and the only way to transport it was by boat, and then along Ridge Street to his own property. Unfortunately"—my father raised his finger, his eyes twinkling—"the farmhouse was too big to be transported all at once. It had to be sawed in half. So then he floats it to a beach on our side of the bar.

"A few days later the residents of Ridge Street are driving home from work and notice that the large trees along the road have all been marked with orange paint. One of the guys on Ridge Street is a garbage collector, he calls someone at the works department and asks whether there is a project scheduled? His friend says, 'I don't know of any project.' So everyone is puzzled. They learn that the so-called conservationist has measured the width of Ridge and then the width of his farmhouse and seen that the street would need to get wider to let the house through—and without telling anyone, he has hired a construction crew to *cut large branches off the trees.*"

"Like Stalin in Moscow," I said.

"Exactly," said my father. "So everyone is furious. They gather on the beach in front of the house. It's been sitting there for a week by this point."

"Sawed in half," I said.

"That's right. And it's illegal, by the way. You can't just put a house on the beach, you know.

"So in the end, after he's confronted by this mob, he's forced to cut the house in half *again.* Both halves! Then, finally, after paying all the fines for keeping it on the beach so long, he gets to take it home in four pieces to his property.

"*Vot tak,*" concluded my father, getting up with his plate and taking mine as well. So there you have it. "Can you believe it? That's

not even a house he's got anymore. That's a—misunderstanding."
My father shook his head in disbelief. That's what the conserva-
tionists get for trying to class up. My father had never had any
interest in classing up.

He looked at me kindly. "You probably want to sleep a little,
yes?"

I did, very much, and I finally went downstairs. And I thought,
on the way down to my room, and on the way down into sleep, of
all the people in the world dragging themselves from old property
to new property, along oceans and highways and Ridge Street,
and arriving, in the end, sawed into pieces. I thought of my kindly,
handsome father, alone in that enormous house, and how he'd
never make up with Misha, though they had both loved my mother.
America was too large; America with its houses, its highways; it
had broken them up, and me as well. No matter what happened
with Arielle (and nothing, I may as well tell you now, happened
with Arielle), I would never have Jillian back, could never have her
back, did not even want her back, which was the whole trouble—
because all the people I'd loved once, or even just knew once, were
scattered, never to be seen again in one place. So that all the feelings
one expended, received, that one felt at the core of one's being, had
turned, in the course of things, to dust.

And outside already it was growing dark.

III

Jenin

And in Jenin, Sam waited for the tanks. On the streets and in the hookah shops and in the Internet cafes, he waited and waited.

Things in America—America itself—hadn't quite worked out for Sam. Perhaps it was just Boston, dreary expensive Boston, or perhaps it was just Sam, but in the weeks and months before his departure he'd been in the process of getting obliterated, broken in half, by the perplexing Katie Riesling, and now he'd run away. Not on a journey of self-discovery—Sam was too old for self-discovery—but on a journey for the discovery of certain facts. The facts on the ground. Was it lame and pathetic on Sam's part to have fled a romantic disaster so he could sort out his feelings about the Occupation? Was it lame and pathetic and even farcical? Maybe. Yeah.

Sam arrived in Tel Aviv and despite the beaches and sunshine immediately took a van from the airport to his cousin Witold's place in Jerusalem. It cost just forty shekels—ten dollars. Actually, thirteen dollars, but it was one of the oddities of human nature that while traveling in a country where the exchange rate was just above three, one always calculated it as being more like four, reducing prices. And Sam was in a hurry.

Cousin Witold lived in a thin-walled little concrete apartment house, in the old mini-socialist style, in a prestigious section of Jerusalem. Witold himself was not prestigious; he was still recently arrived from Poland, a member of the strange Polish branch of the Mitnick family. Seven years older than Sam, a little taller, more wiry, he had the kind of thin potato face you really see only in Polish films, flat nose and wide cheekbones and hair cropped close, a younger, thinner version of his brother Walech, who lived in New Jersey and built mathematical models of the stock exchange. "You have to think of the stock exchange as an expanding sphere," the older brother once told Sam. It sounded like a prelude to stock advice, so Sam's ears pricked up, but he was unable to follow the parable that Walech then unspooled. Walech kept his stock advice to himself.

Witold was more open. Like Sam he had recently been through a bad breakup, with a girl of Yemenese descent, and he was so depressed, he told Sam, that he couldn't fulfill his army reserve duties. His commanding officer would call, Witold wouldn't answer the phone, his commanding officer would leave a message asking Witold to come to drills that weekend, and Witold wouldn't call him back for a week or two, pretending he'd been away.

"How long will this work?" Sam asked. They were drinking tea in Witold's miniature kitchen.

"I don't know," admitted Witold.

On the other hand, he carried a gun, a Glock from Austria, and knew how to use it. He tucked it into these hideous green shorts he wore everywhere, not that he and Sam went very far from Witold's kitchen—which was, when Sam studied it a bit more carefully, filled to capacity with whole grains and herbs and grainy spices, the diet of a survivalist, which was what Witold was. When Sam had declared, upon emerging from the shower not long after emerging from his airport taxi, that they should get dinner at a fancy restaurant, at Sam's expense, because it was Sam's first night in the Holy Land, Witold had demurred, saying that a fancy restaurant just around the corner had been blown up by a suicide bomber a few weeks earlier. "All right," said Sam. "Can we at least get a falafel? It's my first night in Israel."

"OK," Witold relented. "I know the best falafel in West Jerusalem."

"And the best falafel in all of Jerusalem?" Sam asked.

"That would be in East Jerusalem," said Witold. "We'd have to shoot our way out."

On the plane, and in the van, and on the thin mattress Witold put down on the floor for him in his tiny apartment, Sam thought of Katie. He rewound their meetings in his mind. Their first date and his disgraceful behavior—how he'd underestimated her then! They'd run into each other a while later, and she'd managed to forgive him somehow without ever quite forgiving him. And suddenly Sam had seen depths to her that he hadn't known were there, and his whole attitude changed overnight. He was in love. She was the one for him. She'd scored what you might call a dialectical reversal: he was under her thumb. He would see her walking down Cambridge Street, loping really, her head traveling great distances up and down as she walked, leaning forward, a lopy carnivorous walk—and his heart would stop. Then it would soar, and think it all over, and soar again.

She'd been suspicious of his trip. "You're not really going to Israel," she said.

"What do you mean?"

"You live here in Cambridge. We get dinner."

"But we don't sleep together!" he burst out. This was the major difficulty. Perhaps it was an expression of other difficulties, but if so it was occluding them. It certainly seemed, as they wrestled like teenagers in her apartment, ending up, somehow, every time, furious with each other, like the main difficulty.

"That's why you're going to Israel?"

"It's as good a reason as any!" he yelled. He always lost his cool, talking to her. He always felt outsmarted, then humiliated. "Plus there's the Occupation."

"You're weird," she said.

Sam clutched Witold's little mattress, crushing it. She was infuriating. And he was a grown man. You can't call a grown man weird. You can call him chubby—Sam was growing chubby—and you can call him bald, or balding, which in Sam's case was debatable and controversial, no one could say for sure, and you can call him callous, distant, clumsy, overbearing—but not *weird*. You just can't. After falafel he'd returned to find an e-mail from her imploring him to be careful. It was a nice e-mail. For a few minutes Sam felt the old feelings again, unreservedly; then he started remembering the conversations; he clutched his mattress now in the dark.

In the morning Witold took Sam on a tour of the city. It was an old city but not a particularly big one—no city really is, deep down, all that big—and they covered the whole thing in less than two hours. Witold told Sam the story of his life in Israel: he had had to work on a kibbutz, carrying fifty-pound bushels of bananas, for eight months before he earned enough money and social benefits to move to Jerusalem. Then he'd served in the army. Now he fixed computers. Witold did not have to tell Sam the story of his life before Israel—of his mother's and grandmother's life during the war, his grandfather's death—they were the only ones from the Mitnick clan to survive the war inside Poland. (Sam's own grandmother had escaped to Russia.) After all that, the children had left Poland as soon as they could, for Jerusalem and New Jersey, where they could feel safe.

Witold did not approve of Sam's plan to head for the territories. "We could go to the Negev," he said. They were sitting outdoors near the main market, eating another falafel. "We could go to Sfat."

"I'm not a tourist," Sam said, slightly affronted.

"Yes you are."

Witold began to talk about his tour of duty with the army; he was occasionally made to go into the territories. This was in the mid-1990s, after the Oslo Accords, before the assassination of Rabin—a golden age, in retrospect. "And still I have to tell you, it was unpleasant there," said Witold. Years earlier, when the First Intifada began with large Palestinian protests in the occupied territories, Israeli soldiers several times fired live ammunition at protesters, killing some. This was bad, internationally, for Israel, so Rabin, then the army's chief of staff, ordered the men to use nonlethal means on the protesters. "Break their bones" was the infamous phrase—and so Israeli soldiers began using their rifle butts and batons to crush people's arms and ribs.

"When I first entered the army," Witold told Sam, "I thought I would not be able to talk to them"—to the ones who broke people's bones. "But then I met them. And I understood: if you are out there, you have five, six men, and there are a thousand angry people—what are you going to do?"

"Leave the territories?" Sam suggested.

Witold sighed. His English was good but it was not good enough to detect when Sam was kidding, or half kidding, or maybe a quarter kidding, if at all—in fact very few people's English was that good, which may have indicated a problem less with their English than with Sam. In any case, Witold simply assumed that every time he spoke, Sam was serious. It was a masterly strategy for dealing with Sam. Now Witold said, of Sam's suggestion that the territories be unoccupied: "Someday." And then: "You will see for yourself."

The next morning Sam woke up, checked his e-mail, packed a duffel bag, checked his e-mail again, and walked to the Three Kings hostel near the walls of the Old City. It served, Sam knew from the Internet, as the unofficial hangout of the Global International Solidarity human rights and occasional human shields group, infamous in the United States for its "breakfast with Arafat" during the Israeli siege of the old man's compound in Ramallah. During those days all Arafat had was his bulky satellite phone and these useful Swedish and American idiots, eating hummus and flat bread and showing up on the BBC.

On the way to the hostel Sam noticed a commotion outside a busy, glassed-in restaurant at the bottom of Cousin Witold's street. Sam stopped to watch on the other side of the street.

Directly in front of the restaurant was a stout middle-aged woman holding a large placard on which a blown-up photo showed a young man's handsome Jewish face. It was her son. The restaurant's two security guards—even the hole-in-the-wall best-falafel-in-West-Jerusalem had a guard, a sour-looking Russian guy—shifted from foot to foot silently before her, as if barring her way. Sam stood watching. There was some Hebrew writing on the sign that he couldn't read, and the glum faces of the men, the security guards, gave nothing away. And nonetheless he knew. The restaurant was just around the corner from Witold's house; a month before, a young Palestinian in a bomb belt had blown himself to pieces right outside the entrance. One of the people killed was this woman's son. And she wanted—what did she want? Now a sharply dressed young man emerged forcefully from the restaurant, presumably the mâitre d' or the manager, and headed for the woman. He said something to her in a slightly pleading way; she said something aggressively back. He raised his hand as if about to start yelling at her and then stopped, and simply stood there with the two tall guards. The woman continued to hold her sign, the photo of her son, in front of the restaurant where he'd been killed, where people continued to eat breakfast or even, by now, an early lunch.

At the Three Kings half an hour later, strewn as it was with backpacks and Swedes, Sam found Roger, an American geographer who was heading out for Jenin, and joined him.

How easy it turned out to be, to get from here to there! (If you were from here. Not so much if you were from there.) They climbed into a minivan cab to reach, in ten minutes, the checkpoint just outside Ramallah, and from there a yellow Mercedes taxicab drove off with them for Jenin. Sam looked around, almost speechless. The West Bank! Here it was, that source of all the world's problems, here it was before his very eyes. As they wound past little hills he looked for tanks, he looked for violent settlers, he expected the earth to open its great maw and roar at all the trouble and the foolishness going on. Sam was so transfixed he forgot momentarily about Katie—her pouty lips, her dramatic gestures, her funny imitations of foreigners.

Roger, a bulky, effeminate WASP in wire-rim glasses, was a treasure chest of anti-Israeli information. Year-round he worked in Cairo for the U.N., examining the various effects of the Nile Delta on the Egyptian population. But in his spare time, he explained, he was preparing a "cartography of oppression."

"What's it look like?" Sam asked.

"Look around," said Roger proudly, as if he himself had charted it.

Sam did as he was told. He looked at the stingy desert hills, covered with little green and brown scrub grass, barely elevated, rolling and rolling on into the horizon.

"Barely even any hills," he said.

"That's exactly right," Roger looked pleased. "These are *minor dominating heights.* It's almost impossible to hide in them—good for a regular army, but suicide for a bunch of dudes with Kalashnikovs and homemade bombs."

"What's that?" Sam said. Atop one hill a neat group of twenty houses stood, with neat orange gable roofs.

"That would be a settlement," Roger said. "See the roofs? The Palestinians keep theirs flat."

Twenty minutes on there appeared, in the middle of the desert, a traffic jam. Or a toll. Three Israeli soldiers stood lazily around, casting cursory glances at documents. They took their time. They really took their time. After a soldier had taken the documents from the first car in line and brought them over to their little post, and then stood chatting with his buddies, obviously not looking at any of the documents, Sam demanded to know of Roger what they were doing.

"Checking them against lists," Roger said. "And looking for weapons."

"I don't see him looking for any weapons."

"Of course not. It's a taxi. It's not carrying weapons. But this—this is geography. You stop people just so they know whose road it is. It fits into their psychic map. The map that's in their heads."

Now a blue Audi flew past them, waved to the guards, and kept going.

"Who was that?" asked Sam, growing increasingly upset.

"That would be a settler."

"Motherfucker," said Sam.

"Yes."

"In Cambridge we have permit parking," said Sam. "It's really hard to park if you don't have a resident permit and sometimes you have to drive around for an hour."

"With the difference that if you actually live in Cambridge, as the Palestinians live here, you get a permit."

"If you can afford the insurance! If you can't, you register somewhere else and then waste your life looking for parking. Just like now I'm wasting my life in this taxi while that guy cruises over to his settlement!"

"That's about right," said Roger. He seemed extraordinarily pleased now.

At Akhmed's father's house, in a small village outside Jenin, Sam waited for the tanks.

Akhmed taught English in the village of Birqin, when school was in session. Whether it was out of session now because it was July or because tanks were always coming into town, Sam didn't know. In the meantime Akhmed had befriended the Global International Solidarity Swedes, and it was thought he'd enjoy Sam's genuine American English, and so Sam was asked to stay at Akhmed's.

Arriving there, Sam found that Akhmed was his age exactly, with a droopy mustache and a slow, deliberate way of framing his sentences. Sweet-tempered, shy, he immediately reminded Sam of the soft-spoken social-democrats he'd seen now and again in

Cambridge, quietly urging their resistance to the upcoming war with Iraq. He greeted Roger and Sam with some ceremony, kissed them on both cheeks (four cheeks), sat them down in a garden behind his father's house while his two younger brothers, Bashar and Mohammed, brought out hummus and pita and grapes. Sam was clearly going to get chubby in Jenin; on the other hand, look at fat Roger. Roger was asking Akhmed about his father. His father was very upset, Akhmed answered. Four young men had been arrested in the next village over, and six had been arrested in Jenin, and two houses had been blown up at night by the Israelis. *Izrah-ilis* is how even the best-spoken Palestinians pronounced it. Finally, said Akhmed, his brother Mohammed "is not very smart. He was almost killed. This close."

Mohammed, who did not speak English, perked up at the sound of his name. "Idiot," Akhmed said to him, or so it seemed to Sam, by the sound of it in Arabic, and Mohammed grinned. His brothers, unlike Akhmed, were athletic and boisterous, and Mohammed wore a white polyester shirt under which you could see his bandaged chest.

"Why did they shoot at him?" Sam asked.

"Why?" said Akhmed. "No why. He was standing. They shot."

"For no reason?" Sam asked again.

"It just slipped him," Akhmed said. "Is this right? Slipped?"

"Grazed," Roger said. "It grazed him."

"Ah," said Akhmed. "Grazed."

"For no reason?" Sam repeated.

But the conversation had moved on, and no one heard him.

Thus began Sam's life in Jenin. In the evenings he would sit with Akhmed and his brothers, sometimes other young men from the town would come by to talk about the Occupation and have a look at Sam—young healthy American Sam turned out to be something of a curiosity around the village of Birqin—sometimes Roger and the Swedes would drop in. At night he slept on a cot on the roof; the Palestinian houses with their flat roofs grew too hot during the day to be slept in at night, and in the mornings he would walk over to Jenin and begin his daylong vigil for the tanks. He wandered around, past the flimsy concrete structures, and only a few streets' worth, not even a city, not really, with dust everywhere; the heat of the sun, the humidity, was awful. In the tropics people would start drinking at twilight so they could fall asleep by nighttime. It was less hot in Jenin, maybe, but on the other hand there was much less alcohol. In fact, there was no alcohol at all.

Sober, the men in the doorways bided their time, the kids in the street ran this way and that, a kind of freelance summer boot camp for when the tanks came and they could throw rocks. Because surely the tanks would come? The shops shuttered with the same metal shutters as anywhere else, Boston or New York, the awnings still hanging humbly, collecting dust on their Arabic script: FURNITURE, they must have said, and HOUSEHOLD GOODS, PHARMACY, 99 CENT STORE. And then at visible points, under all the awnings, at corners, on street lamps where you could see the bullet holes still, everywhere the cheap xeroxed photos of "martyrs"—holding Kalashnikovs, some of them, with their faces covered in the romantic Hamas style, a kerchief, and a splash of Hamas green when they could afford it—but mostly it was just their ID photos. Martyr, martyr, martyr, said the door shutters and walls and broken street lamps of Jenin.

Really, really, really? said Sam. They were just standing around? And the tanks just shot? It was one thing to read about this in the *Nation;* it was one thing to read about it on the *Ha'aretz* Web site, sitting in Cambridge, in between checking your e-mail. But here in Jenin—come on. Look at Cousin Witold, in his goofy green shorts—true, just now he was avoiding the draft, but there were many like him, in green shorts equally goofy, and Cousin Witold wouldn't just shoot you. He'd shoot you, that is, very accurately, but only, Sam thought, if you'd done something bad.

He checked his e-mail. Katie had been reading up on the machine-gun rounds currently being employed by the Israeli Merkava tanks, and she was very concerned. "The biggest trouble now is the incommensurability of advanced firepower with the still pretty unadvanced state of human skin and bone," she wrote. "A round can go through six or seven people. I think you should stay out of the way. Or put eight or nine people at least between you and the tank. More than that if the people are skinny." Sam smiled at the computer screen—she was so tender now that he was so far away. The oldest paradox. But still. An appointment just then—he had to meet Roger and his sidekick Lukas at the hookah joint—kept him from responding, and anyway it wouldn't do to seem too eager.

In the hookah joint, on the second floor, in a wood-paneled bar that served no alcohol, they ate ice cream and smoked apple tobacco from the water pipe and gazed out over the quiet main intersection of Jenin. Roger explained the symbolic difference between an actual crossroads and a T formation, as here: the head of the T, where they sat, necessarily became a military target. On his way into the bar, Sam had noted the main traffic light leaning against the building in which they now sat, holes from large-caliber rounds all through its long trunk. Cars occasionally passed by below, slowing down momentarily out of respect for the traffic signal that once was, then moving on again.

"Now, Gaza," Roger said, filling his lungs expertly from the pipe. "Gaza is much worse."

Sam was immediately annoyed. "You said yesterday that Beirut was worse. And the day before that Mogadishu was."

"They are worse," Roger confirmed.

"OK, but this place is pretty bad." Sam couldn't help the slightly hopeful note in his voice as he said this.

"No, my friend," said Roger. "This is a picnic. This is Club Med. I come here to relax and eat ice cream. But Gaza is the real thing."

"I heard that too," said Lukas. He was a tall lanky college student from Stockholm who hung out with Roger because the other Swedes were actually off doing humanitarian work. Lukas was as it happened eating an ice cream just then; Sam wanted one too, but now he was too angry. He had come a long way to be in Jenin! When he'd asked the other Swedes about helping out, they said there wasn't anything to do; it was enough, they said, that he "bear witness." OK, OK, but he was bearing witness to nothing; there weren't any tanks; he was bearing witness to checking his e-mail.

Speaking of which, he thought now, and stood up decisively from his seat—if that's how it was, then that's how it would be. He bought an ice cream to take with him and walked down the main thoroughfare, taking little bites and trying to keep it from getting all over him as he made his way down to the Internet cafe, where he wrote Katie an e-mail of startling, rambling, fabulously discursive length.

When he was done he tried to call Witold from a pay phone, but no one answered.

At night after washing his sweaty jeans, Sam would lie in his cot, with its damp, unclean sheets, and talk with Akhmed about peace, about the retreat of leftist hopes in the face of a religious revival in the Arab world, about the disastrous collapse at Camp David ("Unacceptable," Akhmed said of the offer, and Sam argued with him, and lost). They talked of the splintering Palestinian cause: even within Akhmed's family, he said, his uncle and father were still strongly pro-Arafat, but Bashar and Mohammed were visibly impatient. "I did not tell you," Akhmed confided of his brothers. "They fought in Jenin Camp." Akhmed for his part was still a socialist; his party's leader had been forced to flee to Damascus, and Akhmed kept a photo of him in his notebook, otherwise the place for unfamiliar English words that somewhere or other he'd heard or read. He showed a few of the words to Sam; they were unfamiliar to him, too.

Sam had not told Akhmed that he was Jewish. Roger in the car to Jenin had asked him not to mention it—"You're not Jewish in the sense that they'd understand anyway," he said. "Meaning?" "Meaning Israeli." And for a while this made sense. What's more, Sam just assumed that everyone knew. He was dark, and hairy, and his brown eyes sparkled, and upon seeing him Arabs always asked if he was Arab. When he said no, they paused a moment and wondered if he was perhaps Spanish? Italian? Bulgarian? It seemed obvious to Sam that someone in this part of the world with black hair and an olive complexion could be only one of two things. Yet somehow no one seemed to grasp that. And as Sam grew closer to the sweet saintly Akhmed, as Akhmed confided in him, he began to feel he was concealing it.

Still, his heart was pure. There'd been situations in Sam's life—connected with women, usually—where he'd felt that if something terrible happened to him just then, that he deserved it. Not so here. It's true he'd been sentimental about a Jewish army and Jewish guns, and Jewish women carrying guns, but he'd never thought the Palestinians should be driven into the Jordan River. Living in the States, he had never discovered any advantage—any angle, any percentage—to his skepticism toward Israel, and still he had worked four straight full-time weeks formatting Excel sheets at Fidelity to earn the money to come here, and in addition he'd given up his apartment for an entire summer, meaning he'd have to stay with Toby in Somerville, or else, maybe, with Katie, though obviously he wasn't going to be the one to suggest it, he liked her apartment, but there was never any food in the refrigerator and she was careless with her things. In short, he'd gone out of his way to come here and see—for certain—just what his brethren were up to. If he was killed for being Jewish, well that would be one thing; but if someone killed him for supposedly supporting the Occupation, that would be totally unfair.

And then on his fourth day at Akhmed's, after another hummus-filled breakfast—Sam loved this stuff and if he was getting a little pudgy, so be it, it was a war zone—Akhmed announced that his uncle would be going into Jenin and could take Sam to the refugee camp, if Sam liked. If Sam liked! What a question. If he couldn't have tanks, he'd at least have the camp where the tanks and bulldozers had been. And he was eager to spend time with an older man. Akhmed's uncle had been educated in Cairo, was active in Fatah, had been briefly jailed, Akhmed told Sam, for organizing marches during the First Intifada. A man of the world, he'd be able to tell right away that Sam was Jewish, and Sam would welcome it. They would get it out in the open, and then come what may.

They set off after breakfast, Sam and the three brothers and their uncle, five men across, on a field trip to see what the Israelis had done to the Palestinians. The Palestinians called it the Jenin massacre. The Portuguese writer José Saramago had compared it to Auschwitz. Sam had been to Auschwitz twice. Now he'd see Jenin Camp.

Sam imagined it would be a series of tents, or even just one enormous tent, but Jenin Camp turned out to be nothing more than a very crowded neighborhood, with concrete houses and kids running around in the street. Akhmed's uncle regaled them with stories as they walked. Like Akhmed's father, he was a short man with a mustache; but where Akhmed's father was quiet, thin, even a little sickly, Akhmed's uncle was plump, voluble, and his huge bushy eyebrows moved up and down expressively when he talked. They covered the mile to the camp in no time, in fact moving perhaps too quickly, and Sam sweated profusely into the jeans he wore to keep his knees away from the eyes of Muslim women. He was so unbearably hot, in fact, that he ducked into a little corner grocery and bought an ice cream sandwich. The others declined.

And then they climbed a few more steps and arrived suddenly at a clearing. The clearing had been, once, a city block of square concrete houses; now it was just a series of little rubble piles. Some of the houses, it's true, remained basically recognizable, where the front walls had been collapsed by the bulldozers, so they were like dollhouses you could open so as to watch the people inside. But there were no people of course, and some of the houses had simply crumpled. After sending in highly trained light infantry—mostly older men, reservists like Witold who would not necessarily or not immediately lose their tempers—against a highly motivated group of urban guerrillas armed with Kalashnikovs, some hand grenades, and a good number of homemade bombs, and losing more men in a week (twenty-three) than in any single battle since the IDF took Beirut in 1982, the Israelis, exhausted, demoralized, had sent in the helicopter gunships and the armored bulldozers, and the tanks. The bulldozers climbed these streets and came to these buildings and took them down, some of them with people still inside.

Sam stood there, with his ice cream sandwich half eaten, wondering what to say. Oh, the Palestinians had asked for it, all right. In this camp they'd manufactured the explosives that they then strapped around the waists of young men, sending them to Israeli cities to kill people who were eating lunch. How disingenuous, how grotesque, to call this a massacre—like the pundits who after

178

September 11 argued that the Pentagon was not a legitimate military target. And the final body count, as things were settling down, looked to be twenty-three Israeli dead against perhaps sixty Palestinian dead. Considering the extreme imbalance in firepower, this was some distance away from a massacre.

But standing here you also knew this: these were people's homes. The Israelis had to defend themselves; in the battle for the camp, especially in its first phase, they acted with significantly more discipline and restraint than any other armed force in the world (the American Rangers and Delta fighters in Mogadishu had lost eighteen men—and killed perhaps a thousand); once here, once given an order to take the camp, they did what they had to do. But these were people's homes. *The Israelis had no business being in Jenin to begin with.*

Akhmed's uncle pointed now to one of the wrecked houses, collapsed, twisted, with mangled metal supports still protruding, and even some crushed furniture visible inside under the white wreckage of the walls. "Here," he said, pointing. "I went here to dig. My friend said his father disappeared. I did not think so. People turned up every time—they had escaped or left town. At first they said four hundred dead! Now it is sixty, maybe seventy. So I did not think he was dead. But we began to dig and then suddenly there is a terrible smell. I have never smelled this." He looked at Sam, whose ice cream sandwich, which he'd not touched since they reached the clearing, was melting into his palm. He was going to confront him now, Sam thought, he would tell the Jew what his people had done. But he did not. "I was sick," said Akhmed's uncle. "I went off and was sick. My friend, I saw him, he was mad. He was crazy. 'My father,' he said. 'My father, my father.'" *Fah-der,* Akhmed's uncle pronounced it. *My fah-der.* "He was pulling him out piece by piece. 'My father. My father.' It was—" Akhmed's uncle stopped, shrugged, looked away from the group.

What was it? It was horrible, that's what. It was just horrible. Sam's ice cream sandwich was gone now, all melted. Akhmed's uncle did not know that he was a Jew. Otherwise he would have said the obvious thing. The fearsome Israeli artillery against the besieged Palestinians, who had armed themselves with whatever they could find; the slow tightening of the noose around them; the final operation to liquidate a city block where the resistance was most fierce, and now, around them, lay in rubble: it was not Auschwitz, not at all. Jesus. It was the liquidation of the Warsaw Ghetto in 1943. The liquidation and the resistance. Sam wiped his hand, covered in ice cream, on his jeans.

On his way to meet Roger and Lukas for Ping-Pong, Sam ducked into the Internet shop (it closed at six). There was an e-mail from Katie. Somehow the warmth that had suffused their correspondence since he'd arrived in Israel was leaking from it again. Sam was beginning to suspect that Katie suspected that he wasn't seeing any tanks. "Take care," she signed off now, a bit automatically, as if Sam was just in Watertown, or New Hampshire, that a man who produced e-mails the length of the e-mails Sam was producing in the many Internet places of Jenin had not, perhaps, really left the country at all.

He found himself mildly annoyed. She had stopped writing her sex column a while ago and taken a job at the *Globe;* she wanted to be a real journalist, she said. Well and here was Sam in Jenin! So maybe there were no tanks, but still, but still. He continued to feel strongly for Katie—her voice on the phone, her messages on the phone, she'd once called him after a big dinner at a friend's house and left a ten-minute voice mail describing all the dishes she'd had, she was some kind of genius—but for the first time in a long time he felt a little off her side.

The Ping-Pong was in the little backyard cafe that Roger had dubbed the gentlemen's club.

In the gentlemen's club, Lukas and Roger and Mohammed and Sam waited for the tanks. The other Swedes were out with Palestinian ambulances so that these would not be harassed by Israeli troops. (The IDF claimed that Palestinians carried weapons in them. The Palestinians denied it, waving their arms; the Swedes were appalled that such an accusation could be made. To Sam it seemed pretty obvious that Palestinians would carry weapons in their Red Cross ambulances—why not? But often they carried sick people too, since their public health system had broken down, and since Israelis occasionally shot them.) Some of the other Swedes, while Sam sat in the gentlemen's club, drinking orange Fanta, escorted farmers to their fields, and some other Swedes did other things. For his part Roger had already sketched out the oppressive cartography of Jenin and the surrounding areas; at this point he really needed to see some tanks, and people moving in the presence of tanks—so he, too, waited for them. He justified the waiting thusly: People were happy to see them; kids ran up in the street to play with the foreigners. "Psycho-topographically?" Roger said. "It assures them there's a world on the other side of the Israeli tanks. It's important." Sam was happy to hear this, it's true; but if they'd been utterly indifferent to him, the Palestinians, that too would have been fine. He'd come to work some Sam things out, here.

And on this sixth day of his vigil in Jenin he played, for the sixth time, some Ping-Pong. He had never lost at Ping-Pong, and he saw no reason to lose now. After yesterday's brutal dispatching of poor Akhmed, his brother Mohammed had come, in the Arab way, to seek revenge—but Sam did not lose at Ping-Pong in Jenin.

At the end of the game Mohammed threw his racket into the grass and cursed in Arabic.

Sweaty Sam retreated to the plastic table at which Lukas and Roger lounged. "Will the tanks be here today?" he said.

"Let's hope not." This was Roger. "They shoot at people."

"So you say."

Imperceptibly, by degrees, but pretty definitely, his relationship with Roger had deteriorated.

Roger turned to Lukas. "He doesn't believe me that the tanks shoot at people."

"Perhaps they are in Palestine to get some sun?" Lukas said.

"I hope," Roger concluded solemnly, "that you never have to see a tank."

"Yeah, OK," said Sam. "I'm not holding my breath."

Sullen Sam wandered over to the pay phone in the corner of the yard. He'd tried Witold the past few days and never received any response. Perhaps the army had finally taken him, perhaps he was even now manning some tank, riding through the desert toward Jenin?

The answering machine picked up. "Witold!" Sam cried. "Hey, pick up, it's me, Sam! I'm calling from Jenin! I'm not your commanding officer!"

And then Witold did pick up. "Where have you been?" he said. "I've been worried about you. Your father would kill me if you got killed."

"I didn't get killed. I've been calling but you don't pick up."

"Oh, sorry. You know I screen the calls. So what's it like? What money do they use? Is there shooting? Is there Hamas? How much does a falafel cost?"

"It's fine," said Sam. "They use shekels. A falafel costs five shekels. It's pretty hot. There's no shooting, and you don't see Hamas. I haven't even seen a tank yet."

"What do you want to see a tank for? Come back and I'll show you a dozen tanks."

"That's typical Occupationist thinking, Witold. Of course you don't care about the tanks, because they're on your side. But in Jenin they're pretty important."

"OK, OK. What do you want me to say to your parents?"

"Nothing. They know I'm here. I e-mailed."

"E-mail? They have e-mail?"

"Yes. I'll write you one."

"OK. Be careful. And forget about the tanks. Lots of tanks here."

"Easy for you to say."

Just then, as they were hanging up, excited Arabic voices came on the radio, which had been playing the news and music softly in the background. Someone turned it up. The men in the gentlemen's club all looked suddenly on fire, listening intently. The radio was practically shouting.

"What's going on?" Sam asked his friends. Each of them shrugged. Sam turned to Mohammed, who was sitting at the same plastic table. "Mohammed, what's on the radio? What's going on?"

Mohammed spoke no English, supposedly. But Sam was fairly sure Mohammed knew what he was being asked, because he looked down at the ground and said nothing.

"AL-QUDS!" the radio blared. The Holy One. Jerusalem.

Sam turned to a group of men at another of the plastic tables. One of them was smiling at Sam, as if he wanted to say something, share the good news. Sam smiled back, because he wanted to share the good news, too. The man held up his hand with the fingers spread out: five. And then he made a throat-slitting motion. And then held up his hand again. Five dead. In Jerusalem. Oh Jesus. That's why he was smiling. Some asshole had blown himself up.

Sam's stomach turned over inside him, it was full of Fanta, and he felt sick. The smile left his lips and he held the man's gaze long enough that the man could know Sam didn't think this was such good news. Eventually the man looked away, embarrassed.

Sam turned to Roger. "How long have you lived in Cairo?" he asked.

"Five years."

"And you can't understand the radio?"

"The dialects are a lot more different than you'd think," Roger said, carefully. "But if you're asking if I understood the gist of that, just now? Yes, I did."

Well: Witold could not have been in that bus or restaurant, because Witold was on the phone with Sam. And he, Sam, was in Jenin, so it couldn't have been Sam among the dead. But as the man he'd stared down now recovered and glared at him, angrily, the whole trip looked suddenly like not such a great idea. He got up from the table without returning the man's stare, and walked purposefully out into the main street. He was angry with Roger, though Roger and he had spoken about the suicide bombings and Roger was clear on their foolishness, simply as strategy, and also on their barbarity. But Roger did not have relatives there, and Sam did not want to be around him just now. Mohammed, you could tell, didn't like what had happened, but what could Mohammed say.

Out in the street there were as always kids running, and dust, a despair that clung to everything, like this would never end. And in Jerusalem five Jews were dead. What was he doing here? When I see a worker confronted with his natural enemy, the policeman, said Orwell, I know whose side I'm on. And if Sam were to see a Palestinian confronted with his natural enemy, the tank, well, he'd know too. But there were no tanks! There were bullet holes in all the big metal doors that fronted the houses, and the man in the street with a cistern of Turkish coffee, for which he charged half a shekel. A good deal. What was Sam *doing*? The Palestinians were sweet, and hospitable, he had really liked Akhmed's uncle, but they were not his brothers. And maybe they were not so sweet. Now, Witold was not Sam's brother either, but at least Witold was his cousin. Their fathers, growing up in Poland and the U.S., respectively, were also not brothers, they were cousins. But *their* fathers, in Warsaw, were brothers. And now Sam and Witold were cousins, like he'd said. And he and Katie were—what?—soul mates. Or near soul mates. And that—he wanted to explain this to her somehow—that may be all you were going to get, in this life.

He needed to leave Jenin right away. And having decided this he went over to the Internet cafe and told Katie he was coming back early and he'd like to stay with her. They'd been involved in this dance, this harmful stalemate, for too long. It was now or never, he wrote. Make up your mind.

That night, on the roof, he thought happily of her for the first time in months. She had outsmarted him at every turn; always, whenever a thought occurred to him, he saw too late that she'd already had it. A month ago he'd decided they should stop seeing each other, if seeing each other was even the word for it—and as soon as he opened his mouth to say so, she said the exact same thing. Aha! Bested again! He was always off balance. She acted naturally where he acted unnaturally; she was on the alert while he was lazy. She had such control of *tone*, in her text messages, she was the Edith Wharton of text messaging. And she believed, after all they'd been through, that she didn't love Sam. "You can't *do* anything about the way you feel," she'd said, excusing herself. But of course you can; of course you can. You have to want to, is all. And maybe he didn't blame her for not loving Sam, who'd done so little, who'd accomplished so few of the things a girl like Katie thought should be accomplished. He thought of the man in the gentlemen's club, glaring angrily, wanting blood. Oh, she could feel what she wanted, if she wanted, if only she wanted to.

There were no tanks, he thought. Or maybe there were tanks but they were there for a reason. These people wanted to kill and kill; they wanted to simmer in the stew of their hatred, and wipe their hands in Jewish blood. He had forgotten, or repressed, or somehow hadn't thought about, the images they'd shown—he'd never seen anything more horrible—of the two soldiers who'd taken a wrong turn in Ramallah the year before and then been torn to pieces, literally, by a mob of Palestinians, who then—this is what they showed on television—held up their bloodied hands, with the blood of Jews on them, held them out the window where they'd done this, and showed them to the cameras. See?

He and Akhmed lay on their cots, arranged perpendicularly so that their heads were close together, looking up at the stars. "Two forty-two," Akhmed was saying. "Four forty-six. Four seventy-eight. Four ninety-seven." These were U.N. resolutions telling Israel to do one thing or another, withdraw to there or disarm then, which Israel naturally ignored. While Bashar and Mohammed, over in another corner of the roof, whispered to each other in Arabic, guffawed and punched each other, Akhmed pronounced the U.N. resolutions with a melancholy precision and finality, the way, on Sam's first night, he'd pronounced the number of people who'd died in Israeli actions, Israeli raids. Sam had noticed this about the Palestinians and their body counts—always a precise number, always well remembered, even when it was wrong. He wondered whether this was because, by remembering all the numbers so precisely, they felt they were still in control—a sort of mathematical ritual of the oppressed. Or whether it was simpler: that they believed there to be a finite number of Palestinians in the world, and now, each time some number of them were killed, that there were that many fewer?

"Six hundred and five," Akhmed said now, naming resolutions. "Six seventy-three. I know you come here to see what it is like, to understand what it is here to be Palestinian. But what is it like *there*? Why don't they ever listen? Why?"

"I don't know, Akhmed. I'm leaving tomorrow."

"Yes. OK," said Akhmed. He was not surprised. "You can tell people about us."

"I'll do that."

"Tell them about the resolutions."

"They know about the resolutions."

"Then why don't they do anything?"

All right, thought Sam. This is it. He had never been in this situation before. He had briefly gone through a period—after reading a lot of Philip Roth novels—when he began to detect anti-Semitism in everything, but that wore off. In high school he'd once lost his mind with rage during a football game when he thought a player on the other team had called him a "dirty Jew." Sam had grabbed his face mask and demanded to know if that's what he'd said. The other player looked very surprised and shook his head confusedly. Afterward Sam realized that it was probably much more likely that he had merely said "Fuck you," and Sam felt bad. But this was different.

He got up on an elbow and turned his head to Akhmed. "You want to know why no one does anything to stop Israel, Akhmed? It's because people keep blowing themselves up. In Jerusalem. And they don't care who they kill as long as they're Jews. And that makes it very difficult for people to care very much about the resolutions when there are Jews being killed who probably opposed the Occupation."

Sam had said this forcefully but not too loudy, because he did not want Bashar and Mohammed to hear. Akhmed was surprised however at his vehemence and also now got up on an elbow, to look at him. "How can a Jew be against the Occupation?" he asked quietly. "What does this mean?"

"I'm a Jew, Akhmed! I'm a Jew against the Occupation."

Sam confessed this angrily, and then he quickly regretted it—the anger and the confession both.

"You are joking," said Akhmed.

"No, I'm not joking. Why do you think I'm here? You think I have black hair and brown eyes and I'm interested in Palestinians because I'm Italian? Come on."

Akhmed lay back down on his pillow and was silent for a long time. "Wow," he said, finally, and without looking Sam could sense that he was smiling. "That is incredible."

Once again they were silent for a long time. It was unfair to have been so angry at Akhmed: the suicide bombers came from Hamas, a party of religious zealots, and increasingly from Fatah, the corrupt ruling party—but not from Akhmed's gentle social-democrats. And Akhmed himself would never hurt anyone. In another life he would have been a professor, or a teacher—why, he was a teacher in *this* life. Perhaps what Sam meant was that in another life Akhmed would have been a Jewish teacher.

"I know a boy who became an *este-shadi*," Akhmed said now in the dark, not raising his head. A suicide bomber. He sounded very sad. "It was a strange thing. He was from this village, from Birqin. We grew up together, and he was a very quiet boy. Then I did not see him for a few years. And then I heard last year he had become a martyr. It was a very strange feeling, that he had done this thing. Someone I knew. It was a strange and terrible thing."

And lying there, next to Sam—healthy, handsome, and now Jewish Sam, who had come here and become *more* healthy, eating hummus, growing more tan, his smile whiter, and possibly even *more* Jewish, and would be going back, the next day or the day after that, to lie on a beach in Tel Aviv before going home to Katie and Cambridge, while Akhmed stayed here, writing English words he didn't know into a little book—Akhmed began to cry. It was very quiet but Sam could hear it. Or maybe he sensed it first, the crying, and then picked up the sounds. Oh, said Akhmed. Oh oh oh. Lying next to Sam, who could do nothing but look up and wait and try not to be shaken from the bedrock conviction he'd reached just a little bit earlier in that day. Said Akhmed, crying: Why why why.

In the end, Sam had to wait another day: a group of Italian medical students was arriving in Jenin, and he could take their taxi back to Jerusalem. So on his last day in Jenin Sam waited, but really without waiting, for the tanks. At Akhmed's house they watched television—Hezbollah had a cooking show that Akhmed enjoyed, and of course Sam was curious. You could tell it was Hezbollah because occasionally they interrupted the cooking for news flashes of total mayhem—riots in France, flooding in Bangladesh, industrial fires in China. It was always the end of days for Hezbollah. And not for them alone.

Sam was wary of Akhmed after their talk, but Akhmed looked at him with loving eyes. A Jew in his house—now, this was psychotopography. That morning Sam had said good-bye, coldly, to Roger and the Swedes—those useful dummies, those exploiters of Palestinian suffering, checked his e-mail for a definitive ruling from Katie (nothing, but it was early), and hurried back to Birqin. That day he and Akhmed, joined intermittently by Bashar and Mohammed and even Akhmed's uncle, who'd heard Sam was leaving, walked around the village; Sam bought them a watermelon, they sat down in Birqin's main square—a charming, Old World square, more or less, with a real outdoor cafe—and drank some Turkish coffee. They sat in the square well into the evening, past curfew. It was so hot that Sam's shirt stuck to his chest. In truth he was distracted: what had Katie written? He wouldn't know now until he got back to Jerusalem, late tomorrow, for though they'd leave in the morning and it was a thirty-mile drive it took a good three hours, with all the checkpoints, to actually make it. At the very least, on this last night, and despite the unspoken prohibition against them, Sam had put on shorts. If the Muslim women could not behave themselves at the sight of Sam's naked knees, so much the worse for Muslim women.

At around nine, Akhmed stood up and turned to Sam. It looked like he'd suggest they all go home and sleep. Instead he said something else: "Would you like—to do Internet?"

"Ah!" said Sam. "My brother." He clasped Akhmed by the shoulder, tenderly. "But where?"

It was Bashar who answered. "We go into Jenin," he said. "It's OK. We know how."

So on his last night, he'd have an adventure. And he would learn his fate with Katie; already his heart lurched a little at the thought of it. But it was fitting and just. Together Sam and the three brothers headed off into the curfewed night. The moon shone bright, they walked, and there was so little sound—the tanks were not rumbling through the desert, they were not in Jenin. Where were they hiding? The men turned off the main road outside Jenin, and Mohammed led them through a back lot to the all-night Internet cafe. Curfew or not, the Internet went on. This one was on the second floor, in what looked like a converted language lab, with twenty computers set up along its perimeter. With dignity—and trembling—Sam sat down at the keyboard. As his Muslim friends looked on, his fingers moved along the keyboard with a demonic precision—he was the white typewriting god. There were seven new messages since he'd last checked: spam, spam, an invitation to a party in New York (Sam was still vestigially on some e-mail lists). And one from Katie.

With great deliberation he deleted his junk mail. He read the party invitation (it was in a week, perhaps he'd make it). Then he opened Katie's. Right away key words registered in his mind before he'd actually read them, and already his face burned, as if the computer had given off a charge of heat. He swallowed hard. Oh, God. He took a breath and began: "Dear Sam," it went.

> i got your note last night before going to bed and i've been up ever since worrying about it and torturing myself. what can i say? i'm so, so sorry. you are so valuable to me. and these last months

He stopped again. He wasn't going to read this. There was enough torture going around. The Americans tortured the Arabs; the Israelis tortured the Palestinians. Something Akhmed told him one night while they lay on their cots, the most awful thing he'd heard: Palestinian men who returned from Israeli prisons after being tortured—being forced to sit in a chair, without sleep, without water except the water thrown on their faces to keep them awake, and without the right to use a bathroom, so that they shat themselves, eventually, and without the right to talk—had a psychic compulsion to repeat their experiences exactly as they had happened, except with the roles reversed. That wasn't yet the awful part. The awful part was that the only people they had around with whom to perform these reenactments were their wives.

Sam deleted Katie's e-mail without finishing it. She wanted to tell him they were alien creatures, not one, that they were not—this was an expression she'd used numerous times—"peas in the

191

same pod." He knew that. And maybe she was right. Or maybe she was wrong. Either way, that was that. It was over. He felt like a great and miserable explosion had occurred in his head, a burst of fire against a wall, he felt heavy and distraught. But also he was free, and alone, and still alive.

He stood up. Akhmed sat in a far corner, probably reading the *Guardian,* his favorite paper. Sam joined Bashar and Mohammed instead. A little window was open on their screen; it showed a bored American girl in a slinky white undershirt. She might have been eighteen, or twenty-two, or sixteen. The camera took a photo every ten seconds, so that in every picture the girl would be in a slightly different position, which one could examine, and consider, until the next photo. "What are you guys up to?" she asked. Mohammed, of course, knew no English, but was a master of font manipulation. While Bashar leaned over him to type, Mohammed turned the letters pink and green and enormous and shook the dialogue box with tremors. "Sweetie," typed Bashar. "You have very prettie eyes." He looked to Sam, who, offscreen, corrected the spelling; Mohammed pressed Send. The girl wanted to know: "Which one of you is typing?" She could see Mohammed and Bashar, but that was all she knew—they were good-looking kids, in their early twenties, in blue jeans and light polyester shirts, and there were no Koranic verses behind their heads, no Kalashnikovs by their sides. They might have been anyone. "I type," wrote Bashar, and waved at the tiny Webcam mounted atop the monitor. "But he love you," he added, and patted Mohammed on the shoulder. Mohammed grinned.

Sam was indignant. "This is the Intifada?" he demanded. "This is how you fight the Occupation? No wonder the tanks never come—all you guys do is try to pick up girls on the Internet."

The girl in the box had stretched her arms over her head and leaned back, so that the slinky undershirt stretched over her breasts.

"Not that I blame you," added Sam.

"You have such pretty eyes," Bashar typed again. "Will u show me another thing?"

"What?" asked the girl.

"I would like," Bashar typed slowly, "if you do not have sheert." He turned to Sam.

"An *i* in shirt," said Sam.

"Ah," Bashar agreed, and corrected it. He told Mohammed what he was saying and told him to Send. This was Mohammed's most ambitious font project yet. He made the font blue and the letters bubbly, and he caused the text box to whirl around and tremble and bounce. But it had taken too long! The girl had disappeared.

"Ah!" said Mohammed, shoving the keyboard in disgust.

"Akh," said Bashar, then shrugged apologetically at Sam.

As if Sam cared! He knit his brow. "This is how you end the Occupation?" he said again.

Bashar turned squarely to Sam. Undernourished as he was, skinnier and shorter than Sam, who was not tall, Bashar stood now to his full height. "I am a good fighter," he said. "Ask Akhmed. Look." He pulled up his jeans to his knee, exposing his ankle, and pointing. Sam saw a small dime-size circular scar on his ankle, and then Bashar turned his leg so that Sam saw a slightly larger one on the other side. "The bullet came here and out there. At Jenin Camp. So I am a good fighter," Bashar concluded.

"OK," said Sam. "But you're still too skinny." And he squeezed his arm while Bashar made a muscle.

Meanwhile Mohammed had moved on to another chat session, this one in Arabic. A girl in Muslim headdress was on the screen in the same spot as the girl in the tank top had been. Mohammed grinned and picked at the keys, not bothering now to adorn them in all the colors of the world.

"His girlfriend," said Bashar. Mohammed overheard and,

perhaps it was one English word he knew, punched his brother in the leg.

Then he grew excited. He typed faster, Sam-like. He typed like the wind. Bashar, reading over his shoulder, became concerned. "She is also in Internet," he explained to Sam. "She is saying there is tank. We cannot go home."

Sam didn't understand.

"We live here," Bashar said, indicating Birqin with a stab of his finger on the monitor of the sleeping computer next to Mohammed's. "And now we are here. And she is here. Tank is here."

There was a tank between them and Akhmed's father's house, and Mohammed's girlfriend could see it from where she was. "So we'll sleep at the GIS apartment," Sam said. But if they hadn't logged on to this chat, if the American girl hadn't become spooked by the twin Arab font geniuses, then what? OK, they should not have been out past curfew—but why was there a curfew? *The Israelis weren't even here.*

They walked back into the night. The Internet place was air-conditioned, if only weakly, and now the humidity surrounded Sam like a blanket. He tried to breathe slowly, walk slowly, like an Arab. In Jerusalem right now it was perfect—dry, balmy, a little breeze on the heights, and probably the safest time to be out, since terrorism was a daytime job. Although only here, the place from which the random violence emanated, could you really feel safe. That is, if you were American. You didn't feel safe here if you were a Palestinian, because Israelis sometimes shot at you. This was how it went: Palestinians felt OK on Israeli buses, and Sam, who was nervous on Israeli buses, felt OK in the territories. It was a very *modern* situation.

They wended through various backstreets and alleyways, inso-far as little Jenin had them, and emerged at last onto the main road, the next turn of which would take them to the GIS apartment and safety. And then, suddenly, right before them, a thing—an enormous, gigantic, hulking metal thing. Perhaps not so gigantic. But bigger than a horse, a lot bigger, and bigger than a pickup truck. A pretty big thing. A tank.

The four of them froze. They were out after curfew and the tank could, theoretically, open fire. Those were the rules. And Sam—Sam was not wearing an orange vest or carrying a laptop or really in any way distinguishable from a native Jeninian military-age male.

Except for his shorts. It would be embarrassing to die in one's shorts, and yet—as the split second for which they'd been frozen ended, and all four dove back into the alleyway—Sam wondered whether it wasn't the shorts that had given the soldiers in the tank pause. Because as soon as they were in the alleyway a series of rounds hit the ground where they had been.

They stood still, their backs pressed to the wall.

"Are they really trying to shoot us?" Sam asked Akhmed.

Akhmed was too out of breath to answer.

"Probably no." Bashar answered for him. "They shoot—just in case." He grinned at Sam.

Sam nodded.

Mohammed had gone farther down the alley, scoping out the situation, but now he flew by them and, without sticking his head out into the street, flung something in the direction of the tank. A rock—Sam saw it leave his hand in the moonlight. "Jesus Christ," he said, incredulous, and then the four of them waited, hushed, cringing, wondering what kind of repercussion this rock, thrown with such nonchalance, by this boy, Mohammed, the master of font manipulation, would have—and then, incredibly, a sharp metallic *plunk*. The rock had hit the tank! What a sound it made! And despite all the hummus he'd eaten, Sam now kept up with the brothers as they raced down the alleyway toward an alternate route back to the GIS apartment, machine-gun rounds from the tank clattering impotently behind them out on the main road.

Sam couldn't help but laugh and laugh and laugh, even as he ran. There was no going back now, even though he'd go back tomorrow, even though he'd spend the weekend on the beach in Tel Aviv. Now, at long last, his arms pumping at his sides, the tank still firing madly behind them, his chest heaving, he knew. The Palestinians were idiots. But the Israelis—well, the Israelis were fuckers. And when Sam saw an idiot faced with his natural enemy, the fucker, he knew whose side he was on.

He slept in a sweaty heap that night at the GIS apartment, on a bunch of sleeping bags laid across the floor. Akhmed was to the left of him; Mohammed and Bashar on the other side, with Mohammed's leg draped periodically over Sam's ankle. Eight months later, in Gaza, a pretty American college student from the GIS was run over by an Israeli bulldozer, whose driver claimed not to have seen her. That same month, also in Gaza, an Israeli sniper put a bullet into the brain of a British GIS member, killing him. And that same month—it was the month the United States was invading Iraq, so the world was very busy—a young American in Jenin, staring down an Israeli armored personnel carrier in broad daylight, had part of his face taken off by a round it fired. Sam recognized the name of the street. But he was in New York by then, where he'd moved shortly after returning to the States, and found a job paralegaling. Sam was preparing for law school. It was important that he knew what he knew, though how exactly it would come into play was impossible to tell. For the moment, on weekends, he kept up with the news, sipped his beer, and thought about the future.

Phenomenology
of the Spirit

I found the Mensheviks kind, intelligent, witty. But everything I saw convinced me that, face to face with the ruth-
lessness of history, they were wrong.

—Victor Serge

Mark's dissertation, in the end, was about Roman
Sidorovich, "the funny Menshevik." Lenin had
called him that, *menshevitskiy khakhmach*, in 1911. Sidorovich was
tickled. "I'd rather be *menshevitskiy khakhmach*," he said (to friends),
"than *bolshevitskiy palach*." I'd rather be the Menshevik funny-man
than the Bolshevik hangman. Oops.

They were all in Switzerland then, having fled the scrutiny of
the tsar's secret police. In 1917, they all, Lenin and Trotsky and
Sidorovich, returned home after the tsar abdicated. Or anyway

Mark thought they did. The truth is, Sidorovich was too minor a figure for anyone to have noticed when exactly he returned, what exactly he was wearing, his friends and his widow gave contradictory accounts, and his personal papers were confiscated in the 1930s. But Mark thought he could see him in the documentary evidence, cracking jokes. It was in fact the task of his dissertation to prove that many of the anonymously attributed humorous remarks of 1917 ("someone joked," "a wit replied") were attributable to Roman Sidorovich.

In 1920, after securing power, Lenin exiled many of the Mensheviks. The Sidoroviches found themselves in Berlin, where Roman briefly succumbed to the temptation to write humorous book reviews for *Rul'*, the liberal paper associated with, among others, Nabokov's father. In 1926, however, Sidorovich grew bored and depressed and asked to be allowed back into the country. He was allowed. Five years later, he was arrested, and his "humorous remarks," the ones Mark spent all his time authenticating, were spat back at him during his interrogation. It turned out the Bolsheviks had a very good memory for humorous remarks.

"I confessed to the good ones right away," Sidorovich said later.

"Then they tortured me, and I confessed to the bad ones, too.

"Then they tortured me some more," he also apparently said, a few times, "and I blamed the bad ones on my friends."

The record of the interrogation had not survived. But it was known that Sidorovich received a five-year sentence in Verkhne-Udalsk. He returned to Moscow in 1936 and was rearrested in early 1941. He was on his way back to Verkhne-Udalsk, or beyond, when the Germans invaded. At this point history lost track of Roman Sidorovich, and so did Mark.

*   *   *

It was now the spring of 2006, and in a flurry of activity over the course of two weekends, Mark had actually finished the dissertation that for so long, over the course of so many days and nights, so many hockey practices and midday jogs, so many arguments with Sasha, poor Sasha—and then after she left, all the wandering through the apartment, all the fruitless trips to the library during which he looked at photos of naked women, if no one was around—that through all this had occupied his mind. It was over. He was done; he had affixed all the proper footnotes, the appendices, the (possibly dubious) methodological explanations, and then he'd affixed all the proper postage and, from the giant post office in Madison Square, mailed the dissertation to his saintly adviser, Jeff. As a kind of joke, Jeff decided to schedule his defense for May 1, International Workers' Day. Now it was getting on toward the end of April. All that remained for Mark to do was produce a short talk in his own defense and take a bus up to Syracuse.

But it was not so simple. Life, Mark's life, had thickened somehow, had expanded greatly in its complexity without expanding simultaneously in capacity and means. He was embroiled in a situation, in short, and afraid to leave New York.

Mark had spent his twenties, even that portion of his twenties that he spent married, preoccupied with the problem of sex. He considered it in the positivist tradition of how to find it, of course, but also, and more significant, in the interpretivist or postmodernist tradition of how to think about it, how to ponder it historically, how to discourse about and critique it. This was, again, both during and after his marriage to Sasha. To be outside of sex, Mark believed, to be outside this great procession, this great unfolding of man's freedom, was to be reactionary, irrelevant. Did he exaggerate the importance of sex because he himself, trapped in marriage and trapped in Syracuse, was so far removed from it? Perhaps. And yet the fact that sex eluded him seemed only to indicate to Mark his historical position. Who was he to argue? He kept his mouth shut and searched the Internet for dates. No wonder he couldn't write his dissertation.

Then—eighteen months ago—he moved to Brooklyn. Historical periods, according to Marx, produce both recognizable types and anti-types, and late capitalism, at around the time Mark was moving to Brooklyn, was producing its own antibodies, its antitheses, in the form of young women who thought that Mark was just fine, that Mark was just dreamy. They loved that he didn't have any money; they adored that he didn't know how to go about getting it. He was so cute! thought the women. Where did you come from? thought Mark. The answer was that the colleges produced them. Then bought them plane tickets, gave them Mark's address. "The workers have no country," wrote Karl Marx—but Mark Grossman did have a country, as it turned out, and that country was New York. In his first two weeks there he met more attractive, articulate women, in person, than he had in the previous four years of multimedia dating in Syracuse. He bought a cell phone and the women of Brooklyn called him on it, texted him on it; he set his ring tone to the opening theme of the television show *Dynasty*, and they caused it to chime from his phone at all hours of the day. What could he do? He canceled his Internet dating profiles, ceased his interminable e-mail negotiations with girls he'd never seen. At the age of thirty, Mark Grossman had finally solved the problem of sex.

Too late, it turned out. Life worked by a series of compensatory measures. You had to wait and wait, and while you waited you worked in libraries on your dissertation and occasionally logged on to the Internet to watch the trailers for the latest pornographic films. And now? Now behold Mark in bed with Gwyn, his beautiful former student. His beautiful twenty-two-year-old former student. An impossibility in Syracuse; an everyday occurrence all across New York. No wonder they charged such rents. But behold Mark staring up at the ceiling queasily. Behold him making inadequate mumbled responses to her questions. Behold Gwyn asking directly if he would please make love to her. Behold Mark saying no!

Oh, if Mark's teenage self had seen him doing this—why, if Mark's self of just eighteen months ago had seen it—those Marks would have shaken their fists at this Mark. They'd have called him terrible names. But they didn't know the situation! thought Mark. "Listen," he wanted to plead with the teenage Mark, "don't spend the bar mitzvah money on a car. Let *Dad* buy you the car. He won't mind. Save the money for when you're thirty years old and living in Brooklyn. You'll need it." "You're pathetic," teenage Mark would no doubt answer. He was a cocky kid. "I need that car to get to hockey practice. Are you going bald?" "I'm not sure," grown-up Mark would say. "It's been like this since I was twenty. Kind of a mystery." Then he thought of something. "Listen!" he called out to disappearing teenage Mark. "Don't go to grad school!" But teenage Mark was already gone, that little snot, leaving grown-up Mark to face the present. In the present things had come to a sorry pass. He was running out of money. He was dating two women, causing him to feel guilty, causing him to spend more money, causing him to experience what Americans call *stress*. Mark was an American himself, and not immune to it.

He woke up a few hours later, late and alone. Gwyn had gone off to her internship, and he had a lunch meeting with his adviser,

Jeff. After that he had to watch the hockey game, it was the play-offs, and tomorrow night he'd have dinner with Celeste—his old beloved Celeste—possibly their last. And he had many e-mails to write in the interim, he knew.

He got up and showered. The door to his roommate Toby's room was closed, meaning Toby was inside looking at computer models of global warming. A novelist by trade—he had sold his novel about Milwaukee to a major publisher, who had then failed to publish it, so that Toby—like the screenwriters in Hollywood who live off options—was now in the process of selling *the very same novel* to another publisher ("No publisher wants to be the publisher who turned down my novel," he explained), and so on—but in the meantime he'd become obsessed with the impending climate catastrophe. He had been a computer wizard once, and now he would spend hours in his room looking at the catastrophic climate models, modeling them. "At this rate," he would sometimes say, meaning the rate of global climate change, "my novel might never even be published." Toby was in a better situation than Mark, because he didn't spend so much money on dates. This wasn't because he didn't go on them—as a matter of fact he went on dates with a girl named Arielle, who was, incidentally, the high school ex-girlfriend of Mark and Toby's mutual friend Sam—but she was a lawyer now, and paid for them.

"Jog later?" Mark called through Toby's closed door.

Toby answered momentarily: "When?"

"Six?"

Toby agreed, and Mark was out the door. On his way down St. John's—the street got leafier, livelier, even the sounds carried more musically, the closer one got to Park Slope—he took out his cell phone and flipped it back and forth in his hand. His first phone had broken after he dropped it to the pavement, but he'd since replaced it with a sturdier Samsung model, and now he happily threw it up in the air and caught it again as he walked, knowing it could survive anything.

But riding the Q train over the Manhattan Bridge, Mark became depressed. There had been a time, upon moving to New York, when he would stand at the Q train window looking in awe and deference at the glory of the downtown skyscrapers, the huge art deco Verizon building, Pier 17, the cars moving, with wild abandon, on the FDR. Also, when he'd sometimes been on a date and forced to take a cab back across the bridge from Manhattan, it had been a consolation for the fifteen dollars he was spending to look out from that bridge after his six or seven drinks. Now the memory of those fifteen-dollar rides cut him to the quick. Syracuse had funded him longer, and more generously, while asking fewer questions and making fewer demands (though forwarding an obscene amount of departmental e-mail) than he could ever have hoped—and still it was about to end. With his defense, or without it, the money would now stop coming. Mark stayed glumly in his seat, counting how much longer he could remain in New York at his current rate of spending. He had $2,000 in the bank, and one more stipend check ($1,200) coming. That was it. And he was thirty years old.

Jeff Sterne, his saintly dissertation adviser, was already at the University Diner when Mark showed up ten minutes late. He had heard the trembling in Mark's e-mails and taken the train down to see him. Jeff was a wonderful man!—a professor who did not like the university, a Democrat who could not stomach the Democrats, and a vegetarian who did not like vegetables. While Mark chomped on a bacon cheeseburger ("Go ahead!" Jeff had said. "You look pallid. It's on me"), Jeff ordered a plate of rice and then coffee after coffee, into each cup of which he bravely poured sugar as he tried to convince Mark that the dissertation defense was nothing to fear.

"All you need to do is sit there," he said, pouring sugar. "Nod when they say you've done something wrong; apologize when they say you've offended them. It's like—a Komsomol court."

"I know," said Mark. "I know. It's just . . . Syracuse."

"Oh, it's not so bad."

"Do I really look pallid?"

"No. You look like a former athlete, gracefully aged."

"Thank you," said Mark.

They talked about Sidorovich, about some of Mark's former fellow graduate students, still trapped in Syracuse, still snorting pharmaceutical medications. Jeff told a funny story about the great Ulinsky. Mark watched him; Mark may not have been pale but Jeff really was. He was also broad-shouldered, gray-eyed, bespectacled, a surprisingly good-looking man, given his reticence, his kindness. "In a way I understand," he said now. "Once you enter the academy, it's hard to get out. They expect things from you. And you might get a job—or, put another way, they might assign you to a post—somewhere that is not New York. That too is like the Soviet education system. And I could see how one wouldn't want to leave."

Jeff looked around. Just then a very attractive forty-year-old woman in a thin leather car coat walked into the diner and made her way over to a booth and kissed—on the cheek—an older, rough-looking man. What was their relationship? Where did such women come from? Mark's adviser sighed. "You forget about death here," he said. "You might even forget about defeat." He spoke with the knowledge of twenty-five long years of political and academic defeat; with the disappointment of having written one good book in his career, about the Mensheviks in exile ("in autumn," he'd called it), which was one good book too few. He had contributed articles to *Debate*, a gentle, intelligent journal of the Left. One time—and one time only—he had been asked by the *New York Review of Books* to write up a biography of Stolypin. But he'd already agreed to do it for *Debate*. It was typical of Mark's adviser that it was not he, but someone else, who had told Mark that story.

Mark was not worthy to sit at the same booth in a diner with this man. Looking down at his plate he saw that he'd devoured the burger but there were still some fries left, and he nudged the plate to the middle of the table to suggest that his adviser have some, too.

"You know," Jeff said finally, folding his arms on the table and leaning in toward Mark. "We always think we can save people. I mean we on the Left. And men too, I guess. We men.

"But I'm your adviser, right? I'm going to give you some advice. I came down here on the pretext that *I* was going to save you. But actually I just wanted to see the city. People are going to do what they do, and aside from a social safety net and not bombing them, it's out of our hands. You have to save yourself, man. Each of us does. Save yourself."

He poured a mound of sugar into his coffee and smiled ruefully.

"Anyway, enough of that," he said. "Tell me about your life here. Are you in love?"

Was Mark in love?

He pondered the question on the ten blocks down from the diner to the NYU library. From Syracuse, over the course of several maddening weeks, he had once claimed, with mounting fervor, to be in love with Celeste. And then, four months ago, he had walked into a party in Park Slope and seen her at the other end of the room. His heart leaped to his throat. There she was! She was laughing. She didn't see him. They hadn't talked since the night she left those messages on his machine while he was—the thought pained him even now—at Leslie's place. Seeing her to his right across a room in Park Slope he turned left, put down his coat, found a drink, drank it, found another drink, and only then, when he suspected she might already have seen him, finally approached. He was no longer the awkward recently divorced graduate student trapped in Syracuse; he was a man with half an apartment on St. John's between Washington and Classon, a real person. And yet he felt like a boy.

She was delighted to see him, however. She'd heard he was in New York. What was more, she managed to add quickly enough, she had broken up with her boyfriend, the very boyfriend Mark had so zealously tried to chase away.

"What happened?" Mark was shocked. In his way he'd developed an attachment to the boyfriend, as the revolutionaries might be said to have developed an attachment to the tsar. Whenever anyone tried to include a clause in the old social-democratic charters, long before the Revolution, banning capital punishment, the cry would go up, "What about Nicholas II?" This was always argument enough. Then the Bolsheviks murdered the entire royal family in a blood-soaked basement in Yekaterinburg and, you know, after sex all animals are sad.

"Oh, God," said Celeste. "It was like dating, I don't know, Peter Pan. No, not like that. It was like dating Kafka!"

Mark didn't understand.

"No, you're right, he wasn't like Kafka. It was just—I'm out of literary allusions. It was like Charlotte's fiancé in *Sex and the City*. Have you seen that one? Anyway, Tom, my ex, he can't stop seeing his mother. He visits her like every weekend. He's a thirty-year-old man. Is that normal?"

"It's not normal."

"I agree. So . . . here I am." She laughed, and appraised him.

"Look at you! You're like the Count of Monte Cristo escaped from prison." She fingered some fabric from his sleeve. "Nice shirt!"

Mark was, in fact, wearing his nice shirt. "Thank you," he said.

And they were off, talking about their lives. Was it too late? Celeste looked—she was Celeste. Her laugh that he had never forgotten, throwing her head back, glamorously; her sense of fashion, both new and old and flattering and unflattering in all the right measures. She was three years older than she'd been when they had spent all those hours on the phone together, but she was alive, she was all and always herself, as none of the women Mark had known since moving to New York had been. She wore a short dress and tall boots; her hair was cut short. She lived in Fort Greene, and they made a plan—it wasn't even like he was asking her out—to meet up and get drinks. Mark walked home from the party with a whole new idea of life, of what life could do. Was it too late? He didn't know. Then they met for drinks and got so drunk! That was the thing about New York. Everyone was drunk all the time. But it was all right. It was discreet. It was upscale. It was not like in Syracuse, or Moscow, the drinking in the middle of the afternoon, the roving bands of drunks and the random violence. People were drunk in couples; they emerged from bars, quickly kissed, hailed a cab: and you never saw them again.

That's what Mark and Celeste did, too, though they were already close to her apartment, and so they walked.

Mark entered the NYU library with his visiting scholar pass and headed straight for the beautiful iMacs in the reference room.

So he had found Celeste. She lived in a large sunny studio on the third floor of a big Fort Greene building and her place was filled with her smells. Her shower curtain was a work of art. There were scattered papers from all her traveling and a backlog of the higher-brow magazines, but otherwise it was a lovely apartment, and as for her moods, which had sometimes been destructive, she had stabilized them masterfully with a dozen mood stabilizers. And so, old and experienced, they dove right in. Celeste did not like the Brooklyn weekend eating scene—"competitive brunching," she called it—and instead on weekend mornings she sent Mark to the gourmet deli on Lafayette for egg sandwiches and in the meantime made French press coffee; then they sat on her big L-shaped couch, next to the window, reading the enormous *New York Times*.

Recently, however, there'd been some kind of shift. Celeste, truth be told, wasn't quite who Mark thought she was, from Syracuse; or rather he wasn't quite who *he* thought he was. Too long a sacrifice, Mark sometimes said to himself, when he began to notice their problems, can make a stone of the heart. But that wasn't really it. Objectively they were in trouble. "We're not twenty-three anymore," Celeste said once as they settled down at Frank's, in Fort Greene, to get drunk. "And I'm tired." She kept having to fly off to Chicago, to Miami, to cover their so-called news. Mark's roommate, Toby, would have known that the only news that mattered was the daily increasing hegemony of the global corporations and their destruction of the earth. But still Celeste had to fly. And her sleeping pills and eating habits, and above all her many mood stabilizers, had some troublesome effects, inhibiting important intimate functions in addition to the depression and anxiety ones. "Can you stop taking them?" asked Mark. "I'd be weepy all the time," said Celeste. Mark said, "That sounds nice." "What about curled up in the corner with a knife?" "Less nice." "OK then." They sat in Frank's and eyed each other semi-warily. The newspapers, the magazines, the television, and Mark's in-box were selling youth elixirs and penis extenders. One possible explanation was late-imperial decadence and corruption: life was too easy. Another explanation tended in the opposite direction. The television sold youth because life was *not* simple and *not* easy; because you did not emerge from your twenties smiley-faced and full of cheer and love for all existence.

"You know," Mark began, "the Mensheviks would have said that—"

"Will you stop it with the Mensheviks? I mean, can we have one conversation where we talk about something else?"

Mark was hurt. "OK," he said meanly, "how many men have you slept with?"

Now Celeste was hurt. "I don't know," she lied. "Four?"

"Yeah," said Mark. "Sure. Me too."

So that was Celeste and Mark, six weeks ago. Not long after, Mark had received an e-mail.

Dear Mark,

Hi, it's Gwyn, from your European history section in the spring of 2004. (In case you don't remember me, I wrote a paper on the Russian Constituent Assembly. Poor Constituent Assembly!) I just graduated and am about to move to New York to intern in publishing. I heard from Professor Sterne that you're living there. I don't know the city very well, so I'm hoping that you might meet me for coffee next week—to help a girl get her bearings in the city. Are you available to meet?

I hope you're doing well.

Best,
Gwyn

Mark was all alone that week—Celeste was in Miami to write about Cubans, and Mark was supposed to be finishing his dissertation—and he must have read the e-mail a hundred times. He looked under it, he looked around it, he sniffed and searched. A girl in the city? Available to meet? It could not mean what it looked like it meant. Gwyn had been so much more attractive—and, in her way, aloof, self-contained, cool—than any student he'd taught at Syracuse that it had never occurred to him that something other than just teaching and learning about the Bolshevik Revolution could go on between them. Her paper on the Constituent Assembly was clear, sharp, dutiful; at times it bordered, when it dealt with a really major text like Ulinsky's, on the worshipful. Maybe it had occurred to Mark, momentarily, that this worship could be redirected. But he'd dismissed the thought, or anyway the thought as it pertained to Mark. And he dismissed it again three years later, despite the e-mail. So great is the power of human self-deception—*ideology*, the old revolutionaries would have called it—that even as Mark sat drinking coffee with Gwyn, her strong half-bare shoulders, her pure perfect skin, her chin like Ava Gardner's chin, her thick sensual lips—a girl from Minnesota—and all of it was shocking, to Mark, at his age, he was ten years older than she was, almost—even then, even as she told him that the publishing house's idea of an internship was that she put on high heels and go around to boutiques in Soho, seeing if they'd agree to sell some of the publisher's books, she had a kind of reserve, he'd really not thought anything could happen, which is why he didn't think it necessary even to mention this meeting to Celeste when she'd called him from Miami earlier in the day. In the coffee shop on Elizabeth they talked about the history of the Mensheviks: "I miss our class," Gwyn said. "I miss the Mensheviks." After coffee they walked out into the afternoon, it was still light out, and Mark—he had learned Old World manners, a little, from reading so much about the Old World—was politely walking her back to her new place on First Avenue, she was new to the city after all and might not find it, when she said, "You know, I kind of want a beer. Would you mind?" So they had gone to a bar. It was five o'clock; it was happy hour. At this point, something began to dawn on Mark. He drank four beers. Actually, he drank five and a half beers, approximately, because he drank so much faster than Gwyn, and she kept playfully topping him off from her own. The whole event cost him $20, plus $6 in tips, $26, barely more than a pair of movie tickets, and by the time they walked out they were both plastered. And somewhere back there he'd begun to suspect that Gwyn was not just innocently soliciting information about neighborhood restaurants from him. After a while her beauty, too, did not seem so incongruous. If you hung around with a very pretty woman in a dark bar during the afternoon, Mark found on this afternoon, you began simply to think that that's what people looked like. And so it was in kind of a spirit of experimentation that Mark leaned forward toward Gwyn on her landing and kissed her.

That was a month ago, and it had inaugurated a period of Mark's life that was bound to end badly. If meeting Celeste post-boyfriend was like arriving in Russia in March 1917, hopeful March after the tsar's abdication, the appointment of the provisional government, the short-lived democratic process, then they were well into anarchic June or even forbidding July. Was Gwyn his Kerensky? His Kornilov? Ekh. Ultimately these historical parallels were of limited use in figuring out your personal life.

Mark checked his e-mail in the NYU library. He had fourteen new messages, though no one had anything in particular they needed to tell Mark—except Celeste, who was checking on

tomorrow's dinner, and Gwyn, who was sending some nice pho-
tos of them together at a bar. He hammered away at the replies,
the loudest typist in the reference room by far. NO E-MAIL ON
THIS COMPUTER said a little piece of paper affixed to his monitor.
GO FUCK YOURSELF, thought Mark. This isn't the Soviet Union.
He would e-mail wherever he felt like it.

So was he in love? Perhaps rather than historically the answer
could be formed mathematically. If he looked inside his heart,
Mark could see that he did not quite love Celeste; and he did not
love Gwyn. He had tender feelings, of different kinds, for both
of them. Celeste was so funny! Gwyn was an angel. If you combined these feelings, they would add up to one unit of love. Possibly *more* than one unit; definitely more than one unit. But—and
this was the sign of Mark's maturity, on which Mark congratu-
lated himself—he also knew that if he ended it with Celeste, or he
ended it with Gwyn, he would still have one unit of love to give,
and he would give it to Gwyn, or Celeste, respectively.

Except how was he going to do this? He didn't want to hurt
anyone's feelings. He did not want to be denounced by anyone,
especially Celeste. Or especially Gwyn. The world was full of so
much pain and the thought of adding to that pain—again—was
hard to bear. Oh, Mark thought as he headed for the subway. If
only he could be as brave in his personal relations as he was in his
defiance of anti–e-mail librarians!

In the history of Menshevism, there were exactly three great
events: the break with Lenin in 1903; the walkout from the Soviet
on the night of October 25, 1917; and, of course, the Constituent
Assembly in January 1918.

Sidorovich was definitely not in Brussels in 1903; he may or
may not have been in Petersburg in October; but he was, finally,

at the Constituent Assembly in January. He had even produced a witticism on the subject. "The Constituent Assembly was like the opera," said Sidorovich. "It was very boring but you felt, given how much it had cost, that you had to stay." It had cost nearly a hundred years of tireless labor; the fight for an all-Russian democratic congress—which is what the Constituent Assembly was—had destroyed the lives of countless men and women. And when it finally came, during the early months of the Bolshevik dictatorship, it lasted exactly one day. When it became clear to the delegates on that day that they would not be allowed to return, they decided not to leave. At 4:00 a.m. they were expelled from the building. And it was over. A Bolshevik, asked by a journalist before the event what would happen if the Mensheviks and others tried to protest against the regime, had made a witticism of his own. "First, we will try to dissuade them," he said. "Then we will shoot."

Sidorovich didn't really have a comeback for that one. Neither did the Mensheviks. Even in Russian, some things aren't all that funny.

Mark emerged from the subway back in Brooklyn to find a voice message on his magic phone. "Hi, it's me," said Gwyn. "Just wondering what you're doing. I'm thinking of going to a movie. Do you want to come? There's this old movie playing at the Film Forum."

How young people loved to watch movies! And how their days had become strangely distended, and his days too, with their cell phones for calling each other on. He called back and told her he had blocked off tonight as defense preparation.

"OK," she said, sounding sad.

"Don't sound sad!"

"Are you almost done with it, though?"

"Yes," said Mark, honestly enough. "I'm almost done."

"Well," she said, "I can't wait to read it."

They hung up and almost immediately the *Dynasty* theme song was playing again. Mark listened to it for a little while. What if Sidorovich had had a cell phone? He could have called home from Berlin in 1926. "Hey! How's the Revolution going? Oh really? That sounds terrible. Gosh. I guess I'll stay here for now."

He looked at the phone. It was Sasha. His dear Sasha.

"Sushok," he said, picking up.

"Hi, Mufka," she said. "What are you doing?"

"Walking down the street," he said. "What about you?"

"I had a bad dream about you, Mufka. Are you OK?"

"I'm OK. Yes. I think so. I'm going to defend my dissertation next week."

"Really? Mufka, that's great! In Syracuse? Do you want me to come watch?"

"Oh, no. In Syracuse? No. That would be too sad."

"Yes, that would be sad."

"Sushok?" They hadn't talked in a while, and though there was still no one person as significant in their lives (or Mark's, anyway), time too had done its work. So had the hurting of others, Mark had found. He was about to hurt Celeste, he feared, and this distanced him from Sasha, whom he'd hurt so long ago. "Sushok, how are things up there?"

"I don't know," she said. "It's pretty here but everyone is stupid. All they talk about is dating. I don't want to do that."

"No. No. Don't date."

"And I don't want to go on the Internet."

"Oh, no. God, no. No Internet." The thought of his ex-wife on the Internet was truly horrible.

"So, there we are."

Mark took a breath, preparing to say something that might offend his sensitive Sushok. "Sushok," he said. "You need to marry a rich man."

"Find me a rich man," Sasha said very seriously, "and I'll consider it."

"Rich men aren't idiots," Mark told her, half believing it. "They'll find you themselves. You're a beautiful woman still, you know." Which was true.

"Well," said Sasha. "We'll see."

Mark was already at his building, and now he got off the phone. Would he really give her away? Really? The thought of them getting back together was blasphemy, it was socially taboo. You made a certain promise when you gathered all your friends and were married, and accepted their gifts, and congratulations, toasts and well wishes. When, in the course of time, you broke that promise, when you divorced and told your friends and gathered them, together or singly, to announce it, and accepted their condolences, their regrets, their well wishes—well, you soon found you'd made another promise, this time that you were apart. Now you had to stay apart.

His roommate Toby's door was still closed when Mark came in, meaning he had been home all this time, growing angry about global warming. Mark knocked anyway and Toby appeared.

"Jog?" said Mark.

"OK," Toby answered wearily. He hadn't shaved.

"It's a nice day out," said Mark.

"Nice day out for you."

"What's that mean?"

"Nice day here means more drought in the Sahara and hurricanes of unprecedented force off the Gulf Coast."

"Look. I've stopped leaving my reading light on at night."

"I know. Thank you."

Toby was right, of course. They were done for. But still they had to live. Mark said, "I have to break up with Celeste tomorrow."

"Why?"

"Because. I don't know. Because of Gwyn."

"Well," said Toby. "There could be worse reasons."

"Thank you. It would help if we could jog."

"OK, OK," said Toby, and retreated into his room to put on his jogging shorts. Mark did the same. "When are you going up to Syracuse?" Toby called out from his room.

"Monday!" Mark called back. "If I go!"

"Of course you'll go!" Toby appeared now in Mark's doorway. His jogging shorts were too long for him. "You should stay there, too. When the floods come, Syracuse might survive. In fact it might become a coastal city. A Marseilles."

"When are the floods?"

"Can't say. Could be thirty years, could be five. Some of these things, they're not predictable." Mark threw Toby the house keys. Toby had a pocket for them.

"What about Brooklyn?"

"No more Brooklyn."

"Parties?"

"No more parties. No more pretty girls. No Mensheviks, no jogging, no delicious Senegalese restaurant for breaking up with your older but more interesting and intelligent girlfriend."

They walked out onto St. John's, two highly trained, highly educated white men. "Of course, Canada is really your safest bet," Toby went on. He used to be a very quiet guy, but the global climate had changed his personality. "It's the Saudi Arabia of freshwater, plus Canadian citizenship will be very valuable when most of the U.S. is under water."

"Sasha's in Canada," said Mark.

"Sasha's a genius," said Toby.

They used to jog on the concrete road that encircled the park. Now, in deference to their aging knees, they jogged straight through—up and back once, then up and back again on the soft Brooklyn grass.

He had to break up with Celeste. He said it to himself in the shower; he repeated it to himself as he spread out his notes for the dissertation presentation, and some beers, and turned on the Rangers first-round playoff game. Their best player, Jaromir Jagr, wore a 68 on his jersey in honor of the Czech uprising against the Soviets. Mark had always found this puzzling, like when football players thanked Jesus for touchdowns. He got a little drunk, watching the Rangers lose, and helplessly wrote both Celeste and Gwyn tender text messages before falling asleep on the couch.

But he had to break up with Celeste; he began catechizing himself again the next day as he rode down Classon on his bike. Break up with Celeste, he said. You are both unhappy. You are not, it turns out, such a great couple. Misanthropes should not marry. At least not each other. And your failure to end it now would be purely the product of fear—and some misguided loyalty to Syracuse Mark, poor lonely stupid Syracuse Mark. In his mind he defended his decision to the dissertation committee: This is a relationship of convenience. We cannot keep it up. We are desperate and we've tugged on this last straw. We don't love each other!

"You loved her before," answered the dissertation committee.

"That was a long time ago. We were both different."

"She's twenty-nine years old."

"I know! That's why we shouldn't drag this out."

"You might not find another girl like her."

"What about Gwyn?"

"She's twenty-two, Mark."

Mark turned the dissertation committee off in his brain. Those people were out to get him. He went into the wine store and bought a bottle of rosé for nine dollars, Celeste had declared it the wine of choice for the coming summer. At first he looped the plastic bag over the handlebar but as the road was uneven and his beautiful if very heavy antique Schwinn, once a birthday present for Sasha—"It's definitely a nice bike," Sasha said, trying to lift it, "for an enormous *muzhik*"—had deteriorated, quite a bit, in the realm of the wheel bearings, causing the front wheel to oscillate on its axis, the wine bottle kept knocking against the bike, and so eventually he just took it in his hand and held it, keeping the other hand for steering. Up ahead a group of teenagers had come across a ripped trash bag that had been set out for recycling, and were now pelting one another with plastic bottles. When he passed they threw one at Mark and he ducked.

Celeste was already at the restaurant, reading the *New Yorker* when he arrived. What a city! She wore a vintage dress, black, with lots of ruffles, or detailing, as they'd say about a car. She smiled when she saw him and got up to kiss him on the cheek. Then she pulled back. "You're so sweaty!" she said.

"Oops," said Mark, looking down. He had begun to sweat a ferocious sweat during his afternoon jog with Toby and he'd never really stopped sweating it, though it took entering muggy Bistro Senegale for him to notice just how wet his shirt had become. "Sorry," he said.

"No," said Celeste, "I like it."

They sat down, she had already ordered some plantains. Mark forked one off her plate.

"You're going up to Syracuse Monday?"

"Yup." It was now Saturday.

"Do you want me to come?"

"Oh no. I mean, I don't think it's worth it. I'm just going to go up, defend my important ideas, and come right back."

"What are you doing tomorrow night? I can probably get Rangers tickets from someone at the office, if you want."

"Oh no. I need to prepare and they're getting embarrassed anyway. Let's just have a party when I get back."

"I'm flying to Seattle Tuesday," she said.

"You're kidding."

"Nope. Microsoft shareholders' meeting."

"But that's halfway across the continent!"

She laughed. Gwyn, he immediately thought, a little unfairly, would have looked at him strangely and told him that, no, Seattle is all the way across the continent.

"So it goes," said Celeste. "I'm hungry."

They ate chicken with peanut butter sauce. "Tell me, Mark," Celeste said suddenly, "what do you do when I'm gone?"

"What do you mean? I work on my dissertation."

"For a man who every time I've asked him what he's been doing over the past, what is it, three years, has always said, 'Working on my dissertation'"—Celeste put a hunk of chicken into her mouth—"you sure as hell haven't produced a very long dissertation."

Mark's dissertation on Sidorovich was, indeed, a slim volume.

"There wasn't a lot of evidence," Mark grumbled.

"I think you're seeing a younger woman," said Celeste, a little experimentally.

"Do you?" said Mark. Celeste didn't really think this, he thought, but she did sense it. It was incredible what women sensed.

"Yup, and I think you're going to give me all sorts of young people diseases."

"Like what?"

"I don't know," said Celeste. "What are the kids into, these days? Syphilis? Chlamydia?"

"Youth, I think, actually," said Mark coolly.

"Maybe you'll give me that, then," said Celeste.

Mark looked up from his plate and smiled as if to say: There is no one but you. Celeste smiled back, as if to say: I will cut off your balls. They watched each other across the square clumsy table. She wore makeup—a little foundation, a little blush, some eyeliner.

"My ex-boyfriend has been calling me a lot," she said.

"Yeah? What's he want?"

"To get back together."

"That's what they all want."

"What do you think about that?"

"I think he should fuck off."

"Oh, Marky-poo. You're sweet."

They sat and ate their dinner and drank their rosé wine. By expressing anger toward Celeste's ex-boyfriend, Mark had confirmed his affection for her. Peace reigned again at their table. And she—oh, she was formidable. Now she began to relay the tale of the upcoming shareholders' meeting in Seattle, doing the voices of the various financial officers, and he listened raptly. She told him about some journalists' conference she'd been to over the weekend in D.C. The English polemicist Christopher Hitchens had been there, she said, smoking and drinking and with his shirt wide open. "I mean, come on," she said now. "Do you think you're Mick Jagger?"

Mark laughed. He was not Mick Jagger either. Celeste was twenty-nine years old. In general, this was a pretty good age to be, a pretty happy age. But in Brooklyn in 2006, with every other weekend a wedding save-the-date from a college friend in her mailbox, it was less so. Celeste concentrated momentarily on her food as Mark watched her. You could hold out against the calendar of the system for only so long; you could remain steadfast for only so long. This was her last chance at something; Mark of all people was her last chance at something, before she crossed into a different phase of her life.

"Don't look at me like that," she said.

"Like what?"

"Like I'm some lost puppy you've taken in! Shithead."

"Sorry."

She reached out her hand to take his, forgiving him. From the restaurant they rode his bike down Fulton to her place, she on the seat holding on to him, laughing. They were tired and sweaty, Mark especially, when they got home, and he took a shower, though Celeste said she couldn't guarantee she'd be awake when he got out. But her shower was so much nicer than his and Toby's, and Mark was a very sweaty man.

Celeste was indeed asleep already when he emerged. He put on a T-shirt and got in bed with her, laying his hand hesitantly on her hip. She woke up momentarily and placed the hand, tenderly, on her stomach. They both fell asleep then, in the Brooklyn night, two people no longer very young, no longer very happy, though still unsettled, still a mess.

The next night, his last before the defense, he met Gwyn in the basement of a bar in the East Village; a friend of hers, from Syracuse, was in a band. Before moving to New York Mark had been to stadium concerts and concerts in protest of wars, but never, to his great regret, to an intimate *show*, like the Sex Pistols' first show, in a basement. Now for his sins he was summoned to one such show every other week. They cost eight dollars for admission and then the bar overcharged for beer. The sound quality was miserable. The bands were bad. Nonetheless he'd convinced Toby to come along by promising to pay his cover, and he shut off his cell phone entirely, so it would seem he'd been on the subway, if Celeste called.

This would be the last time he did this, however, as he was going to end it finally tonight. He was going to try to make it work with Celeste. He was not a boy, after all, or a publishing assistant, to be attending rock shows and paying five dollars for bottles of Rolling Rock. This wasn't why he'd spent the past eight years of his life looking up references to Mensheviks in all the triumphalist Bolshevik literature. And he was tired.

At the same time Gwyn was strikingly good-looking, unquestionably the best-looking girl he'd ever gone out with—and she was so young. She was so young. She believed in the Mensheviks and she believed, it seemed, in rock and roll. And she reminded him of Sasha, the Sasha he'd known. She believed, just as Sasha and he had once believed, in saving money—she thought it was fun. And also like Sasha, because she was young, and because she was so beautiful, she really didn't mind, it really didn't matter, that she didn't have any clothes to wear.

One year while Mark was in high school, the hockey team had practiced at an outdoor rink next to a river. And several times during that year the weather had been such—warm, Mark supposed now—that the air coming off the river and the outdoor ice combined to create a thick fog on the ice surface, so you couldn't see more than ten feet ahead of you. Coach Rezzutti loved those practices: "You'll develop your hockey sense," he said. *Hah-key*, he said it. And it was true: without seeing the puck at all, merely hearing it off sticks and only barely at that, Mark could sense not only where the play was just then but often the direction in which it was heading.

In the same way, he could always spot Gwyn upon entering a

room. The attention of the room, the direction of its attention, plus a kind of phalanx of men, one or two talking to her, and several hanging around waiting, told him exactly where she was. This was because she was handsome, yes; but it was also because, having looked this way for a while now, she had learned that she could keep men's attention by encouraging them. So, for example, as he entered this basement Mark saw her put her hand on the shoulder of a tall young man in black pants and a black T-shirt with hair falling down around his ears. This was annoying, especially as Toby saw it, too.

But that's what you get! Mark handed Toby a ten for beer (not quite enough, he knew) and maneuvered over to Gwyn—he always overdressed, in a nice blue shirt and his one brown sport jacket, when going out with her, so that it was clear he wasn't about to start apologizing for being older than everyone—and put his arm around her waist. "Oh hello!" she said, and reached up with the hand that had just been on the young man's shoulder to put it around Mark's neck and pull herself up to him in a hug. She introduced him to the young hipster, who didn't seem to have much to say to Mark, or to Gwyn now that Mark was there, and soon slunk off into the corner.

Yet this was enough. Mark could not possibly stop seeing Gwyn. It wasn't that he couldn't live without her. He could probably live without her. Or maybe he couldn't. That wasn't the point. The point was that he couldn't possibly stand to see her with that dipshit.

"Can we leave?" he asked Gwyn. Her friend's band had stopped playing.

"Do you want to?" she said.

"Yeah," he said. "I'd like us to have some time together tonight and I have to get up pretty early in the morning."

"I'll go if you want to. I'm a little drunk."

She had her arm around his neck. "You're the most beautiful girl I've ever seen," he said.

"No I'm not."

He kissed her. She kissed him back. They kept their lips closed—Gwyn was a nice girl, from Minnesota, and Mark was almost ten years older than she—but she kissed him with such an intensity of kissing, such an abandon to it, that he began to think that maybe he could just do it all over again. Gwyn was a little straitlaced, like Sasha, and she was a little awkward, like her, and also like Sasha and very much unlike Celeste she was meant, clearly, for existing *with* someone in the world—and perhaps all the things he'd done wrong with Sasha, all the mistakes he'd made, all the money he didn't spend on taxicabs, on dinners, on better coffee, that of course in retrospect he should have spent (poor Sasha, and all those nights that they'd spent on subways instead), all the things he said no to that he should have said yes to, all the years in Syracuse they wasted, and all the words, yes, the unkind words that, because of his stupidity, his inexperience, his callowness, he'd allowed to slip through his lips—not to mention his sexual inexperience, had he neglected to mention this? He was just a boy! Boys should not marry! Oh. They should not marry. But now—he wondered now, as his lips unlocked from Gwyn's and only their foreheads touched, looking down on her lips, her chin, he wondered if perhaps he couldn't do right all that he'd once done wrong.

He thought.

"Let's stay a little longer," Gwyn whispered.

"OK," said Mark, as he always did.

At the end of the night, they took the subway back to Brooklyn. Toby had disappeared to somewhere, so they were alone. Mark looked out at the bridge again, wondering if this was his last all-time date, the date that ended it, if he might finally just give this a shot. "What are you thinking?" Gwyn asked him.

"Oh," said Mark. "I missed the Rangers game."

"Ah," said Gwyn, disappointed.

By the time they arrived at his place it was past three, and they fell asleep in positions of cuddling, with their clothes on.

And then it was May Day. Mark opened his eyes—Gwyn was already gone to her internship, she'd washed her face and brushed her teeth and looked as fresh as a cut flower—and jumped out of bed. All right, he thought. Bring on the dissertation committee.

Instead, out in the kitchen, sat the social committee: Toby and Arielle, at his father's big green kitchen table, drinking coffee.

"Good morning," said Mark.

"With all due respect," Toby began immediately, "but is it likely that in any other American city you would get so much as a hand job on a regular basis?"

"It's not likely," Mark admitted.

"Which is a poor reflection on other American cities."

"Yes, it is."

It was like a Socratic dialogue.

"We saw Gwyn on her way out," Arielle said.

"Ah," said Mark. "She's very young."

"And gorgeous."

"Yes."

"But what happened to Celeste?"

"Nothing."

"You could learn a lot from Celeste. Just the way she dresses."

"I know."

"Is it just that Gwyn is younger? How much? Five years? What's five years?"

Five years was the length of Sidorovich's jail sentence in 1931.

Five years was the amount of time he lived with Sasha.

225

Four years was the number of years they'd now been apart.

"Eight," he said. "It's eight years."

"Jesus," said Arielle.

They sat for a moment in silence at Mark's father's green table.

"You wouldn't do that to me, would you?" Arielle asked Toby.

"It would never occur to me!"

"You're nice," said Arielle, and laughed skeptically.

Mark watched them. He was very moved. What if Arielle ended up with Toby? Old Sam wouldn't mind, he didn't think. He should write Sam, Mark now realized, when all this dissertation business was over. Sam was in New Haven now for law school, apparently, it wasn't far, and Mark had already forgotten what it was they'd fought about that time. Was it really Israel? In any case, Toby and Arielle—yes, it would give all their lives a pleasant circularity.

"Excuse me," he said, and got up from the table to check his e-mail and his phone messages from the night before.

"Mark!" Arielle called after him. "Choose wisely!"

"Hey." Toby cut in again.

"No, I need to say this," Arielle insisted. "I've known guys like you, Mark. You think girls need to be saved. But we don't. We're OK. Save yourself!"

Mark was already listening to his phone messages. There were three.

The first was from Jeff, thanking Mark for having lunch and gently imploring him to show up tomorrow (now today). So far so good.

The next was from Celeste, at around ten last night. "Hey, Marky-poo, just got home from a fun Sunday at work. Call me if you get this, I'll be up."

Ah, thought Mark, very quickly. A strategic error. It meant she couldn't call again without seeming like a crazy person, and he could claim he didn't get the message until too late. Poor Celeste.

Except the next message, received just after 1:00 a.m., was also from her. "Mark," it said. "If you're fucking that little tramp of yours, I will cut your dick off, do you hear me? Just kidding. Where are you? Call me!"

And of course he hadn't gotten the message, and he hadn't called.

We hurt one another. We go through life dressing up in new clothes and covering up our true motives. We meet up lightly, we drink rosé wine, and then we give each other pain. We don't want to! What we want to do, what one really wants to do is put out one's hands—like some dancer, in a trance, just put out one's hands—and touch all the people and tell them: I'm sorry. I love you. Thank you for your e-mail. Thank you for coming to see me. Thank you. But we can't. We can't. On the little life raft of Mark only one other person could fit. Just one! And so, thwarted, we inflict pain. That's what we do. We do not keep each other company. We do not send each other cute text messages. Or, rather, when we do these things, we do them merely to postpone the moment when we'll push these people off, and beat forward, beat forward on our little raft, alone.

Mark was on the bus up to Syracuse as he thought this. There was a moment, not long after the bus emerged from the Lincoln Tunnel, and then took a sharp turn, upward out of the tunnel so that it was heading back momentarily toward the city, and the entire vista of midtown Manhattan opened up before you: you just knew things, then, the truth of things.

He had been so early for the ten o'clock bus, so uncharacteristically early, that he'd walked over to Celeste's office and called her from the street.

"Hi!" she said a little quizzically.

"Hi," Mark had said, miserably. "Can you come down? I'm downstairs."

"What do you mean?"

"I'm out on the street. My defense is today. I'm on the way to the bus. It's May Day, baby."

She came out a minute later in her business suit, looking smart, her hair pulled back. She wore a little blush on her cheekbones. It was a slightly cool day, for May 1, but she did not put on a coat.

Mark stood against the building with his enormous backpack, looking, as he'd often looked in his life, like a homeless person.

Celeste began to say exactly this but then saw the look on his face.

"Oh, you," she said. "You're sleeping with someone."

Mark nodded miserably.

"I can't believe this. You're sleeping with someone! And you're breaking up with me!"

Mark nodded again.

"Say something then! Don't just stand there!"

"I'm sad," he said.

"You're a shithead! How much longer do you think you can do this?"

"We weren't doing that great, baby."

"Oh, fuck you! You think I don't know that?"

Suddenly her face scrunched up and she put her head into his shoulder, hiding it. "I have to go back to work like this," she said. "You couldn't have picked a time when I wasn't at work?"

"Baby" was all Mark could say.

"Are you sure?" she asked his shoulder.

Mark nodded with his entire body, his arms around her now.

"OK," said Celeste. She pulled away from Mark slightly, composed her face, blew her nose into his sweatshirt, and placed her palm tenderly on his cheek. She expelled a breath. "Good luck," said Celeste. That was all. Then she turned on her heel and walked back into the skyscraper.

In the bus Mark played the scene repeatedly in his mind. Celeste—and Sasha. These were the most impressive people he'd known in his life and now they were gone. He got a call from Gwyn but he didn't take it. She sent a text—"I miss you."—but he didn't take that either. He took a nap instead.

Four hours later he was in the Syracuse bus station. It was—here was the joke—the cleanest, most modern, best-lit and comfortable bus station he'd ever been in. It gave you the wrong idea about Syracuse, boy. Of course, that's what bus stations were supposed to do, throughout history. Give travelers the wrong idea.

He checked the city bus schedule—he had twenty minutes until a bus would take him to campus. He bought a muffin and a coffee at the station Dunkin' Donuts and sat down on the handsome blue metal mesh seats. The station may have been incongruously nice for Syracuse but it was not incongruously crowded, that is to say it was empty, and Mark's backpack also got a seat, next to him.

He sometimes wondered what happened to Sidorovich in 1941. Had he died in a train station, like Tolstoy? Or had he left the train somewhere, say in Sverdlovsk, and simply walked into the city and disappeared? Perhaps he taught at the university? Or at a high school? He couldn't teach history, with his views on history, but why not geography? The names of the rivers, the cities, the cathedrals—he knew them all. Maybe Sidorovich taught geography and coached hockey, in Sverdlovsk, thought Mark.

He looked up at the board of departures. There was a bus for Buffalo, a bus back to New York, and a bus to Montreal. It left in fifteen minutes. Just as he looked up they announced it over the intercom: "The bus for Montreal is now seating passengers at Gate Three. Gate Three."

Sasha was in Montreal. He could go up there, say hello. Maybe Sasha would know what he should do. She'd read a million books. She was very wise. And Canada gives people a nice perspective on things.

Now the bus that could take him to campus pulled up outside the station, a little ahead of schedule. Or maybe the time on Mark's cell phone was off—maybe it was confused, being this far north.

Or maybe he should just get back on the bus to New York.

He hadn't yet finished his coffee and muffin. They had cost $2.74, for the love of God.

He had left Sasha, he had allowed Sasha to leave, because he could no longer abide the person he had become with her. He lied and lied and when the lies had mounted festering in the corner he covered them with further lies. Then he had suffered in Syracuse alone. Or rather the loneliness was the suffering. He had dated. He had Internet dated. And even when he'd solved all these problems of dating he—well, continued to date. As if only the women he dated could tell him who Mark was. As if he would not be a full person, a full Mark, until he'd found the perfect complement. Except every woman he dated took a chunk of Mark with her. And vice versa. So that if you looked, if you walked around New York and looked properly, if you walked around America and looked properly, what you saw was a group of wandering disaggregated people, torn apart and carrying with them, in their hands, like supplicants, the pieces of flesh they'd won from others in their time. And who now would take them in?

Mark hadn't yet finished his coffee and muffin. He was like the knight errant in the tale. If he went north he would see Sasha. If he went into Syracuse he would find Jeff and his dissertation committee. Go back south and there'd be Gwyn.

Save yourself, they had told him. Save yourself, Mark. Save yourself.

2008

A nd then I too moved to New York. I was not, after all, an idiot.

The city had changed, but I had also changed, and neither of us had changed very much. New York had grown richer and glitzier, and so had I; deep down it was unchanged, and so was I. For all the new glass condominiums and coffee shops in Brooklyn, the BQE was still an awful road, full of monstrous gaping holes, and as I bounced around on it in my U-Haul, past the warehouses of Sunset Park, I worried the wheels would fall off the truck, I worried that I'd get lost here and be all alone, and, just like every other time I'd visited, I was afraid.

I got over it. I had just spent several years abroad, mostly in Moscow, watching a government slowly strangle an entire nation. I had seen what the world looked like before you covered it up with two hundred years of accumulated wealth (it wasn't pretty). I probably could have stayed there, writing long, indignant dispatches for American magazines, but I came back. Life was here.

I had not fallen behind while away; in fact the others had fallen behind, and I had grown stronger, my vision was wider, and I saw more clearly than my contemporaries. In Brooklyn I quickly finished my book about the Bush administration's foreign policy (*The Damage Done*, I called it—it was an angry book) and found an agent, a fancy agent, and she took me to lunch at the Museum of Modern Art. Then, magically, she sold my book and told me to take a vacation. I did not take a vacation. I rented another U-Haul, bid farewell to Brooklyn, and moved my stuff to a little corner of the city tucked just under the Queensboro Bridge. My parents had had friends who lived in Jackson Heights, and when we'd visited them, and then driven to Manhattan at night, we had always gone over this bridge. It remains the most dramatic way to enter the city: one second you are in the grimiest section of Queens, where they drop off prisoners from Rikers, and the next second you are told that a left will get you FDR Drive, but a right, my friend, a right will put you at 61st and First. And that's where I found a place, 61st and First.

My friends during these years were all busy becoming lawyers and getting married, getting married and becoming lawyers. Ferdinand, a lawyer, got married to another lawyer; Josh, a community organizer, got married to a social worker; Ravi Winikoff, now a lawyer, married a banker. It had recently been proposed, at the monthly discussion hosted by the journal *Debate* about "what went wrong with the Left" that the Left had failed to replace the deep culture of religion with a culture of its own. "When I attend the funerals of my social-democratic friends," the elderly editor of the journal had said, "no one knows what to *do*. Whereas at the funerals of religious friends, everything is minutely prescribed. It's very comforting." Well, the weddings I attended were neither social-democratic nor religious—they were rich! Money was the form their oaths had taken—and love, I think. A kind of yearning, and relief. As for myself, while I dutifully attended all these weddings, I had other plans. I spent most of my time alone, walking through my neighborhood, past the famous strip club Scores, around the giant Bloomingdale's flagship store, as big as an aircraft carrier, and writing my long pieces of political analysis. Of course in a way it was all pretty academic. The Bush years were winding down disgracefully, the Iraq war was lost, the Middle East was lost, the environment was lost: YOU DO NOT SUBJECT YOUR COUNTRY TO SIX YEARS OF MISRULE BY FANATICAL INCOMPETENTS AND EMERGE SMELLING LIKE ROSES. But what can you do? The trash was still getting picked up on Mondays, water came out of my faucets, hot and cold, and the subway trains ran through the night. In the mornings sometimes I saw pretty girls on those trains reading the *New Yorker* and opposing—too late—the war in Iraq.

Toward the end of the time I'm describing I too met a pretty girl, named Gwyn, who worked at a famous book review for which I wrote. She was younger than I was, by a lot, and she still worshipped, or so she told me and I had no cause to disbelieve her, the life of the mind. Gwyn was quiet and studious in person—like Jillian—but wrote sharp, affectionate e-mails from work and sometimes, or at least often enough, laughed at my jokes when we were home alone in bed or walking down the street together holding hands. She was only a year out of college, and the difference in our ages seemed a scandal to me, at first, but I got over it. She often stayed late at the review, messing up our evening's plans, but in return she brought me review copies, hundreds of review copies, an entire underground publishing economy filtering directly in to me. Gwyn was filled with bright hope for the future and also uncertainty, of course, as to what would become of her and who she really was. (She kept asking me.) And even with her youth, life had not entirely missed her—she'd been involved with an older guy, like me, a graduate student in history, who'd gone off one day to Syracuse and never, apparently, returned.

On Saturday afternoons I met up with some friends—the unmarried ones—to play touch football in the park. Touch football is a limited game, frankly, a shadow cast on the wall by the real thing, and I kept losing at it. I played with some writers and magazine editors, we kept our teams the same each week, and my team always lost. Week after week this happened, for reasons that were beyond me, and week after week, after we had a few pitchers of beer at Oscar's, I walked home to my place on First Avenue (where more often than not now Gwyn would be waiting), wondering what had gone wrong.

Everyone was getting married; it was like some kind of cold people were catching. Ferdinand's wedding was lavish and in another country; Ravi's was lavish in New York. Arielle was getting married! After years of picking up men and discarding them, half alive, she picked one up and let him stay.

Then Jillian got engaged. I had seen her a few times, with varying degrees of pain and discomfort, when she'd come down from Boston. She was doing her medical residency there and it occupied all her time. When we'd seen each other there was no more talk, as there had been for a while before I'd left the country, of us getting back together, though we still clung to each other in the vast universe of other people.

Then one day she called, sounding very nervous, as I sat in my Starbucks reading the political pages of the so-called liberal *New American*. To be connected to the world through a cell phone means getting all sorts of news in very strange places, and it was in the Starbucks on 60th Street that Jillian gave me the news about her engagement.

I said, "To a doctor?"

"What does that matter?" she said. "But yes, to a doctor."

Wow, I thought, almost involuntarily. A doctor.

"Are you OK?" she asked. "I mean, are you OK with it? You're not mad?"

"No," I said, then rummaged about in myself for a moment to make sure. I found no anger there. I was relieved, happy, in shock. So that was that. The end of Jillian and me. "How could I possibly be mad," I said. And then, knowing I got to ask this only once: "Is he a nice person?"

"Yes," she said very seriously. "He is."

"OK." We were silent for a moment. "I'm proud of you," I said.

And I was. It was almost like a victory for us together, that she had managed to move on and find someone nice. And for me it was a dispensation, an annulment. It was the end of something, even if of course everything one does reverberates through the universe eternally, so that there is no end to anything, technically speaking. Jillian was getting married. For her, at least, I was glad.

And then, in November 2006, the Democrats won races for the Senate and House in many states and districts. They took back the Congress. The newly constituted committees began to exercise the privilege—and what a privilege it now seemed!—of congressional oversight. In the spring of 2007, if you'd walked into the Starbucks on First Avenue and 60th Street, you'd have seen a jaded thirty-one-year-old man reading first the *New York Times*, and then, if you'd stuck around and sipped your latte, the *Wall Street Journal*, and, in a crooked, lopsided, jaded way, grinning like a little boy. I was reading about the House Committee on Government Reform. I was reading about the Senate Judiciary Committee. Occasionally I logged on to the better political blogs—there were still some left—and grinned along with them. It was not a happy time, exactly, it was not party-time, exactly, and eventually the Democrats would cave on Iraq, but still something was changing. Things were going to change.

I was sitting in Starbucks one day happily reading my papers when I got a call from Gwyn's book review.

"Hello?" I said, because there was a slight chance that it was the editor, not Gwyn.

"Hi, baby," Gwyn whispered. "What are you doing?"

"I'm reading the outtakes from the Judiciary Committee," I whispered back. "It's awesome."

"Baby, I'm late."

I knew right away what she meant. "How late?"

"More than a week. I had the dates wrong."

"That time . . ."

"Yes. That's the one. I mean, maybe. But really maybe."

I formed, in the Starbucks, the most neutral expression I could summon and tried to channel this, my God-like neutrality, through the phone to Gwyn. Now, she was too young to be having babies, and I, I was too old. But I believed in history, as always, and if history had declared this, then that was history talking.

"Baby," I said. "My baby."

"I bought a test," she whispered. "Can I come over tonight and we'll take it together?"

"Yes, of course," I said. "My sweet. You can pee on the test in my apartment."

She laughed, a little nervously. "Thank you," she said.

We hung up. It was not a great joke but it could have been worse. Now I sat in the Starbucks and suddenly noticed, until then I'd only cared about the perfidies of the Bush administration, that I was surrounded by women and baby carriages. It was 2:00

p.m.—the women-and-baby-carriage hour. The women cooed at their little baby carriages, and exchanged horror stories of baby fevers and baby puking. So I was to be among them, with my own little baby carriage? I made a little cooing noise, to myself, to practice. *Coooooo. Cooo-coooo.*

Of course Gwyn was too young to have a baby, and I, spiritually, was too old. I had done too much damage—to my own life, and to Jillian's, as Jillian had occasionally pointed out. Gwyn would see that. At the same time, if she didn't, I wasn't going to pack her off to the abortion doctor. Was I? I looked back at the papers. The Russians were threatening to cut off EU gas. E-mails were being released proving that the Bush people had suppressed scientific evidence of global warming. Another suicide bombing in Iraq. Another suicide bombing in Iraq. The Sunni and Shia were going to slaughter one another. Gwyn knew about all this; she worked at a great book review. We were going to bring a little baby into this world, *this* world? No, believe me, I loved babies. But you were going to have to find me another world.

I spent the day worrying and thinking.

It was warm out now. The winter had been so strange—January was hot, then February and March were cold, biting cold, and now it was April, and it was raining, and warm, and life was back to normal. I wandered around in the shadow of the Queensboro Bridge. One of the nice things about my life, I thought, if also one of the sad things, was that I'd managed to remain unattached—to places, and other people, and even, aside from my despair at 2000 and the gerrymandering of the districts, to long-term political causes. I was still moving, I was still a few steps ahead. And to think that having finally achieved a separate peace with everyone, including

Jillian, I was going to commit myself to fifty years of Gwyn—that was tough to take, for me, right then. After all the things I'd done wrong, it seemed a little foolish to go and do one more.

I thought too of all the lives I could have had—could still have. I could have stayed in Russia. I could have stayed with Jillian. I could have gone to Israel. I could have gone to graduate school—and graduate school sometimes takes you to strange places. I could have moved back to Clarksville and lived in an attic and coached high school football, as I'd once wanted to do.

There were so many things I'd once wanted to do! The trouble is that when you're young you don't know enough; you are constantly being lied to, in a hundred ways, so your ideas of what the world is like are jumbled; when you imagine the life you want for yourself, you imagine things that don't exist. If I could have gone back and explained to my younger self what the real options were, what the real consequences for certain decisions were going to be, my younger self would have known what to choose. But at the time I didn't know; and now, when I knew, my mind was too filled up with useless auxiliary information, and beholden to special interests, and I was confused.

I wandered around in the warm spring air. Gwyn was pregnant—I knew it in my bones, and her testing positive that evening in my apartment, which she did, which she spectacularly did, was a formality. She was pregnant. We spent the night in shock and professing, over and over, that it was up to the other person.

"We'll do whatever you want," I said.

"We'll do whatever *you* want," answered Gwyn.

The next day we played football.

What was I supposed to do? Gwyn was pregnant and I played football. I ran crossing routes, buttonhooks, end routes, and deep routes, and then some routes that surely were not routes at all. For moments—during the sharp passes, the soft passes, the passes laid right into outstretched hands and the passes that fell, ineffectually, out of reach—I forgot about the predicament I was in. Then I remembered again. I caught a pass lying on my back. The guy I covered—he was a novelist, actually, and he was the one engaged to marry Arielle—caught one, improbably, after it bounced off his shoulder. Balls were swatted down, batted up, redirected. Fingers were caught and crushed. I jammed my thumb. I was called for pass interference, after putting my elbow into someone's stomach—I should have put it in his throat. We played on. Blunders were committed, I dropped an interception, I failed to get open in the end zone, I lost track of the end zone and caught a pass on the one-yard line on fourth down and was tagged. We lost. So it went. We lost.

Sitting in Oscar's afterward, I went over all the promises I'd made myself after Jillian left. No more rushing into things, I had said. No more proceeding on the basis of hope. And, thinking over all the time that had passed, how I wished that I could be other than I was! How I wished that I could be younger for Gwyn; that we had met ten years earlier, or even five. That the things that had happened had not actually happened, or had happened to someone else, or had, barring that, happened to us together.

But they had, and hadn't, and hadn't, and here I was.

Here I was, and walking out from Oscar's slightly drunk into the warmth of the day, because it was still day, I realized all at once that I'd been gone four hours. And it occurred to me, now that I was walking back, that Gwyn, my Gwyn, my quiet Gwyn, may quietly have let herself out, while I was gone, and made her way, alone, to the clinic on 70th Street, then sat quietly in the waiting room with the other women, until they called her name. And I began to walk faster, and then, my bag with cleats and clothing

241

awkwardly beside me, I began to run. Because it wasn't over yet, I thought, remembering my friends at *Debate*, my gentle social-democratic friends—there was still work to be done. A cabal of liars and hypocrites had stolen the White House, launched a criminal war, bankrupted our treasury, and authorized torture in our prisons. And now it was too late, as I have said—but also, you know, not too late. We had to live. And there were enough of us, I thought, if we just stuck together. We would take back the White House, and the statehouses and city halls and town councils. We'd keep the Congress. And in order to ensure a permanent left major-ity, Gwyn, we'd have many left-wing babies. My love.

I turned the corner finally, unlocked the door, and bounded up the stairs.

Permission Credits

Portions of this book first appeared in *Agni: Best New American Voices 2005* (Harcourt), Francine Prose, guest editor; and in *n+1*.

Excerpt from "Da Baddest Poet" by Sole (Tim Holland). By permission of Tim Holland.